Till The Day Go Down

by

Jen Black

Copyright © Jen Black, 2009

Jen Black has asserted her moral rights
under the Copyright, Designs and Patents Act 1988.
All rights reserved. No part of this publication may be reproduced,
stored in a retrieval system or transmitted, in any form or by any means,
without the prior permission of Quaestor2000 Ltd, or as expressly
permitted by law or under the terms agreed with the appropriate
reprographic rights organisation. Enquiries concerning reproduction
which may not be covered by the above should be addressed to
Quaestor2000 Ltd at the address below.

Quaestor2000 Ltd, 15 Turner Close CW1 3WZ
Website: http://www.quaestor2000.com
British Library Cataloguing in Publication Data
Data Available

ISBN: 978-1-906836-17-7 (paperback)
ISBN: 978-1-906836-18-4 (large print)

Printed and bound in Great Britain by
Marston Book Services Limited, Oxford
and in the United States by
Lightning Source Inc., La Vergne, Tennessee

To Bill

Chapter One

Corbrige, Northumberland, June 1543

Harry Wharton strolled across the cobbles of the square and smiled at the farm girls who eyed him speculatively across the market stalls. Flirtatious matrons offered tempting morsels of honeycomb along with bawdy suggestions and Harry, grinning at their good-humoured audacity, shook his head at them all and kept his eyes open for a local man who could tell him the secret ways through the Border. The quicker he got to Edinburgh, the sooner he could accomplish the business, return and claim his reward.

How hard could it be?

First, he must find a guide. Getting lost in the boggy, trackless wastes was not the way he wished to start his mission.

The minty green scent of recently pulled cabbages and peas fresh in the pod fought the more earthy smells of livestock penned since early morning. From somewhere close at hand drifted the mouth-watering aroma of hot eel pie. Harry's nostrils flared, his stomach rumbled and he fumbled for the purse at his belt.

"But Mama, we need more ale. There's little left. Buy a keg or two, do!"

The clear feminine voice wavered between wheedle and command and did not belong to a farm girl. Harry turned, uttered a soundless whistle and forgot about eel pie.

A black velvet bonnet tilted rakishly to one side of her head. High cheekbones, a neat nose and open brown eyes in a clear complexion. Wisps and strands of chestnut hair tangled about her ears, and as she turned he glimpsed a thick, lustrous brown plait between her shoulder blades. The square-necked green gown hugged her waist, flared over the curve of her hip and a frill of white showed at the tight cuff of her plain, practical sleeves. The long tasselled tabs of an embroidered girdle hung from her waist.

She radiated energy and purpose. Something shifted under Harry's diaphragm, which was odd because he considered himself well used to ladies of quality. Less than three weeks ago he had flirted with court beauties on a daily basis, even bedded one or two during his service in the duke's household.

"*Please*, Mama. Why do you hesitate?" Pleasant toned and with a fluency lacking in the rough accents around him, her voice held Harry's attention as she turned to the servant beside her. "Joseph will take it to the cart, won't you, Joseph?"

Joseph, a stalwart man in his fifties, hastily nodded agreement. The young woman swung back to her parent. Joseph kept his gaze on the cobbles and looked as if he struggled to maintain a respectful expression.

Harry smiled. She stood out among the ill-dressed crowds in the market square as if a shaft of sunshine followed her every movement and he was willing to bet life would never be dull with that young lady around.

"Very well, dear." The older woman sighed and gave up the struggle. "Two kegs, Joseph, if you please."

Joseph bowed his head and turned away to make the transaction.

Dark lashes shadowed fine eyes. Harry traced the swooping line of her brows, so clear against her pale skin. An unexpected tightness in his throat caused him to swallow hard and look away.

"Now, Mama, what about needles and yarn for those quilts we are to make this winter?"

He turned back in time to see the young woman gesture towards the stall at his side, which offered hanks of wool, yarns and silk threads in an array of colours. His first inclination was to move out of the away. Nay, he thought, stay. An hour's banter before riding on to Edinburgh may prove an entertainment to beguile a boring day.

The familiar pleasure of the chase surged through his veins. He pretended to study the goods on offer, allowed a frown to cloud his brow and stared at the display in what he hoped was an artful show of great perplexity. A flash of green fabric swirled against his booted leg and his senses, already sharp, tightened another notch as the scent of roses reached him.

"Why, sir, do you hesitate over needles?" The soft gurgle of laughter at his elbow made him lift his head. Her smile was like quicksilver. "Mama and I could help you make a selection if you find it beyond you."

"Alina! Hold your tongue!" The sharp words drew Harry's gaze to the girl's mother, who frowned at him.

He bowed to them both, and kept his head down for several respectful moments. Alina. Alina. Harry savoured the name and decided he liked it.

"The gentleman obviously needs assistance, Mama."

"The stall owner is present, daughter, and will offer all the assistance he needs."

At the snapped rejoinder, Harry stood straight and tall once more, and noticed Alina tilted her head to meet his gaze. Her smile took his breath away.

"I, er…I thought to take a small gift home for my sister, but…"

Jesu! He could not frame the simplest sentence, and her laughing brown eyes mocked his efforts. He shook his head, defeated. "I know nothing of needles."

"See, Mama." The young woman half-turned to her annoyed parent. "He does need our help. I thought he might." The sun sparkled on the vagabond curls tangled like gold wires about her ears.

Harry rallied his scattered wits. What was the matter with him? He cleared his throat to give himself time to think.

But she was too swift for him. "You still look puzzled, sir. They are only needles and pins, not something the Good Lord has dropped from the sky."

Ye Gods! She spoke as if he were a simpleton. The skin of Harry's face prickled and burned. It was years since he had blushed at something a woman said to him. He inhaled through his nose, ignored her and turned his attention to the older woman. "I would be most grateful for your help, ma'am. I must admit pins and spindles have not figured overmuch in my education."

The mother had been a beauty in her time. The square-necked black velvet gown did nothing to lighten the sallow hue of her complexion and the severe gable hood, still popular among those who once supported Queen Catherine, did nothing to brighten her countenance. Still, Harry saw a likeness to her daughter in the eloquent brown eyes and the line of her jaw even though the good woman's expression remained stern.

She turned a quelling glance on Alina, as if warning her daughter to remain silent. "I suggest, sir, a package of needles such as—" she indicated a small silk-wrapped bundle with a gloved hand—"would be welcome to most young ladies."

Harry offered a second casual yet elegant bow. "Thank you, ma'am. I appreciate your advice."

She inclined her head. A jewel at her throat caught the light and the gauzy stuff of the hood hid her neck as she turned to the stallholder.

"Use a ribbon, Mary, since it is to be a gift." She cast a calculating eye over Harry's dark woollen doublet and rakish cap. "I am sure the young man has coin enough."

Harry bristled under her sharp scrutiny. His brows lifted, and a retort sprang to his lips, but he caught sight of Alina's commiserating smile behind her mother's shoulder and forgot what he had been about to say.

The stallholder, who had remained silent throughout the exchange, beamed and bobbed a small curtsy.

Alina's mother continued to regard Harry with condescension, and then glanced towards the stallholder once more. "We shall return to make our selection later, Mary." She directed a regal nod to Harry. "Good day, young man."

She shepherded her daughter away. It was obvious she intended to return when he was out of the way. Harry gritted his teeth, offered his most elegant bow and watched them go. He received a swift glance over her shoulder from the younger lady before the crowd took her away.

He turned to the stallholder. "Who was that?"

Shrewd blue eyes regarded him. "Fancy ye chances, lad? That was the lady of Aydon Hall. Margery Carnaby and her daughter Alina. They're a-carin' for Sir Reynold, him that's ill and like to die soon."

"Aydon? Just north of here?"

"Aye. Right by the Ay Burn. Ye'll be a stranger to these parts yourself, sir?"

Harry saw no need to deny it. "Travelling north to Edinburgh."

"Oh, aye. And ye'd be from Lonnun, then, sir?"

Harry practised his famous smile. There was no harm in letting everyone think he was from the south. In fact, it was to his advantage. "How'd ye guess?"

The woman relaxed, as they all did when he concentrated on them. The heavy wool shawl draping her shoulders moved as she shrugged. "Ye don't sound as if ye come from these parts. Ye sound more like gentry. I thought o' Lonnun, that's all."

"It is quieter hereabouts than London."

Mary handed him a neatly wrapped package and named her price. He counted out coins into her palm, aware she eyed him up and down. "Quiet, d'ye think, lad? It's but a hundred miles to Edinburgh, and ye'll travel some o' the most dangerous land in the country to get there."

Harry's hands stopped moving, and his gaze rose from the coins to the woman's rosy, thread-veined face and dark curls.

"Dangerous for everyone, or just for me?"

Mary choked back a laugh. "There's outlaws and broken men up in't hills, my bonny lad, and they'll shake loose the Border whenever they take a fancy to dee it. They'll not stop to ask ye name, never mind ye destination, before they slit ye throat and ride off wi ye purse." She looked him up and down. "They'll no' forget ye sword nor ye dagger, either, nor that bonny jewel in your cap. Nekkid as a babe ye'll be, when those limmers leave ye."

He resumed counting out coins into her plump hand. "I'd best take care how I ride then," he said. "For ride I will."

Her blue eyes twinkled. "Luck be wi ye, sir."

Harry slid the small package inside his doublet and wandered on. The woman's words rang through his head and made his task seem more a dangerous enterprise than a grand adventure. He whistled silently through his teeth, wondered if he should have asked about guides and then shook his head. He didn't want every village idiot knowing his business, and he'd prefer to use his own judgement in finding a man who knew the routes through the hills.

He eyed and rejected various stalwart fellows as unlikely to have travelled further than Stagshaw Fair on a good day. Those with a dishonest, shifty look about them he ignored. Stallholders offered their goods as he strolled by, and he shook his head, smiling, at the offer of ribbons, lace, gowns, cloaks, whistles, carved wooden dogs and live piglets in swift succession. But the odour of leather drew him to the saddler's merchandise in the corner of the square where the land dropped to the river.

The merchandise was good. He couldn't buy, of course. His current pose as sturdy soldier-cum-messenger precluded using fancy harness just as it prevented him wearing his fashionable fine cut velvets and expensive jewelled rings. The stone in his bonnet was of poor quality and would fool no one of consequence. But any man, whatever his station, would gaze with longing at the dark leather bridle, embossed and studded with silver, hanging on display.

The overpowering smell of livestock came on the breeze through the cut from Hill Street as he fingered the smooth, glossy leatherwork. He was dimly aware of cows and calves moaning and bawling in their temporary pens on the other side of the stone church as his fingers caressed the fifteen silver studs on each rein, and three silver stars on each cheek piece.

"Yon's a fine bridle, sir." The merchant, no doubt anxious to guard costly goods against pilfering, hovered at his side. "Would—"

A bellow broke the air. Harry and the leather merchant turned to seek the cause. Hoarse yells and a mounting series of shrieks and screams echoed between the houses and people scrambled to get out of the way. A young red and white bull hurtled on a zigzag course through the narrow street by the Vicar's Peel Tower and erupted, still bellowing, into the market place.

Half a dozen farmhands pounded after it, wooden rakes and hayforks prodding the air.

The bull kicked out at an unseen foe, a stall rocked and cheap crockery shattered as it hit the cobbles. The furious stallholder threw a pot at the beast's head. It ducked and wheeled towards the church.

"A bee stung 'im!" One of the farmhands yelled. "He's madder'n the de'il!"

Harry laughed.

"'ere, you won't be laughing, me lad," the leather merchant muttered, "if yon beast catches you on those ugly great 'orns of 'is."

The bull swung back, ducked, pivoted and dashed off in the opposite direction. Women squealed and grabbed their children. Stallholders regrouped to defend their precious wares with waving arms and missiles, but not one of them was stupid enough to stand his ground when the animal turned on him.

Tail in the air, head down, the beast pounded across the cobbles. In pain and threatened on every side, it saw no escape and swung round once more, snorting. Everyone stood very still.

The farmhands, wooden hayforks held before them, came on slowly.

The sharp, curving horns turned towards the end of the market. One forefoot pawed the cobbles.

Harry followed the beast's gaze. A cluster of empty wagons and farm carts blocked the point where Watling Street entered the market square. A lithe shape in long green dress backed out from between two carts, her attention on some object in her hands.

Harry stopped laughing, took an inadvertent step forward and yelled at the top of his voice. "Alina, run! Get out of the way!"

"'ere, that be Mistress Carnaby's daughter."

"I know that." Harry looked back at the bull. Lunging to dodge a hayfork, the beast knocked one man aside. With a quick flick of its head it tore a long, bloody rent in another man's hose. Hooves scrabbling for grip on the cobbles, it plunged forward, heading straight for Alina.

Harry ran. He grabbed a cloak from a stall as he passed, converged on the bull and raced alongside as it pounded by. The great head turned, horns flicked in his direction. The heat and miasma of several hundred pounds of bovine horn, bone and muscle assaulted his senses. He strained to keep up as the beast thundered across the cobbles. Somehow he flipped the cloak open to its full extent and tossed it over the sharp horns.

The beast bellowed, fearful of the dark cloud settling over its head, and the cloven hooves splayed as it skidded to a halt.

Harry raced over the last few yards as the bull tried to free itself from the enveloping folds of heavy velvet. He leapt onto the platform of the nearest cart and skipped across to the corner where Alina huddled between two solid wooden carts.

"Give me your hands!"

White as the bleached linen of her chemise peeping above the neckline of her gown, she looked as if she did not understand plain English. She never took her gaze from the tormented animal with the cloth flapping about its head.

"Alina, give me your hands!" Harry bawled. "The cloak could fall at any moment."

She flinched, stretched out one hand towards him. Harry seized it. "Your other hand as well."

She shook her head. The velvet bonnet fell off into the mire. "I can't."

Harry glanced at her hands. "Put the blasted cat in your pocket and give me your hand, you idiot!"

She opened her mouth to remonstrate, then thought better of it. She eased the tiny kitten into a pocket, and put one foot on the wheel hub. With one furious glance she raised her hand and let him swing her onto the cart. Harry registered her annoyance, but ignored it. Nice words and action rarely went together. At least now she was moving. He hustled her from one cart to another until they reached the church wall. Harry hoisted himself onto the top of the wall, and leaned towards her.

"Once over the wall, we'll be safe." Harry glanced over her head to the snorting, bellowing bull. "If he flips off the cloak, he'll soon scatter these carts. Give me your hand again."

This time Alina made no complaint. Pulling one side of her gown high to protect the kitten hidden in the pocket, she offered her hand, and with a swift tug from Harry's strong arm and an agile twist of her own, she sat on the sun-warmed stones beside him.

Breathing hard, Harry watched the farmhands surround the heaving animal and pull the blindfold tighter. There was a flurry of movement beside him as Alina slid from the wall to the grass of the churchyard.

"We'll be safer still here." She was not looking at him but delved into the pocket she had protected with such care and extracted a tiny bundle of grey fur with a short, stiff stub of a tail.

Harry looked down into the churchyard. All seemed peaceful beneath the shade of the big sycamore tree.

"It's a kitten." She cradled it in both hands and spoke without looking at Harry. "It was lost. We need more cats." Her breathing was back to normal. He liked that for it suggested she must be an active person. He liked the fact she was calm, too. Some girls would have been fainting or throwing hysterical fits after facing an angry bull. "Uncle Reynold hates them, so there's only one and it can't keep down all the mice and rats."

Harry slid off the wall and joined her on the grass. He gazed at the creature's round blue eyes and then back at the girl.

"It'll never be big enough to catch a rat. It's the rats will be chasing that ball of thistledown."

She ignored him and murmured soothing nonsense to the kitten. Close to, her skin reminded him of cream on the top of the milk, and something in the sharp curve of her lips tugged at his senses. An urge to pull her into his arms and hold her close ran through him. He couldn't, of course. She was no village girl to fondle behind a convenient byre. She wasn't married, certainly, or her hair would have been hidden beneath a headdress, but there was likely an affianced gentleman somewhere in the offing.

Harry looked up as a fracas beyond the gateway caught his attention. Farmhands led the bull away and an irate stallholder followed them, anxious they should not disappear with his expensive merchandise.

"Hey! Who's to pay me, then? That's a good velvet cloak, that is! Fit for a gentleman, and ruined on that brute's horns!"

The last farmhand, clutching a bloody thigh, stabbed a red finger in the direction of the churchyard. "Ask 'im, he took it."

Their moments of privacy were numbered. Harry looked at Alina. "Where's your mother?"

"In church." She coaxed the kitten, and received a yawn and a blink in response. "Talking to Lady Alice." She flicked a glance at Harry and he was surprised to see her mouth turn down. "I wouldn't be surprised if she wasn't making plans for my wedding. It's bound to be soon. Father's been grousing about it lately."

Well, he'd been right in so far as she wasn't married yet, but it looked as if she soon would be. She seemed dispirited at the prospect. Harry opened his mouth, heard the rattle of the iron sneck and looked round.

"Here, you!" The stallholder, a sacking apron tied around his ample form, waddled through the churchyard gate and glared at Harry from bulbous eyes. "Ye'll be paying me for that cloak, then?"

Harry laughed, and put a hand under Alina's elbow to help her to her feet. "What cloak? Do you see a cloak about my person?"

Alina's sharp elbow nudged Harry's ribs in rebuke. She shook her head at him then turned and smiled at the angry merchant. "Good day, Master Rutherford. I shall pay for your cloak, since it saved me from being gored to death. Pray tell Joseph how much I owe you, and he will bring it to you later in the day."

Muttering and grumbling but unable to reject such a handsome offer, Rutherford trundled back out into the market place. Alina looked up at Harry, her brown eyes sober. "It was a brave thing you did, sir. I am in your debt much more than to Master Rutherford. Is there a way in which I may repay you?"

The kitten mewled in her hands.

When she raised her chin, the white ruffle of her chemise framed the line of her jaw and enhanced the purity of her complexion. He caught his breath at the sight. She was beautiful. He thought for a moment of demanding a kiss as payment, and immediately rejected the idea. She would never allow it, and besides, there was something about this maid he wanted to cherish.

"You did not have to do that." Harry's tone was sharp. "I will pay the man. As your lady mother said earlier, I have coin enough."

Her expressive dark eyes regarded him with curiosity. The tip of her tongue swept her lower lip, then the corners of her mouth turned up and amusement flickered through her face. "Aye, Mama can be severe when she has a mind to be. But we cannot let you pay for the cloak after having saved my life. That would not be just, or fair."

Harry let out a faint snort of laughter. "My father always says life is unfair and the sooner I realise it, the better off I'll be."

"That is a hard maxim." She tilted her head and gave him a warm, considering glance from beneath long black lashes as her fingers continued to soothe the kitten. Her gaze descended from his eyes to his mouth, lingered there before returning to his eyes. One of her eyebrows tilted, as if questioning him. "But I suppose it is true, especially in these parts." She lifted the puny creature and let it rest on the soft swell of her bosom.

The kitten's pale claws flexed against the rounded curve of her breast where the chemise disappeared beneath her green gown. The court ladies wore stomachers to gave a straight line to their expensive gowns, but not so this girl. No doubt she hoped the sound of her heartbeat would soothe the animal, but Harry thought only of what lay beneath the kitten's claws. He shuffled his feet, looked at the grass and cleared his throat. She must be aware of the effect she had on him.

"A stallholder warned me I may lose my life on the road to Edinburgh. Are things so bad in the Borders?"

Alina's smile disappeared. Her brow furrowed. "Yes."

"I must go," he said, when she said nothing more. "The journey is one I…it is important."

He bit his tongue. He must not compromise his mission. He certainly could not say *why* he was travelling north.

She sighed. "Then go you must, but it is a bad road and you must take care."

"Then I shall take another road."

Her smile informed him she thought him a simpleton. "Whichever road you take through the Borders will be dangerous, sir." The kitten, tucked in beneath her chin, stared at him, too. "Will you tell me your name?"

The two pairs of eyes regarded him so seriously Harry couldn't prevent his smile breaking out once more. "Harry Scott at your service, lady. That creature's probably got fleas, you know." A fine gold chain supported a tiny gold cross at her throat, and it twinkled in the sunlight as she moved.

"Your family name is Scott?" Her brows arrowed down at the inner corners like daggers, and all laughter fled as her eyes searched his face.

He had chosen the surname at random. Why did she look at him as if he was an enemy? Perhaps he should have chosen a decent English name like Smith or Wilson.

He nodded, determined to make nothing of it. Scott was a common enough name, after all. "And your name, lady? I may pass this way on my return."

"Alina Carnaby. I live at Aydon Hall now." She turned her attention to the kitten, one forefinger parting the fluffy grey hairs. "My father hates every Scott ever born."

So casually did she say it that it took a moment for the words to register in Harry's mind. "Ah. I wonder why?" He hid his concern behind banter. "But whatever the reason, I suppose you will not be taking me to meet him?"

"I could." She studied him. "But he may kill you before you say a word. The most hated name along the English side of the Border is undoubtedly Elliot, but within my family, the name Scott is hated far more."

Harry recalled his father's tales of endless feuds between families on both sides of the Border, and he had no reason to doubt what she said. Plague take it, why had he plucked the name Scott out of the air?

The thought that it was just as well stole into his mind. At least now he would not be drawn into a relationship he neither wanted nor needed. He required a rich bride with a title to a fine manor and vast acreages to her name.

He stiffened his shoulders. The choice before him was obvious. At least he could bid her a gentle goodbye.

"Then I regret this shall be but a brief encounter. Farewell, my lady."

Chapter Two

Harry rode north out of Corbrige confident in the knowledge that he had directions for Edinburgh memorised, given by a man who regularly walked the distance with naught but a pack pony and a sack of knick-knacks for company.

'Stay till night comes ower the ground,' he'd said to Harry over a meal of ale and ham. 'Tis safer that way, lessen o' course the Armstrongs be ridin.'

Harry bided his time. Dusk came late in summer but at last the birds sought their roosts as the clear day sank to a cloudless evening. When the swelling moon rose over the hills to the south, he set out, shifting comfortably in his saddle as he headed up the gentle rise to the old Port Gate.

Cotts and cabins straggled along either side of the dusty lane from the stable yard, but before he'd covered a hundred paces he rode into open country. Listening to the gentle huff of wind that came down from the ridge, he rode on between high hawthorn hedges. Solid black shadows hid their roots and Harry gave thanks that the moon shone over his shoulder and picked out the dried mud of the track slanting gently uphill ahead of him.

He heard the burble of water before he saw the burn flow across the path. Bessie hesitated. Harry looked east. A dark mass of trees reached out across the hillside and swallowed up the stream. He wondered if this was the Ay burn that led to Aydon, Alina's home. He considered for a moment, then turned Bessie to the east and allowed the mare to pace slowly along the grassy bank.

The trees were single specimens strung out beside the water, their trunks black and silver in the moonlight; but soon comrades filled the opposite bank and swooped in from the slopes around him. In no time at all, Bessie walked through woodland, and Harry ducked now and then to avoid a low branch.

At one point he asked himself why he was doing this foolish thing, and shook his head. He knew why he had followed the stream east instead of heading north.

He could label it all sorts of thing, but in truth nothing more than idle curiosity and a simple wish to see where Alina lived sent him this way. Folk would call him mad to wander through an unknown wood in the dark on nothing more than a whim, but he pressed on over last year's leaf fall, moving slowly and carefully between tall, fat-girthed trees. Moonlight fought its way through the summer foliage, spattered the ground and sparkled now and then on the rush and splash of the stream. The land rose swiftly on his right and rapidly became a cliff face to which trees clung with roots like gnarled hands. Soon the land on his left matched it and Harry halted, staring ahead at a stream gushing down through a narrow ravine.

A small tributary dashed in from the left. Harry followed it up the slope and it brought him to open land. Smooth meadows rose twenty or thirty feet and then levelled out. Above them, a dark outline stood stark against the indigo sky. That must be Aydon Hall, perched on the headland above the ravine.

No lights showed at the windows so high above. But then, it had taken him an hour or more to follow the winding stream through the meadows, and longer still through the woods. Harry grinned in the dark. Father would call him a romantic idiot for turning aside for a pretty girl. Father excelled at strategy, in confusing his enemies, in always being in the right place at the right time, and despised pointless excursions that brought no reward. Harry knew his own talents veered towards seizing opportune moments and following gut instinct.

Harry shifted in his saddle. He wasn't worried. Father must have been romantic once in his life, for he doted, in his stern, unbending way, on Harry's mother. Harry clicked his tongue and urged Bessie on. This wasn't romance, but sheer, bloody-minded nosiness. He drew rein and stood beneath Aydon Hall in the darkest half of the night.

He had time to waste. If he didn't get beyond the old wall tonight, it would not matter. His mission would take all of three weeks, possibly more. What difference could a few hours make?

Harry's father had ignored his battalions of spies and chosen to engage his middle son in a daring, secret foray across the border. *He knows I'll succeed.* Harry smiled, and shrugged off the possibility of danger. After a whole two years of boredom confined in the stuffy, tension ridden rooms of the king's court where the heady mix of perfumes and fright made a man's head ache, what could be better than being out in the cool night air, with an adventure about to begin? Better by far than hanging about at court waiting for greedy men to decide if they should petition the king before dinner, after it or wait until morning.

He looked up at the hall. It was imposing, though not overlarge, and also crenellated, which was not unusual in these times. Marauding Scots and greedy reivers pushed a man into being sensible. To defend his property, a man needed a parapet and something to hide behind while he aimed his arrows.

Harry expected to own something better one day. With the benefits of a good education behind him, a strong physique and his father's support, he should manage it before he was much older. Wharton Hall, along with Nateby and Healaugh would go to George, and while he didn't begrudge his eldest brother the inheritance, Harry wanted something better than the ancient peel tower that would eventually come to him. He snorted in derision. He intended to have something far finer than Old Lammerside as his dwelling, and he was prepared to risk his neck to get it.

If he rode up the slope he would get a better view, see how big a place it was. There had to be a lane leading to the main entry gate, for no supplies could be brought in the way he had travelled tonight.

Urging Bessie up the slope, he wondered if there would be guards peering through the crenels. He didn't want an arrow in his back. Suddenly wary, he studied the parapet as he moved closer. Bessie heaved up the last of the incline and stood on almost level ground. Now he could see the length of high wall running away from him into darkness where the trees rose up on the other side of the ravine. Not a guard in sight. He rode on, and halted Bessie before the massive gateway. A beast bellowed in the byre behind him, and another answered.

He looked around. All was in shadow but for moonlight hitting the rounded curve of a high drum tower midway along the wall. He could learn nothing more about Aydon or its young mistress tonight.

Time to give up and ride on.

Probably just as well. Charming as Alina was, she was not the rich heiress of his dreams. Smiling at the foolish whimsy that had brought him here, he turned Bessie, followed the lane from the gateway and rounded the corner of a farm hind's cottage. Shadowy grey in the moonlight, the lane stretched away into the distance. Beyond the thick hawthorn hedges, fields rose to the ridge where the Romans built their wall so long ago.

A muted cry reached him, and another.

Harry pulled his horse to a stand. Frowning, he looked around.

He heard the faint sound of hooves thudding against the earth, the moan and bellow of disturbed beasts.

Harry scanned the fields, and finally saw the moving black dots trotting across the slope, heading diagonally towards the wall. The words of his guide resonated in his mind. *'Lessen o' course the Armstrongs be ridin.'*

It might not be the Armstrongs, but somebody was riding tonight. Harry stared, all thought suspended. Was he watching a raid take place? It seemed he was. Fascinated, he watched six or seven men round up the beasts and chivvy them into one dark, moving mass.

He ought to rouse the owner of Aydon Hall. He turned Bessie and urged her back to the hall. Strangely reluctant to head back the way she had come, she pranced on the spot. "Come *on*, Bessie!"

The mare made up her mind and lunged towards the castle. Harry looked over his shoulder. The moving black circle was much further across the hillside now. Pushing Bessie into a canter, he covered the half mile back to the hall, rounded the corner of the hind's cottage and ran smack into a bunch of horsemen and cattle blocking the lane.

Bessie flung up her head and stopped of her own accord. Harry scanned the group warily. In the shadows, faces were no more than grey blobs but Harry was certain of three men, though less sure of the cattle that milled around him. The wide door of the byre stood open behind them.

"Get 'im, Will!"

The order was given in a whisper, but it sent a chill down Harry's spine. He heard the short sound of steel drawn from a scabbard, and wondered if he would get a dagger in the chest. Abruptly he wheeled Bessie and threw her into a gallop back along the dusty lane. He heeled sharply around the hind's cottage, saw a fence looming and set Bessie at it.

Christ! This was madness! He had no idea what lay on the other side of the fence. But he had a short start while his adversary forged his way through the cattle, and wasn't about to present himself as a clear target for the man's knife. Bessie landed in what looked like a cabbage patch. Ahead lay a run of rickety planks, a dilapidated fence streaked by moonlight, all that stood between him and open fields. Bessie snorted, cleared it with ease and ran on. Harry glanced back and saw his pursuer's shaggy pony leap nimbly over the rails.

Thank the Lord for moonlight. He set Bessie for the distant woods, threw his weight back in the saddle as she skidded down the incline, hunched over her shoulders as she stumbled and steadied at the bottom. He set her at a dead run and glanced back. Bessie would surely beat the pony on level ground. Trouble was, the trees drew closer. He would have to slow down or ride straight into them. And that would pitch the mare straight into the ravine.

Impossible.

He looked back.

The rider came on. The pony covered the ground at an amazing speed. The rider's arm drew back, something silver flashed in his hand, something that streaked past Harry's shoulder and buried itself in the turf to the left of Bessie's front hooves. Quicker than thought, she shied to the right. Harry flew out of the saddle.

He sucked in a breath but there was no time to cry out. He hurtled through the air, crashed into the tree and dropped to the ground.

***

Alina lounged against the cool stone merlon of the crenellated parapet, tipped her face to the early morning sun and thanked the Lord that no one could read her thoughts. If Harry Scott's dancing blue eyes had run through her dreams all night long, no one knew of it. Nor did they know that now, after the upheaval of overnight raiders and stolen cattle, thoughts of the handsome stranger still filled her mind.

She remembered his warning shout, and the athleticism with which he had leapt onto the cart. He had truly put his own life in danger to save her. The memory of his devastating smile flashed a spasm of excitement through her innards. He'd also bawled at her like an idiot when she moved too slowly to suit him.

Biting back a smile, she wished for the thousandth time his name had not been Harry Scott. She doubted she would ever see him again. When she told him of her father's hatred for the entire family Scott she'd not seen a moment's distress cross his face. Thinking back over his reaction, she suspected he had been relieved he would not be meeting her family.

Opening her eyes, Alina stared at the pigeons hugging the Aydon roofline. By now Harry would be riding through the Borders towards Edinburgh, and who knew where he would go after that? Better if she forgot all about him and concentrated on settling down to be a good wife and mother. It was a sobering thought.

The chosen bridegroom would likely be John Errington, the younger son of the family over at Sandhoe. John had played with her and Lionel on fair days and at local gatherings, but once the boys' education began in earnest, she'd not seen him. In her father's eyes, John was ideal husband material. His family connections were good, with lots of links to the lords of Langleydale and Allendale, and he would undoubtedly keep her in comfort for the rest of her life.

But did he own the quickness of mind and body to save her from a charging bull? She doubted it. Would her stomach tighten at the sight of him walking through the courtyard? Probably not.

"Look! They're ready to go."

Her brother's voice sounded odd. Roused from her daydream, Alina glanced along the length of the alure and clicked her tongue in alarm. Lance and Cuddy, like most boisterous lads of thirteen and seven, lay belly down across the grey stones of the battlements so they could peer down into the outer yard.

In spite of the danger, the sight of two pairs of brown woollen hose and sturdy boots made her smile and shake her head. Moving swiftly, she grasped the youngest boy's belt for fear he'd disappear headfirst over the wall and crash to the ground sixteen feet below. Cuddy's head twisted around, and his bright seven-year-old face beamed at her. "They'll thoon catch the reivers and bring back the cattle, won't they, Ally?"

"I hope so, Cuddy."

Keeping her grasp of his belt, she leaned over Cuddy's shoulder and looked through the crenel into the outer courtyard of Aydon Hall. Her father, astride his sweating gelding, held the reins in one hand and an eight-foot lance in the other. His steel cap and coat of plate reflected the sunshine in a dazzle of light as he twisted and turned in the saddle to view his motley collection of followers. Impatience jangled through every line of his hard, stocky body.

He opened his mouth and roared. "*In line!* In line *behind* me, you idiots!"

Pigeons took off in a clatter of wings from the roof ridge. Alina bit her lip to hide a smile as the troop tied itself in knots trying to form a double line behind her father. She should not laugh, for the men were farmers, not soldiers.

"There's Lionel!" Lance yelled from the other side of the merlon.

Alina followed Lance's pointing finger and saw their brother jockeying for position with Matho Spirston. "If he doesn't watch out," Lance said with a snigger, "Matho'll have pride of place behind Father."

"Take care you don't fall and join him," Alina warned.

Lionel would be mortified if the head stockman's son beat him to the front of the line. As the eldest of the Carnaby boys, he was now eighteen, wearing his new jack and conscious of his importance. Alina looked at Matho with affection. Mother Spirston still lived in a tiny cottage up on the hill at Halton, and Alina sometimes visited the old lady when she went to church. Some three years older than Lionel, Matho had always been the undisputed leader of the gang of children who fought and played together among the scattered farms, cotts and cabins that composed the Aydon Township. With the advantage of three years growth over Lionel, Matho usually found it easy to grin and shove the younger boy out of the way, but now Lionel was catching up fast. She hoped the old friendships would not change too much as Lionel came of age and took on more responsibility alongside his father.

The sound of heavy breathing announced her mother's arrival, panting at the unaccustomed exertion of mounting so many stairs up to the wall-walk.. Alina turned in time to see horror cross her mother's face at the sight of Lance's boots waggling so high in the air.

"Alina!" she gasped, stretching out to grasp her son's tunic. "What were you *thinking?*"

"I have a firm grip of Cuddy, Mama."

Mistress Carnaby hauled Lance back, kept her grip of his tunic and peered over his head into the grassy courtyard below.

"Dear Lord," she murmured, gazing on her husband. "How does he think to pursue raiders with but fourteen men, none of them with any armour?"

Cuthbert Carnaby, unaware of his wife's worries, chose that moment to brandish his lance in the air. Face flushed with heat and excitement, he roared out an order, then, with a final flourish in the direction of his family, wheeled his horse and headed for the gateway. The ragged column of riders followed.

"They are strong and healthy, Mama. All will be well." Alina waved and saw Lionel glance back as he rode out under the stone arch with Matho seemingly resigned to third place. A fierce grin stamped her brother's lean, craggy face. He knew his own importance now.

As the last horse trotted beneath the stone arch, Lance wriggled back to the walk-way and tugged his tunic down over his long woollen hose. "Can we follow them, Mama?"

"You may go no further than the gateway."

Alina helped Cuddy, still small for his age, shuffle back down to the alure and once his boots hit the stone both boys raced towards the narrow doorway that led down to the inner courtyard. The lady of Aydon watched them go and let out a vast, gusty sigh. Her shoulders slumped. "Alina, Alina…what if he fails to come home? What then? He should not go when Reynold is so like to die."

Alina hesitated. In normal times Uncle Reynold, as lord of the manor of Aydon, would have led the men after the raiders. But since he was confined to his bed in the downstairs hall, Father, in charge of everything while his brother lay dying, must follow the reivers' trail.

"Father wants to go, Mama." She struggled to keep impatience out of her voice. "So does Lionel, and so do the lads. They love the chance to tear off on a Trod, you know that."

The unwritten laws of the Hot Trod decreed a man might follow the reivers with hound and horn in order to recover stolen goods. Neighbourhood men between the ages of sixteen and sixty had a duty to aid and attend the victim by chasing the raiders. Should a man refuse, he would be lucky if he wasn't thought to be in league with the enemy and made a fugitive at the horn himself.

If some of the Aydon tenants and farmhands weren't exactly eager, they knew their duty. Once they noticed the absence of cattle in the byres and yards after daybreak, they sighed or grinned according to their nature, and headed for Aydon Hall knowing what was expected of them. Now they rode out on borrowed horses to chase the thieves, and it didn't really matter if the miscreants proved to be Scots or English.

It didn't signify. The reivers of upper Tynedale were every bit as vicious as the thugs of Liddesdale, and stole from the English as often as they stole from the Scots.

"Our boys are but farmhands and stable lads," her mother complained, clutching the heavy cross at her throat. "How can they be successful against lawless men who live by shifting and thievery?"

Alina thought of Matho Spirston, with his flaming red hair and temper to match, prepared to jostle her brother Lionel for second place behind her father. He could likely hold his own with any of the thugs that roamed the border. So could Gilbert Reynoldson and Robert Cooper. If men like John Wilson and Geordie Pike were less forthright and hardy, they were still keen to ride out with the others.

"They must get the livestock back, for that is our livelihood and sustenance through the winter. Do not worry, Mama. Father will soon catch and deal with the thieves and he will be home before we have time to miss him."

Her mother sighed. Alina walked slowly along the wall-walk.

"I often wonder which fool built access to the alure through the kitchen, don't you, Mama?" She spoke lightly, hoping to distract her mother from the dismal prospect of an injured husband. "But I suppose the watch-guards like it because they can creep in and get warm by the fire when they come off duty on a cold night." Alina shuffled sideways, watched her farthingale bend through the narrow door and jumped the few steps down into the kitchen. "I should go to the Horse-field," she added, "and make sure they did not take Dragon."

Her mother sniffed. Her hoops were wider than those of her daughter and had to be carefully eased between the narrow stone door jambs. "You care more for that old mare than you do me."

Alina paused to offer assistance as her mother negotiated the stone steps. There was good reason to worry, for not every man came back unscathed from a Hot Trod. Some didn't return at all. She smiled to soften her reply. "Nay, Mama you know that is not true. I do not think they will have taken her, for she is too old, but I must be sure. I shall ask Marian to make you a posset as we go through the kitchen."

"I should not have to ask a servant girl when I have a daughter to attend me."

Alina put a comforting arm around her mother's thin shoulders. Normal good sense would return, she knew, as soon as her mother got over watching her man ride out to do battle. "Then I shall do it when I come back, but I must know if my old horse is safe. I shall go straight to the field and back." She ducked her head to check her mother's expression. "You shall not truly mind, I think?"

Mistress Carnaby did not smile, but she waved a hand in a gesture Alina took as agreement.

Alina paused as she passed by the stone sink, asked the maid working there for a claret posset to be prepared for her mother and headed for the main stairs. Across the courtyard she spied both Lance and Cuddy at the gate in the curtain wall, staring after the troop of men and horses. She looked north and saw nothing but a plume of dust in the sky to show where sixteen horses and riders rode the mile towards the square stone tower of Halton where her grandfather lived.

Fourteen farmhands, full of excitement, bearing weapons pulled out of the armoury that morning. At least they were young, fit men, and would be joined by her grandfather's more seasoned campaigners once they reached Halton. A band thirty strong would soon set out after the raiders.

Lance demanded to know where she was going and pulled a face when she told him. "Come with me if you like."

For a moment she thought the boys would follow her, but they shrugged and stayed where they were.

She left them kicking their toes in the dust. No doubt they wished they were old enough to ride out with Father and Lionel. The raiders put everyone at risk. An image of Harry Scott flitted unbidden into her mind. She hoped he managed to avoid the reiver band as he rode north. Even if she never saw him again, she hoped he would stay safe.

She hurried through the Stack-garth and the heavy dew of the Night-fold knowing she ought to forget Harry Scott. He was naught but a passing stranger. But strangers were a rarity in Corbrige where the whole district seemed related by marriage or blood ties, and bloodlines could be traced back four generations or more.

At the hurdle gate she hesitated. An icy hand touched her heart when she saw no calm brown mare among the buttercups of the

Horse-field. She bit her lip in anxiety, for the mare could not travel at the pace reivers would enforce. Sliding between the wall and the hurdle, she sent up a swift prayer, lifted her skirt and petticoats and increased her pace as she hurried down the grassy slope. She scanned the alders and birches that bordered the burn trickling through the meadows towards the deeper ravine that held Aydon Hall in the crook of its arm.

Her horse stood half-asleep in the shade of an ancient oak. "Dragon!"

The mare blinked as her mistress approached. Alina pressed her cheek against the horse's warm neck. "Dear old Dragon."

A soft whicker reached her, and for a moment Alina took no notice. Then she realised the sound had not come from Dragon, and lifted her head. At the stream's edge, half-hidden in the dappled shade provided by the old oak tree stood a tall, handsome chestnut, saddled and bridled, but minus a rider.

Chapter Three

Alina bit back a gasp at the sight of the strange horse. Her fingers tightened on Dragon's mane. She scanned the mass of trees along the edge of the ravine, for they formed a dark, shadowy world where any number of men could hide. Had raiders stayed nearby? They might plan to attack again, now the Aydon men had ridden away. She cast an uneasy glance along the banks of the Halton burn, and regarded the horse once more. It was a gentleman's horse or one of the good quality animals used by officials and messengers. The saddle, shiny with use, looked old, and the rolled pack tied behind it was not large.

The horse nosed something in the grass.

Something that looked suspiciously like a body.

She stood on tiptoe and peered over Dragon's warm back. Whoever lay there did not move.

Curiosity drew Alina forward, one hand outstretched, crooning to the mare. The chestnut allowed her to approach, blew over her knuckles and then swung its head round and down to nuzzle at the body sprawled close beneath its hooves.

He looked dead. Alina caught her lower lip in her teeth. It might be a ploy. He might leap up and attack her. She debated running back to the hall to get assistance, but the figure looked oddly familiar. On impulse, she crouched beside him, poised to flee if the need arose.

His back and chest moved as he breathed. There was no blood visible, nor a wound of any kind. One gauntleted hand lay close to the side of his head, fingers relaxed, but the other stretched out as if pointing to something. His legs, in plain hose and tall riding boots, seemed straight and undamaged.

A hoof clicked against a stone as his horse moved off to join Dragon.

She ought to go and rouse the servants, and have the rider thrown in the dungeon jovially referred to as Aydon's goal. She paused. All the fit men rode with her father. She rose, stepped over the stranger and glanced at his profile. Her heart thudded an extra, heavy beat, and she took a hasty step to catch her balance.

The man who chased through her dreams half the night lay at her feet.

She crouched at his side and drank in every detail of his shape and form. Warmth bloomed in her skin, her heart beat increased and the world narrowed to the dark, spreading bruise marring the clean perfection of his forehead.

Dark stubble thrust through the unblemished skin along the strong jaw and thick black lashes shadowed his sun-browned cheek. His nose was short and straight, and his mouth looked ready to release the wonderful smile she remembered so well. Black hair fell over his brow, and his broad velvet cap clung precariously to the crown of his head.

A brooch winked and gleamed at the brow band.

She removed the cap and studied it. He would not want to lose the jewel.

A late primrose peeped out from beneath his chin, and vetches and mosses tickled his nostrils. A small spider travelled over the leather glove and on into the long grass. The vigour and energy, so much a part of Harry in Corbrige's crowded market place, slept now. Her hand hovered over his face and then hesitated.

What was he doing here?

Attacked and left for dead, or was there a more mundane explanation? He lay underneath one of the old oak's thick, low branches. Both sword and dagger were sheathed at his waist, so he had not expected a struggle. The ground showed no flattened grass, no strange hoof prints in the mud of the stream and his horse, now cropping grass beside Dragon, showed no signs of a long chase.

"Well, the reivers would have stolen his weapons and this jewel if they found him," she murmured, eyeing the blue stone in his cap with a critical eye. It was not a sapphire of the first order, for there was a flaw through the centre of the stone. Not that raiders would have noticed had they found him in the dark. She looked up at the thick, gnarled branch that swooped towards the ground. "I suppose, then, he rode into the branch and knocked himself off his horse. Silly creature."

She remembered Harry's athletic ability in Corbrige, and found it hard to believe such a simple thing might have felled him. Still, horses were nervous creatures. If a rabbit ran under its nose in the dark, in strange territory, it was possible the horse jinked aside and dislodged its rider. "What do you say, Dragon?"

Her mare flicked her tail in response.

Alina's gaze returned to the young man. He wore the serviceable doublet she remembered from yesterday with a leather jack, which looked new, over the top. Her brother Lionel owned one like it. The leather would be stuffed with wool and likely have horn plates stitched inside for protection. Her eyes widened on the lace attached to the edge of his collar.

She had not noticed lace yesterday, but then she had been looking at him rather than his clothes. A thread of silver wound through the silk of his shirt cords, and the ends were tipped with silver aiglets. His doublet and breeches were of good heavy woollen cloth, though plain and not new, for the sleeve was worn at the cuff. Beneath the dust and mud his boots, too, were of fine-grained brown leather.

Her father and older brother wore clothes like this when they worked around the estate, saving their expensive velvets for more formal occasions. She looked at the young man's peaceful face. This was no farm boy, but a gentleman come to grief.

He had been here for some time, for a line of moisture crept up the fabric of his clothes from contact with the dew-wet grass. She ran her palm over his back and disturbed the gauzy layer of moisture on the surface of the leather jack.

What if he rode with the raiders? If Father saw him, he would assume Harry to be part of last night's raid and would have spiked him through without a qualm. Was she safe crouching over him like this? If he was a raider, he would have no guilt about killing her in order to escape.

"Are you come to kill me, or help me?"

The croaky, laboured voice caused her to drop his cap and jerk backwards. Her heart loosed a single mighty thump against her chest wall. Poised to rise and flee, she saw that the man made no effort to move. She frowned. He hadn't sounded like Harry at all. His eyes were open, but only as mere slits. Careful to stay out of reach of his arm, she bent low to peer into his face. It *was* the same man.

She prodded his shoulder. "Harry?"

His eyes closed again.

"Sir? Sir?"

His lids lifted with a great effort. "Yes?"

Alina shuffled to one side, so he did not have to adjust his line of vision to see her. "What are you doing here?"

His lids closed once more. "My head...hurts."

"You have a swelling. There."

"Ahhhhhh!"

She whipped her finger back from his brow. "I'm sorry. I did not mean to cause pain."

One of his eyes opened to the merest slit and regarded her with displeasure. "My horse has a gentler touch than you, Madam."

"Well!" Alina could not decide if she should laugh or be affronted.

"No," he said. "Since you ask, I am not well."

"I didn't ask."

"Then you should have done." He closed his eyes again.

Alina stared at him. What was she to do? His name was Harry Scott, and hurt or not, her family would shun him or kill him. But he had cared enough to save her from the bull, so she owed him something. She would never forgive herself if she walked away and left him.

Yesterday the intensity of his gaze made her heart flutter.

Today he behaved as if she were a stranger.

Birdsong flooded from the branches above. Dragon dozed in the sunshine. The stranger's horse moved a pace or two out into the meadow and continued to graze. Could she keep him hidden? Father was away, but could return at any moment. She turned back to the prone figure.

"Can you move?"

His dark brows drew in towards his nose while he considered the matter. "I doubt it."

"I can't move you on my own."

"No need to move me. Just let me be. Sleep...would be...good." His voice slurred on the words and his eyes closed.

Alina leaned over and shook his arm. "You can't sleep here. Someone will find you, and then it will be all over. There was a raid last night, and folk will think you were a part of it." He took no notice, so she shook him again and raised her voice. "Do you want to die today?"

He groaned, and his hand lifted, fingers splayed, to stop her rough shaking. "Enough, I am awake."

She sat back on her heels and surveyed him. "I shall have to go and get Auld John to help me. I hope you are not too heavy, Harry."

He stirred at her movement. His hand grasped the fabric of her skirt in a strong grip and his voice sharpened. "You know me? Know my name? Wait. Help me sit up."

Alina snapped out one word. "Please."

It was the kind of reply she gave Lionel when he tried his new found authority on her. Lionel didn't like it when she stood up to him, but she was the elder and had no intention of being brow beaten by her brother. Harry, however, was unmoved. He stared at the damp hem of her brown skirt as if fascinated by it.

"You are correct," he said. "I am sorry. Would you *please* help me sit up? I shall do my best to assist." Resigned amusement flavoured his apology.

Lionel never reacted like this. Alina made no move to help him, but studied the lines of his face and remembered the oddness of his earlier remark. What did he mean when he asked if she knew his name? "How do I know you won't attack me?"

He groaned. "By the Rood! How will I manage to attack you when I can't sit up? You could fell me with a hazel twig at the moment."

She smiled at the frustrated resignation that rang through his voice. "Can you turn over? It will be easier if you are on your back."

"I can but try." His mouth lifted in a crooked smile.

She observed his careful sequence of movements with a critical eye. Each limb seemed sound, and when he rolled over and stared at the spreading canopy of green leaves above him, she could not help but gasp, for his eyes glowed like sapphires in the soft light beneath the tree.

"Where are you?"

"Here." She moved closer, confident he would not hurt her. "Can't you see me?"

"I can now you've moved." His eyes flickered and squinted as he struggled to focus on her. "What lovely eyes you have. I hope they are kind eyes. If I move my head it makes me dizzy, so just now I prefer not to, if you don't mind."

Full face, he was as attractive as in profile. Her heart gave an odd little jerk. "Then how am I to move you?"

His eyes moved slowly. "We seem to be in a meadow out of sight of any dwelling. If I stay here awhile, the dizziness will pass away." His gaze settled on something behind her right shoulder. "My horse? Is that my horse?"

Alina glanced at the leggy chestnut. "Yes. Were you attacked?"

He frowned. "I have a vague memory of avoiding someone or something. Beyond that, I cannot remember much at all. Where are we?"

"We're in Horse-field below Aydon Hall. All our fields have names," she added before he could ask.

But Harry focussed on essentials. "Aydon Hall?" He squinted. "Who are you?"

Shocked, she stared at him. A pang shot through her. Had he forgotten her already?

"I told you yesterday," she snapped. "I'm Alina Carnaby." Piqued that he did not remember her, she tried not to show it. "My father is Cuthbert Carnaby, and my uncle is Sir Reynold of Aydon Hall."

"Yesterday? We met yesterday? The name Aydon rings no bells with me. Where is the nearest township?"

"Corbrige." Alina frowned. She disliked the sharp tone of his voice. What was the matter with him? Was he lying? All her worries returned.

He raised a hand to his brow in a puzzled manner. When he offered no answer, she asked what seemed to her a silly question, but one that needed to be asked. "Who are you?"

He gave her a charming, rueful smile. "I wish I knew."

"Come, sir, this is no time to play games with me. You gave me your name yesterday." Irritated, she shifted to ease her knees.

The glance he slanted at her was a complicated mix of wry amusement and concern. "Would that I could tell you, Alina. I cannot remember anything beyond riding in the dark, though why I do not know." His gaze travelled beyond her to the heavy branches of the old oak. "Though it is a venerable tree, I doubt it holds any answers."

"I expect you clouted your head on it as you came up the slope. Can you not remember your own name?"

He flinched as his fingers found the sore place on his brow. "Much as I hate to admit it, the tree seems to be the answer." Without any hint of shiftiness or the crafty leers she was used to among the common men of the market place, he held her gaze for a long moment. "In good faith, I cannot tell you my name."

Astounded, she stared at him while the breeze moved over her skin. What must it be like to not remember who you were? She sat back on her heels, using her hands to keep her farthingale down. "You told me your name was Harry Scott, and you were riding to Edinburgh," she reminded him. "You were in Corbrige yesterday, and you saved me from the bull. Do you not remember *any* of it?"

His eyes widened. "I saved you from a bull? I'm sorry, but no. There's nothing in my head but a headache. In a way, it's an interesting experience…you must tell me the whole story sometime…"

"Why were you riding in the dark? What were you doing here? You can't have business with my father? No one opens their gates after dark."

The young man raised a hand to stop the flow of questions. "Good Lord," he said weakly. "You go at a gallop, do you not?" He placed one gloved palm flat on the grass, and tried to push himself upright. She grasped his other arm and steadied him. With a huge effort he sat with knees wide and legs crossed at the ankle. He gripped his shins, shut his eyes and rolled his lips inwards.

"Are you all right? How do you feel?"

"Dizzy," he said. "I should step back if I were you. I might spew."

Alina scrambled to her feet. He might be handsome and make her heart beat faster, but she had no wish to be in the line of fire, so to speak. He did look a strange green colour. She stooped, picked up his cap, shoved it in her pocket and glanced over her shoulder. There was no one about. Her glance passed over the wooden shelter Dragon used in the winter. She frowned, then considered it more carefully. Perhaps it would do. It was snug, built of old oak planks, tucked in beneath the high curtain wall. There was clean dry straw inside, for she had ordered one of Auld John's lads to the task yesterday. Rats were all too easily attracted to old straw.

She glanced at the stranger, and back at the shelter. Perhaps it stood too close to the hall for his safety. Auld John might lean over the wall as he sometimes did when he wanted a breather from shovelling dung from the byre, or shifting the odious piles that built up with monotonous regularity beneath the garderobes on this side of the hall.

She could think of nowhere else. She studied Harry until the green shade receded from his skin.

"There is an old stable up the hill," she suggested. "You can hide there until you feel better. Do you think you can walk? Or ride, perhaps?"

He laughed behind the palms that covered his face. He removed his leather gauntlets, and a sapphire flashed on the smallest finger of one hand. It matched his eyes. His hands, she saw, were as beautiful as the rest of him. She felt an absurd longing to take his hand and hold it to her face.

"Ride?" His voice verged on incredulous laughter. "I doubt it. But I could hang on to the stirrup and let the horse drag me along."

The effort of hauling a six-foot, well built man onto his feet made her breathless, and staggering ten paces proved an exercise in frustration. But it was strangely exciting to touch him and feel his weight on her shoulder. She had never been this close to a man who was not a relative.

She glared at him, panting. He sat, head in his hands, after his third fall. "I had no idea it would be such trouble to hide you. This is hopeless. Can you not call your horse?"

Somehow she got him on his feet again. Sweating with effort, buried beneath his broad shoulder, she twisted her head and growled at him. "Call!"

Swaying, he gazed at the mare. "I can't remember her name."

"Then whistle!"

It took him a moment to gather enough breath to do it. They were both relieved when the chestnut lifted her head and ambled over. "Now, grab onto the stirrup leather," Alina guided his hand. "I'll stay by your side. No, that's no good. She won't know where to go."

Alina detached herself from Harry's grip, went to the chestnut's head and hooked her finger through the bridle. She looked over her shoulder. "Ready?"

Harry's fingers tightened on the stirrup leather. Alina clicked her tongue and the horse walked forward. Harry lurched, staggered and fell without a sound. Alina groaned in despair. The mare stopped and looked round.

"Stay where you are." Anger laced his voice and kept her by the animal's head.

He sounded as frustrated as she was herself. He grasped the mare's foreleg and clambered to his feet, then hung onto the saddle until he caught his balance.

"How lucky she's a good tempered mare," Alina remarked, stroking the velvety neck. "Now all you have to do is move your feet. She will pull you along."

Harry lifted his head. "Easier said than done. And the sarcasm doesn't help, by the way."

Startled, she shot him a wide-eyed glance. "I wasn't being sarcastic. We'll have to do it, Harry. I have to get back soon or someone will come looking for me and then you'll be discovered."

"Then I presume they'll throw me in the dungeon. Not a good idea."

She liked his sense of humour, and smiled in encouragement. He gathered himself for a final effort. He looked rather green again. Hoping he would not notice, she moved to the other side of the mare. Sympathy was all very well, but if he vomited over her gown it would be difficult to hide his presence from her nosy brothers. Or her mother.

Somehow he matched his feet to the stride of the horse and they found themselves at the door to the stable.

"There! I knew we could do it. Give me your hand."

"Don't sound so cocky, young lady. Where…"

He let go and clutched the worn doorpost as if the world swayed around him. Alina swooped forward and kicked straw into a deep bed against the wall. "Don't worry, it's clean. Dragon sleeps outside when it's warm."

"I couldn't care, at this moment, if it was alive with rodents." His eyes closed. He took one step, pitched forward and she only managed to steady him for two paces before he fell into the straw.

"Oh, Harry!"

It was no good. He was beyond her irritation and instructions. He was now either asleep or unconscious and she could only leave him to sleep it off. Lionel had been like this once, she remembered. He missed the mark at tilting practice and forgot to duck when the sandbag swung round on the long arm of the quintain and caught him on the back of the neck. It knocked him unconscious. Everyone laughed at her fears, said he would be all right come morning.

He had, of course, so perhaps she worried needlessly.

Alina heaved Harry's legs onto the straw. She took an old blanket from a peg on the wall, shook it out and draped it over him. Mama would say he ought to be stripped, washed and have hot bricks packed around him but she did not have the means to do it. Thank goodness it was summer. She had no idea how she would feed him, but she would worry about that later. Now, she must hide the strange horse, and hurry back to the hall before she was missed.

She removed the chestnut's saddle and bridle and dumped them in the shelter, then hobbled the animal out of sight of the castle. "Look after your master. I must go."

She found Harry's gauntlets in the grass and threw them into the shadows by his makeshift bed in the stable. The only sound from the occupant was deep, steady breathing. She listened for a moment, then turned and ran back up the hill.

For better, for worse, she had taken the risk of hiding him. Now she had to ensure no harm came to any one because of it.

Chapter Four

Aydon Hall, June 1543

The hasty scramble up the slope from the Horse-field made Alina's heart pound, and she paused at the head of the stairs to take several deep breaths before she entered the hall. Mama, not in the best of moods today, would not be pleased to see her daughter panting like a squire fresh from exercise.

Her glance roamed the quiet courtyard. A stack of new ashlar blocks lay shaped and ready to replace the worn, two-hundred-year-old wooden staircase on which she stood. The stonemasons rode with her father today, and the resulting silence, after days of hammer and chisel on stone, was wonderful.

Mama would be horrified to know that her daughter harboured a strange male in Dragon's stable. Facing the thought head-on, Alina wondered if she had been unwise. Harry was so different to the local lads. Already her ear was attuned to the timbre of his voice and knew she would recognise it among a thousand others. When she looked at him all sorts of unfamiliar feelings stirred: shock, admiration and a twist of…not fear exactly, but excitement, certainly.

Rather like finding a wolf in the sheep pen.

She liked everything about him.

Except that his name was Scott. That name so hated by her father and grandfather.

Alina shrugged, turned and entered the building. She had made the decision and now she had to deal with the problem. *Put him to the back of your mind and go and talk to Mama. Do nothing to endanger him, or bring trouble upon the family.*

Head held high, she walked with straight shoulders and a graceful stride. No need to give Mama the chance to complain about poor posture.

Mama sat ramrod stiff within the pool of sunlight flooding the lancet window. A basket of cardings stood at her feet and a smaller basket of spun wool lodged on the table at her elbow. Alina's spindle lay on the smooth wood like an unspoken rebuke.

"You have had time enough to ride to Corbrige and back."

Alina sighed, and knew from the irritation in her mother's voice that she had been gone too long. "I beg your pardon, Mama."

Her mother rattled her fingers against the side of the smaller basket. "I have spun all this wool."

The unspoken words *'without your help,'* rang in Alina's mind. A twinge of guilt flared and died. "I am here now, Mama." Alina's linen skirt billowed around her as she sank to her accustomed stool, took up her spindle and a clump of wool from the basket and set to work.

Almost at once her thoughts flew to Harry, now hopefully sound asleep in Dragon's shelter. Perhaps after a good night's sleep he would remember his identity.

"Well? Shall you work today, or not?"

Alina started at her mother's sharp words, and lifted the spindle once more.

"There are grass stains on your skirt, Alina." Mama sniffed. "Is it not enough that I fear for your father and every able-bodied man has ridden off on this wretched Hot Trod and left us unguarded? Must I worry about you, daughter?"

Alina concentrated on the spindle in her hand. "There's no need to worry about me, Mama."

"And the grass stains?"

Alina looked down. The long green stain was so obvious against the brown fabric she did not know how she had missed it. It must have happened when Harry's weight felled her to the ground. Sudden memory swamped her and she recalled the smell of leather in her nostrils, his weight across her shoulder and the feel of his wrist in her fingers. He had been so much heavier than she expected.

"What is the matter with you, girl?"

The impatient voice brought her back to reality. "I thought to hide my clumsiness, but now I see I cannot avoid it. I stumbled going down the hill."

"Alina, your childhood is behind you. Soon you will be married, if your father's negotiations are successful, and Dear Lord," she added, raising her eyes to the ceiling, "let us hope that they are. How will you instruct servants and run a household if your staff laugh at you behind your back? You must learn to behave with dignity and decorum."

The complaint had become habitual over the last three or four years and now had little impact. Alina stole a glance at her mother. The clear light lit every line engraved on Mama's face and deepened the frown ridges carved across her brow. Her eyes were pink-rimmed, as if she had been weeping. Alina felt a twinge of sympathy. It could not be easy to have a husband ride off on a Hot Trod and worry, with some justification, that he may never return.

Her natural optimism expected Father to ride back into Aydon unscathed, but until Cuthbert Carnaby greeted his wife once again, Mama would fear for his life. Alina sought a topic to distract Mama from her worries.

"Do you know the man I am to marry?" She kept her voice light. "Has Father decided once and for all on John Errington? Or has he changed his mind again and forgotten to tell me?"

Mama studied her work in order to avoid Alina's eye. "Get on with your spinning. It is not for me to say. Your father will do so when he is ready."

Alina leaned forward. "But you could give me a hint, Mama. In what direction does he ride when he has my marriage in mind? If he rode west it would mean the Erringtons."

Her mother's lips tightened to suppress a smile.

"A hint, Mama? A tiny hint? Does he go east or west? North or south?" Alina lifted a hand to her mouth and pretended shock. "Not *north*, Mama? Surely not one of the Tynedale families? He would not, would he?"

"Do not be so foolish, girl." Mama flicked a glance at Alina, saw she was being teased and almost smiled. She shook her head. "You shall not get around me like that. You know your father would never marry you off north of the border. Neither would he consider one of the infamous riding families in Redesdale."

Alina frowned as if deep in thought. "Then he must be looking east or west, for there are not many who live south of the Tyne. The Erringtons would be best of course, for they have so many good connections, but he may prefer one of the Blackett boys. He surely does not look as high as the *Shaftoes*?"

Her mother put down her spindle. "You can wheedle all you like, daughter, but I shall not reveal your father's plans. Indeed, I do not think they are complete yet."

"I suppose I am not likely to be married in the next two weeks, then." Alina tossed her long plait back over her shoulder with a cheerful smile. "After all, you would want time to make a new gown for my wedding, would you not?"

The sun shining through the tall windows warmed Alina's skin. The grey kitten wobbled across the floor, mewing until she bent and scooped it onto her lap. "I'll have to keep you away from the big yard cat." She tickled its clean pink tummy, and the kitten yawned. "That old tom might do you an injury."

Her mother nodded towards the tiny creature. "Your father will not tolerate the animal around his feet for long. I know you doused it to get rid of fleas, but it will have to go outside."

"I know. But she will soon grow, and when she can fend for herself, she can go outside. Until then I shall keep her in my room and she can chase mice around the attics."

Her mother lapsed into silence, and Alina's thoughts slid back to Harry. Had she been unwise to hide him? It posed a considerable risk, knowing her father's hatred of all Scotts. His temper had been uncertain all this summer.

"Your father's life has been difficult this last year or two."

Guiltily, Alina looked up. Had Mama read her mind? "I know. Johnny Woodrington's death last year was a blow to his plans for marrying me off."

Mama heaved a sigh. "Johnny would have been an ideal match for you, daughter. Same age, same station in life, good rich lands that would come to him in time." She shook her head. "And then he catches the sweating sickness and dies three days later. So much planning and negotiation. Almost two years gone to waste."

Biting her lip, Alina hid a smile. "I'm sure Johnny didn't do it deliberately to annoy you and Father."

"That sounded hard and cold, Alina. I have warned you before about your flippant attitude."

"I am sorry, Mama, I did not mean it so." She ducked her head. "But I hardly knew Johnny. I suppose we must give thanks the disease did not come to Aydon."

Mama regarded her doubtfully. "Indeed. But it meant your father must begin negotiation all over again and it was not easy, let me tell you, though you do nothing but laugh about it. Most of the young men were already spoken for. I know Cuthbert found it trying when he received naught but refusals." She picked up her spindle. "By now you should have had a child in your arms."

"I don't mind, Mama. I am in no hurry to marry."

"Alina, you are no green girl but you still have your head full of nonsense. It is long past time you were married. A grandchild in the house would have been nice," Mama added in a wistful tone, and then shrugged. "But since the Good Lord has seen fit to send illness to your uncle, it is something of a blessing that you are still here to take over some of my tasks." She shook her head. "That was another thing that upset your father. It meant he had to take over all Reynold's duties here as well as his own."

"I know uncle's illness upsets him."

"And as if that was not enough," Mama went on, "there were the responsibilities of rank. Meetings and endless attendance on the Wardens whenever they demand it. Thank the Lord there are only three of them, though at times it seems like there must be three times that number. Setting watches, organising rotas, writing reports, calls to arms. Alina, you have no idea how your father hates it all."

"He seems to be more accepting of it these days." Alina spoke carefully, gauging her mother's state of mind. "I remember he was actually smiling when he returned from the Lord Warden's last summons."

Her mother frowned. "He was, wasn't he? Something to do with John Foster being fooled by a couple of naughty rogues from Coquetdale."

Alina went on spinning. Mama was right. Father had a lot on his mind these days.

It would probably be safer for Harry and everyone else if he left as soon as he could ride. It would not do for Father to discover that she had been hiding a Scott almost on the premises. Father was unlikely to do her bodily harm, but she could not be sure he would be as forgiving with Harry.

The kitten's head twitched, wide blue eyes focussed on the wool twisting into a single strand over its head. It lunged for the wool, missed and toppled to one side. Alina chuckled, and settled it safely in the valley between her thighs, thankful her thick skirt and petticoat shielded her from the sharp claws.

Harry might well sleep through the rest of the day undisturbed, and possibly the night too.

Her mother sighed. Alina looked up. Mama, her eyes tight shut, clutched the spindle against her stomacher.

"Please do not worry, Mama. Father will be hot on their heels by now."

"It should not have been your father's responsibility. This…this ugly old house is Reynold's property." Mama glared around the stone walls as if they were to blame for her current situation.

"But it will soon become father's property if Uncle Reynold does not recover."

Her mother's hands fell to her lap, and the strands of wool, lacking tension, unwound. Tut-tutting at her own carelessness, Mama shook her head. "He took ill early in May, and here we are, mid-way through June. I doubt he will recover now."

"I expect you wish we were at still home, Mama. Grey House is more comfortable than this old place."

"Aye, I would be more comfortable there, to be sure. But we could not in all conscience leave your uncle Reynold to servants, and I imagine they would have applied to your father about the raid even if we had been still at home." She looked up. "And Reynold set the stonemasons to do all this work, and your father insists it must go on. The noise they make is enough to drive one demented."

"It is good to have day's silence without them."

Any moment now Mama would mention, as she often did, that since Sir Reynold's wife had died two summers ago, the responsibility of caring for him in his illness had fallen on her. Alina breathed a sign of relief that his three young daughters had been taken to live with their maternal grandmother at Shortflatt, but a few gentle miles to the north east. Their presence would have been an added burden on Mama.

The kitten reached out for the twisting strands with a tentative paw, and tumbled off Alina's knees. Claws dug in, held on and this time reached her flesh. Alina winced at the sudden pain, scooped the kitten up in one hand and placed it on the floor.

A sniff made her look up. A tear trembled on her mother's lashes. "Don't cry, Mama. Father will return safely, you shall see. The men are loyal and brave, and he has Lionel to support him."

It was the wrong thing to say, for her mother clutched both hands tight to the dark velvet at her breast. "Oh, Lionel!"

Alina sighed. "Lionel is eighteen, almost nineteen, and it is high time he rode out with Father. If he refused, the men would laugh at him behind his back. You know that, Mama."

Margery applied a scrap of linen to her eyes and then cast a sharp glance at her daughter. "You, I suppose, are glad he has gone. You would not care if he was hurt, or…"

"Of course I should care, Mama."

Her mother bit her lip. "I remember once you threatened to smother him with a feather pillow if he did not stop tormenting you."

Alina laughed and lifted the wool out of the kitten's reach. "That was years ago. There was a time I would have given anything to have been born a boy so I could knock out his teeth for teasing me. It doesn't mean I do not love him."

Margery sniffed and allowed herself a small smile behind the scrap of linen. "Come, girl. I must look in on Reynold for a little while. I suppose I must keep him apprised of Cuthbert's decision to ride out."

Almost there, Alina thought. Her mother would soon be back to her normal, cheerful self.

Later that afternoon, when the sun sank below the tree tops, a servant came in to light candles and replenish the fire in the stone hearth. Alina put down her spindle, got to her feet and kissed her mother's cheek.

"Where to now?" Her mother's gaze followed her to the door.

"I need activity or I shall run mad. I promised Dragon an apple. I shall come straight back."

She often slipped out after the last meal to feed Dragon a small handful of grain filched from the sacks stored in the lower hall, mainly because it was one of the few opportunities she could be sure of time to herself. No one would think it strange if she did it tonight. She could easily conceal a small flask of water beneath her skirt, and some bread. Better than have him wandering down to the stream to drink come morning.

The lady of Aydon snorted. "As if a horse understands a promise."

Alina turned, one hand clasping the door. "You know Dragon understands my every word, Mama. Besides, I must keep any promise I make, even if it is to a horse."

She made her way to the Horse-field. Taking food to Harry had seemed such a small thing in the candlelit warmth of the solar, but quite another once she was out in the deepening twilight beneath the safety of the walls. Would she have dared attempt it under Father's wrathful eye? She doubted it, and knew how angry he would be if he could see her now.

Dragon's old stable was a patch of dense shadow. What if Harry had gone? What if he had died, alone and without a hand to hold? What if some other vagrant had slipped in and waited to seize her?

Alina shuddered, breathed deep and marched to the doorway. "Harry?" She halted, one hand on the door jamb. The smell of hay and horses met her nostrils, plus another scent she knew must be him.

"Come in, Alina." His voice was quiet, but she welcomed it.

"How did you know it was me?"

A gleam of white flickered in the shadows. "I know your voice, of course. And you need to be more careful if you want to creep up on people."

She turned aside, scrabbled beneath her skirts and brought out the small leather water flask. "I've brought bread and a hunk of cheese. It was all I could get tonight."

"My mouth waters at the thought."

"Where shall I put them? I cannot see." She groped a step forward. "It is so dark in here."

"Here, beside me. Better if I don't move around too much."

She took a second and third step towards the sound of his voice, stooped and then hesitated, unsure. His hand, clamping about her wrist, made her jump. "Why are you doing this?"

"I don't know." She'd asked herself that question. "Yes, I do. You saved me from the bull."

"Ah. So you feel obligated, and over an incident I cannot remember." There was a short silence. "Consider your debt discharged. Helping me may place you in jeopardy, and I cannot allow that."

She could make him out now, a vague shape in the dim light. She plonked the cheese at his side.

"I know the risks. I want to help." She wished she could see him more clearly. Was he smiling, or not? "Would you rather I handed you over to the Lord Warden? Always assuming you have not forgotten what a Lord Warden is."

There was a small silence. Straw rustled as he moved. "I remember the post but not the incumbent. He would be…?"

"Sir John Forster, Lord Warden of the Middle March. Or the Deputy Lord Warden at Carlisle. His name is Wharton."

"Wharton?" He shook his head. "I feel I ought to know the man, but…." Alina heard the sound of his fist thumping against the straw bed beneath him. "I cannot even tell them my name. And why would you hand me over to them?"

"In this part of the world, not knowing your name could be as much an asset as a drawback. Can you recall *nothing?*"

Alina saw his shoulders rise and fall. "Very little. It is an odd feeling."

"I don't want anyone to know you are here, so I won't be handing you over. You can ride away tomorrow."

"You said there was a raid here last night?"

"They took all our cattle, and Father is out after them now."

"He did not wait for the Warden?"

"Father believes in doing the job himself. A Hot Trod is lawful pursuit of reivers. He has the men, the horses, and would rather be after the rogues at first light than scurrying off trying to find Sir John while the trail goes cold."

"He has but six days to recover whatever stolen goods he may."

"You can remember that?"

Harry tipped his head back against the wooden wall. "I do, oddly enough."

"He might not be away the whole six days. The thieves know every fold and wrinkle of the hills, and Father may lose them. He could be back at first light."

"And already you regret helping me?" His voice held a warm, teasing note, as if he smiled. "You could deny all knowledge of me." He shifted his shoulders against the wall. "I could have found this old stable without your help."

"How could I ignore you? You were hurt, and you saved my life. I don't regret helping you. I haven't done much beyond bring you bread and cheese." She hesitated. "I could say I never saw you, but Mama would find that hard to believe. She is already curious about the time I spend with my horse. She doesn't like to be alone when Father is away, and it is worse because my brother Lionel rides with him for the first time. She fears for both, and wants me with her always."

"So she will remember how much time you spend out in the fields. You had better return at once." His gaze moved beyond her to the doorway. There was a new, authoritative tone to his voice that she had not heard before. He spoke like a man used to command others.

"It grows dark, too. I do not want you to take more risks, Alina. You have done enough. Go now."

Chapter Five

Alina rushed through her tasks next day and tried to give the impression that she had nothing more exciting in mind than a pleasant hour's reading in the orchard. Mama ensured the household tasks were understood, left the servants scurrying about and ventured downstairs to tend her sick brother-in-law at her usual time. Alina gave her a few moments to settle and then whisked out through the storeroom and down to the fields.

Already the sparkle of dew on the grass and hedgerows had disappeared in the heat of the sun. She ran into Dragon's stable and dumped half a stotty cake and a wizened apple beside Harry. "It's fresh made and there's cheese inside. How do you feel this morning?"

"More cheese." He grinned as he opened the cloth.

"Beggars cannot be choosers." She regarded him steadily in the daylight filtering through the door of the cabin. His hair flopped over his brow, his beard had come in overnight and he looked older with the dark fuzz along his jaw. Older and much more mature; a man, not a boy. A small hot dart flickered through her innards and vanished.

He bit into the round of bread and cheese. "Better." The word came out muffled, but his blue eyes sparkled as he looked at her.

Alina ran her palms down the blue linen of her skirt and wondered if he would notice how much care she had taken with her appearance today. The pleats of her fine linen chemise had taken some time to arrange so that they showed to her satisfaction in the wide neckline of the dress and the small gold cross, a last minute addition, hopefully drew attention to them.

She tossed his bonnet to him. "I found that in my pocket last night." She did not add that she had slept with it under her pillow in case someone should find it and ask awkward questions.

He nodded, and went on eating with furious energy. But then, he'd had little yesterday, and she knew from experience how desperate her brothers became if not fed every few hours.

"There's nothing wrong with your appetite," she observed. "Good."

He met her gaze and held it as he chewed and swallowed. "You look pretty this morning. I experimented, too. I walked to the stream and back without falling once." He took another bite, found the cheese and groaned in appreciation. "This is good."

Apprehension hit her like a blow to the stomach and eclipsed his remark about her looks. "I hope no one saw you. I brought you water last night. You had no need to wander outside."

Still chewing, he shook his head. "I checked first, Alina. No one saw me. Now I know I can walk, I shall leave tonight, under cover of darkness. I do not care to bring trouble upon you."

She sniffed, unhappy about his decision. However dangerous it was, she wanted him to stay, but knew that such a thing was not sensible. "We agreed that's how you hit your head in the first place, by travelling in the dark. Where will you go when you cannot remember who you are?"

"Because I rode into the branch once doesn't mean I'll do it every time I ride in the dark. It doesn't really matter where I go."

He thought of her safety before his own. She mulled that over for a while, and found she liked him for it. "There's an old sunken track through the fields," she said at last. "Follow it and you'll reach Dere Street, the old road north."

He wolfed down the last of the bread and cheese and got to his feet. "Show me."

She'd forgotten how tall he was. Even though he steadied himself with one hand on the wall, he positively towered over her.

"You're not exactly fit yet, are you?"

"Fit enough." He got to the door and bit back a soft exclamation. His hand clenched on the doorjamb and he squinted at Alina over his shoulder. "Who are these two?"

A hand clamped around her heart. Surely they had not been discovered? Then common sense reasserted itself and she guessed who stood there. Alina rushed to the door and gazed down at her younger brothers.

"Lance! Cuddy! What are you doing here?"

The boys' hazel eyes, true Carnaby eyes, flickered from Alina to the stranger and away again. Lance backed a step or two, grabbed his brother's arm and dragged Cuddy with him.

"We c-came to see if we c-could have a r-r-ride," Lance stuttered. Cuddy peeped around Lance's shoulder. "On Dragon." Lance collected his wits and glared at his sister. "Who's he?"

Behind her brothers the sun lit the meadow with a green radiance, and the blue sky hung like a huge bowl behind the Halton trees. A few yards away, Dragon cropped the grass, her tail rhythmically swishing away flies. Everything seemed peaceful, but Alina knew her secret was out. Her mouth dry, she walked out of the stable, stood beside the two boys and placed a hand on Lance's shoulder, which he immediately twitched away, and a protective arm around Cuddy.

"These are my brothers," she said to Harry. "Lance is almost fourteen and Cuthbert is seven. Now what do we do?"

Harry stared at them, and the boys, wide eyed, stared back. After a moment, a wicked grin curled the ends of Harry's mouth. "Can you keep a secret, lads?"

Cuddy looked at Lance, who did not hesitate. "Of course." He said it with a hint of a sneer.

Alina bit her lip. "It's hardly fair to involve them. Father has a swift temper, and he'll whip them if he finds out they knew you were here and said nothing."

Harry shrugged. "But they know I'm here now, so what else can we do?" His blue eyes met hers. "Unless I go now, this minute."

"But it's not safe, someone will see you!"

"Then we don't have much choice, do we?" His eyes crinkled with amusement, and his smile was warm.

She did not like his logic, but could not argue with it.

Lance stepped forward. "We can keep a secret." His scowl dared his sister to contradict him. "And we've been whipped before. We know what it's like. What's the secret?"

Cuthbert, his eyes as round as those of an owl, nodded several times.

An absurd rush of pride in them made Alina smile. "Good for you," she whispered.

Harry bent his long legs, slid down the doorjamb and sat in the sunshine. "Sit, lads and let me tell you a story."

Immediately the two boys squatted in front of him. Cuddy's thick brown hose wrinkled sadly about the knees and his fingers immediately went to his round-toed shoes, nervously bending them forward and back. Lance, stalwart as ever, sat and stared at Harry. They were good lads. Three heads turned simultaneously, and she realised all three were waiting for her. Lance frowned. "Sit, Ally."

She saw they liked Harry. In that strange way of children, they had somehow judged him and accepted him. They wanted to help. She wasn't sure if it was wise to involve them, but after a swift glance around to see that they were unobserved, she sat, her back to the doorjamb and remained silent. She was as curious as they to hear whatever Harry decided to tell them.

"You'll laugh at this, lads, but remember my feelings and don't laugh too loud. I rode out a couple of nights ago, and lost my way in the forest." He gestured to the ravine behind them.

The boys nodded as if they knew the many tracks down the ravine to Corbrige better than any one. They probably did, Alina thought.

"Then, to make things worse, I rode into a tree branch and cracked my skull. There, do ye see the bruise?" He pulled his hair back to show them the purple swelling on his forehead.

Cuddy's round hazel eyes widened. "Doth it hurt?" Alina smiled at him affectionately. He only lisped when he was nervous.

"Don't be daft. Of course it hurts." Lance wriggled as he turned to Harry. "Go on."

Harry nodded solemnly. "It laid me out unconscious for the best part of the night. Bessie must have been going at a fair lick up the hill when I connected with the old oak tree by the stream."

He hesitated, and Alina met his swift, considering look. He hadn't been able to remember the name of his mare yesterday, but now he had. He looked vaguely surprised, and shook his head as if to sort out whatever memories existed within his mind.

A warm glow enveloped her as she watched him. He handled the boys well, in spite of his worries. Perhaps lack of memory meant no worries at all. Whichever it was, she found herself content to sit back and listen. His voice was mellow, and if her gaze lingered on his mouth, travelled now and then to his muscular throat, sometimes settled on his long limbs, why should it not?

She liked the way he used his hands to help shape the picture he put together for her brothers, admired the way he sounded his words so clearly and in such contrast to the slurred speech around her every day. She could listen to him forever and never grow bored.

Lance gazed out over the field. "But where—"

"Bessie is hobbled along the stream. Out of sight of prying eyes like yours," Alina told him.

They all looked at Harry.

"So...there I was, sleeping like a baby when your sister found me next morning. Your father rode off after the raiders and she helped me into the stable. I've been asleep ever since."

Lance looked at her with mingled respect and puzzlement. "Why didn't you bring him to the house?"

"I couldn't, Lance." Already, away from her mother's sharp ears, she heard herself echoing her brothers' casual speech patterns.

"Why not? Mother loves guests, you know that."

"His name is Harry Scott."

"Oh." Lance looked from Alina to Harry and back again. "Really? Like the Scott family across the Border?" His lip curled back from his teeth. "You're one of *them*?"

His tone indicated exactly how the Carnabys thought of the unfortunate Scott family.

"I'm afraid he might be," Alina said. "And you know how Father feels about the Scotts."

Lance grimaced and ran his forefinger across his throat.

"Why does he hate them?" Harry linked his fingers together and stretched them in front of him. The joints cracked, and Cuddy flinched.

"You, you mean. Why does he hate you? You're one of them," Lance challenged.

"It's a long story." Alina rushed to cover the awkward moment. "Uncle Reynold made himself unpopular with a reiver called Archie Scott. Archie led a revenge raid against Uncle's lands at Halton and Whittington. He caused a lot of damage. When Uncle followed, they led him into a trap, and it cost a fortune to free him. Then last year a gang of the Scott family assaulted him and his father at the Stagshaw Midsummer Fair."

"Uncle Reynold never went out again after reivers." Lance took up the story. "Now Father's gone instead. He says it's because Uncle Reynold's too ill to go, but I think it's because Uncle's scared of the Scotts."

Alina hastily intervened. "However much you think it, you should not say it, Lance. Especially not in front of strangers. Uncle Reynold is really very ill."

"That's right, Lance. You don't know who I am." Harry stopped short, as if he'd remembered something unpalatable. He waved his hands in the air. "*I* don't know who I am."

Alina hadn't expected his comment any more than the boys. They absorbed his words and then glanced at each other. "You mean hitting the tree branch knocked your brains out?" Lance, as the older, voiced what they were both thinking.

Harry chuckled. "No. It means my memory isn't working very well at the moment. It's a temporary state, I hope."

"What will you do if it dothn't ever work again?" Cuddy's voice reminded Alina of a reed whistle.

"Oh, Cuddy, don't ask such silly questions." Alina frowned. "Of course his memory will come back."

Lance swung round on his sister. "But how long will it take?"

"I don't know. It could take a few minutes or a few hours. Maybe a few days, but I hope not."

Lance stared at Harry with new respect and curiosity, as if willing his memory back again. "Can't you remember *anything*?"

She remembered asking that question yesterday. It seemed so long ago, and her feelings for him had grown so much since then. When Harry sent a quick, amused glance in her direction, the warm glow expanded inside her.

Harry tilted his head. "Well, I can remember how to talk, for a start. And I can remember how to ride, and my horse's name. She'll take me to Edinburgh without any bother, and—"

In the sudden vast, empty silence, Alina leant forward, her teeth sunk in her lip. What had he remembered? He'd obviously recalled something.

Harry sat immobile, his expression frozen, his gaze on Lance as if the boy had given him all the answers he needed. Lance opened his mouth, but Alina shushed him with a movement of her hand. A bee flew by Cuddy's ear. He flinched, but did not move. Both boys sat cross-legged on the grass, hazel eyes fixed on Harry.

Alina watched him, too. She had the nastiest feeling he was about to thank her kindly and tell her he was leaving. She didn't want that. Though the risk increased a thousandfold should her father arrive home, she wanted Harry to stay much, much longer.

"Phew!" Harry drew his fingers down his cheeks so hard she could see the pink inner rims of his eyes.

His hands ran over the top of his head, and his fingers clasped at the nape of his neck. As he tensed his spine against the pull of his clasped hands, he laughed in delight and Alina realised how much the memory loss must have worried him. When he let go and looked at them all, there was a new, brighter sparkle in his eyes and all the lines of his face curved up, rendering him more handsome than ever.

Alina could not match his joy. She could not summon even the briefest smile. If he had remembered everything, he'd leave at once.

"What's the matter?" Lance asked Harry.

"I know who I am."

"You've remembered? Your memory'th come back?" Cuddy beamed.

Harry nodded and turned to Alina. "You told me my name was Harry Scott, and of course I believed you. But now I *know* it, I know it all…I can remember my father, my home and why I am going to Edinburgh—I can remember everything."

***

Once the fuzz cleared from his mind, Harry kept his thoughts private. He talked with the boys, assured them that though his name was Scott he was not related to those dastardly Scotts north of the border, and all the time he knew he must ride north and forget about their sister. He should never have been this close to Aydon.

He cursed the imp of mischief that had made him guide his horse in this direction. She was an attractive girl, and would make some country gentleman a suitable wife one day soon.

Unlike the wife of his dreams, who must be rich.

He had wasted two whole days when he should have concentrated on his mission. Frustration beat hard within him.

Alina, he noted, said nothing. She obviously wanted rid of him.

Come full dark, she would have her wish.

***

Mid-afternoon, Lance pounded across the hall and burst around the solar door. "Father's riding in!"

Mama dropped her spindle with an exclamation of joy. "Thank the Lord! Come Alina!" Rising, she crossed herself and hurried towards the door.

"Coming, Mama." Alina rose more slowly. Relief flowed through her at the news of her father's safe return, but doubts gnawed at her. It was much too soon. Harry had not yet left. How was she to keep him secret with her father's men swarming over the place?

Lance checked that his mother was out of ear-shot. "Lionel's strutting all over the place like the farmyard rooster, but Father's ill-tempered."

Alina anchored her spindle and faced her brother. "Why? Did he not bring back the cattle?"

"Some of them, but not all. I don't know why, and I haven't asked Lionel."

"Lance, is anyone in the hall?"

He peered around the door and shook his head.

"Then I think you should sneak out of the postern gate, and warn Harry. Be very quick. Tell him to go at once. I'll make sure no one notices you've gone missing for a few minutes."

While her brother sped off on his mission, Alina walked out through the hall to greet her father. "I am glad you are safe home, sir."

His face held the haunted, harassed look that had become habitual of late. He favoured her with a brief smile. "Thank you, Alina. How does my brother Reynold?"

"Little changed, sir, since you saw him last."

A grunt was his only answer. He swept by her, one palm holding his sword flat to his thigh as he leapt up the staircase two at a time.

Alina stared after him. Was it possible Father grieved more over his brother's illness than he ever admitted? She glanced around, saw Matho and smiled, glad to see him safely returned. Matho winked and lifted his hand in salute.

Lionel, his hair flattened to his skull by his steel cap and a streak of dirt down one cheek, bent and kissed Mama's brow. "The men called it a runabout raid," he said. "There wasn't one trail to follow, but dozens. They must have split up the beasts and gone in different directions once they got beyond the wall."

Alina listened, mildly amused at his nonchalant attitude. How he had changed in the last few months! Mama let go of Alina's arm in order to lift her skirt over the steps. A flash of movement caught Alina's eye. She looked back and caught sight of Lance as he darted through the gate. He nodded and smiled.

Hopefully Harry would get away from Aydon before anyone discovered him.

Behind her, Lionel excused himself in order to go and see his horse safely bedded down." He stalked away, heading for the stable. Lance and Cuddy exchanged glances and flew after him.

"They will plague him for details of the trod," Alina said, laughing. Privately she thought that if she did not hurry down to the field now, she may never see Harry again. She glanced at her mother, slowly mounting the steps. Her duty lay there, but Father was home now and surely it would not matter if she stole a few moments for herself to see Harry one last time.

The urge grew stronger. She turned towards the gate.

"Alina. Alina!"

No, oh no, not now, Mama. Alina schooled the disappointment out of her face.

Mama smiled and beckoned from the head of the stairs. "Come, Alina, I need you. There is much to be done."

Chapter Six

When Cuthbert Carnaby entered the solar, bathed and splendid in clean linen, crimson velvet, pale hose and round-toed shoes, Alina looked at her father with newly awoken appreciation. With his dark hair, high cheekbones and hooked nose, he was still a handsome man with a fine length of leg. No wonder Mama adored him.

Father strode to the hearth, turned and warmed his backside before the flames. The sun shone through the west window, where Lionel lounged in the window seat, warmed the stone walls to a soft grey and streamed across the floor to reach Alina tucked up on the eastern window seat. The family relaxed in the knowledge that, barring a catastrophe of some kind, no one would interrupt them.

Suddenly aware that Father watched her, she glanced up and found him studying her in the same calculating way he gazed at a prize ram in September. Almost as if he gauged the quality of the progeny to come. Unease prickled along her spine and turned her mouth dry. She raised her brows in exaggerated query at her elder brother.

Lionel, bathed and changed into an old velvet doublet rapidly becoming too small for him, frowned and shook his head. That was a bad sign. Her sense of unease grew with each heartbeat.

"I spoke to Errington today." Her father paused, gauged everyone's reaction. Alina heard the name and her stomach plunged. Father eased up and back on the toes of his soft leather shoes, always a sure sign that he was pleased about something. "I rode home by way of Sandhoe," he added, and glanced at his two younger sons, seated close by on wooden stools. "You know who lives there, boys?"

"The Erringtons, Father." The flames turned their cheeks rosy and glistened on the moist whites of their eyes as they chanted the answer in unison.

Lionel stared at the floor and would not meet her gaze. Alina's skin prickled and crawled beneath her gown.

"Correct." Father beamed at the two boys. "It is a large family, related to the Lords of Langleydale. Do you remember where Sandhoe is?"

"On the other side of Dere Street," Lance said. "It's the tower house that looks down on the river, Father."

Alina raised her brows and mouthed one silent word in Lionel's direction. *What?*

Her brother offered a turned down mouth in a gesture that said all too clearly she wasn't going to like what was coming.

Her father swung to her. "It is a family of some standing, and they have made an offer for you, daughter."

"What?" The offer of marriage was not exactly a surprise, but with her head full of dreams of Harry, Alina had no idea how to react. Her fingers grasped the edge of the stone seat while Father's dark eyes regarded her with something close to satisfaction.

"They have made an offer of marriage, a good match that makes up for all the time lost with the Woodringtons."

"Happy news at last." Mama spoke from her chair by the fireside, and exchanged pleased glances with her husband. Lionel offered a small shrug and a pitying half-smile. The two younger boys merely looked surprised. Alina stared at her father.

He was waiting for her to bow her head and thank him. She remained silent, words locked in her throat.

"Well?" The one harsh word warned Alina he grew impatient for her response. Her mother got up and held a spill to the fire, then moved slowly, her hand shielding the flame, to the candles in the dark inner corners of the room.

Alina moistened her lower lip, and cleared her throat. "Will it be Thomas, or John, Father?" It surely could not be Ralph, for he was far too young.

"John. As you will remember, he is much the same age as Lionel."

"But younger than me, Father. Thomas is five years older—"

"Thomas is betrothed to an heiress in York. While we wasted time with the Woodrington boy, the match was made for Thomas."

John, suddenly, was not an entrancing prospect. Her father waited. Alina watched exasperation alter his expression. She ought to speak and say something that would please him.

Lance shuffled on his stool. "Does this mean a wedding, Father? Here, in our hall?"

The boy's question relieved the growing tension. Their mother, satisfied with the soft, shifting golden light of the newly-lit candles, retreated to her chair. Carnaby beamed once more. "It does indeed, son. Your mother will arrange things, and it will take place soon. As soon as can be arranged, in fact. Probably within a month."

Mama contemplated her embroidered slippers. "The hall must be lime-washed to hide the stains and soot marks before we have important guests. This would be a good time for a pattern to be painted on the plaster, husband."

Carnaby glanced at his silent daughter. "Would you like that, Alina?"

"It would make the hall look better, Father."

If he thought a pattern of vine leaves painted on a wall would make up for being married to John Errington, then he had no idea of her feelings. She glanced at her mother. Mama would never openly oppose her husband, but she might be persuaded to delay things.

"I hoped to be married from Grey House, where I grew up."

"You can forget that notion," her father snapped. "There will be tenants in there soon. Now that I have so many more duties I need a man to work the farm for me. This will become our home and I shall continue Reynold's improvements." A slow smile spread over his swarthy face. "John will come a-visiting tomorrow, so you'd better look your best, daughter."

Alina tried not to let her dismay show. "Yes, Father."

She swallowed hard against the constriction of her throat. She looked out of the window. A rabbit nibbled grass in the orchard. Such a small, defenceless animal. Where her father was concerned, Alina was as defenceless as the rabbit. It was no good pleading with him, and she was not stupid enough to mention that she wanted to wait and to see if Harry came back after completing his mission.

Chapter Six

Changed to a newer gown of brown velvet and a russet underskirt, her hair drawn back in plaits around her head, Alina joined her mother in the solar. Happiness gave Mama a glow that made her look younger tonight. Walking forward, she tucked her arm through the crook of her daughter's elbow. "I am so happy now they're both safe home, but I'm very much afraid we may never stop Lionel talking about the Trod. Come, daughter, let us go into the hall." She cast a critical glance at Alina's gown. "Why did you not wear the amber pendant I gave you? It would match so well to that gown."

Alina's hand went to her bosom. At dinner it was customary to wear a lighter chemise under a gown that left an expanse of exposed skin on view, and usually she enjoyed selecting a chain or pendant to fill the gap. "I forgot it, Mama. Should I go back?" Alina summoned a smile. At least one of them was happy.

Her mother shook her head. "No time now. You know how your father hates to be kept waiting."

Long boards on trestles ran alongside both north and south walls of Aydon hall, and servants not engaged in serving were already seated. Logs blazed in the large fire basket on the raised stone hearth in the centre, and the scent of pine and smoke mixed with the honey scent of thick beeswax candles.

Candlestands stood at each end of the cross table against the solar wall, for Cuthbert Carnaby liked to see what he was eating. As a precaution against outbursts of temper, two smaller candles squatted on the table to shine directly onto his dish. Red and blue wall hangings glittered in the firelight behind his tall carved chair, and pewter goblets and dishes gleamed in the mix of light.

Carnaby stalked in, sat down and glared around the hall. His wife took her place at his side without a word, and Alina slid onto the stool next to her mother's chair. Lionel sat on his father's left while the younger boys sat at the head of one of the two side tables, wedged on the bench between Father John, the boys' sword-master, and their grey-haired tutor.

Servants brought in food and everyone smiled, chattered quietly and kept a wary eye on their master. Carnaby ate a few mouthfuls of mutton, and glared around the room.

"Blasted raiders," he muttered to the room at large. He swallowed half a cup of rich red Bordeaux wine. "Tynedale men, and the ragtag and bobtail of the Borders hanging on for whatever they could get."

Men sipped ale, and smiled cautiously.

"You got most of the cattle back, dear, and everyone is safe." His wife's warm tone showed her relief.

Cuthbert's dark head swung round to his wife. Candlelight caught the tight frizzled curls and dark eyes that betrayed his Norman origins. "Robert Cooper might take issue with you on that. He got a nasty slash across his arm." His harsh tone softened. "His woman will take care of it."

"Was it a thord?" Cuddy's piping voice caught everyone's attention.

"Indeed it was, son."

"How big wath the cut?"

"From there to there." Carnaby touched his elbow and midway along his lower arm.

Cuddy shuddered.

"Is this boy going to be a warrior or a weakling?" Carnaby grinned at his wife, and turned back to Cuddy. "Am I going to have to hand you over to Father John for the Church, boy?"

"No, thir." Cuddy's eyes became huge with worry.

"He is but a few days beyond his sixth year, husband. Time enough for him to become a warrior."

"Cuddy doesn't like the sight of blood, sir." Lance stuck up for his brother. "But he's good with a sword for his age. Even Harry says so."

Alina stopped chewing and stared across the open space between the two tables. Lance didn't realise what he'd said. There was a sudden lull in the conversation as everyone tried to remember who Harry might be, and she saw comprehension dawn in her brother's eyes. In sudden frightened realisation of what he'd said, he swung round and met her wide frozen gaze.

Carnaby frowned. "Oh, well if Harry says so, then Cuddy must be good indeed." Enjoying his own sarcasm, he looked around the hall. "Who is this Harry?"

Anxiety ruined Alina's appetite. She could not swallow the lump of half-chewed, tasteless meat. She spat it quietly into her palm, and fed it to one of the dogs that nosed beneath the tables. The boys must have visited Harry without her. How else could he know of their prowess with a sword?

Lance squirmed on his bench. "Just a lad who lives in the village, Father. He's older than us."

"Then we'll take no notice of what he says, eh? You have a sword master and I pay him a good deal of money for his services." The sword master opened his mouth, but Carnaby cut him off. "I'll listen to what he tells me of young Cuddy's progress in the morning."

"I'm sure you'll hear a good report, sir." Margery smiled at her sons. "The boys work hard at their lessons. I hear them at practice every morning."

Alina knew that was a lie, for the simple reason that the stonemason's work drowned out the sound of the boys' sword play these days. She shot a glance at her mother, and sent up a prayer of thanks that her parents enjoyed a warm relationship. Would Mama's defence sway Father?

Carnaby grunted, speared a slice of mutton and ate it with relish.

Lance stopped squirming and let out a soundless whistle of relief. The incident seemed to be over. Alina stared down at her platter and wondered where her appetite had gone.

"Harry doesn't live in the village, Lance. He sleepth in the stable with Dragon." Cuddy's piercing treble filled the small silence.

Alina's heart leapt against her breastbone. Oh, Cuddy. Her skin turned cold and her mind went blank. Disaster was upon them. Everyone looked at the boys and then, because Lance stared at her, at Alina. Always one to voice her thoughts, tonight she could not think of a single thing to say that might avert what was about to happen.

"We have a stranger living in that wreck of a stable, Alina?" Father's voice was quiet, but she was not fooled. His anger was merely contained. He looked from Cuddy and Lance to Alina.

She smiled, but could not stop her mouth trembling. Blood prickled as it flowed into her face, and she gripped the heavy cloth of her skirts and,,out of sight beneath the table, scrunched it into a ball. She must protect Harry, but how? She looked at Lance and nodded towards the door, hoping desperately that he would have enough sense to slip out unnoticed and warn Harry he'd better leave at once if he hadn't gone already

"Alina!"

She jumped and met her father's hot brown glare. "Yes, sir?" She racked her brains to think of what she might say that would save Harry. From the corner of her eye she saw Lance push up from his bench. Good, he was going to warn Harry.

"Don't play silly games with me, girl. Who lives in the stable with that old horse of yours?" He saw Lance stepping over the bench. "Sit down, and finish your dinner, boy." Lance looked uncertainly at Alina.

"Sit, boy!" Carnaby roared.

Lance's eyes flickered as if he considered mutiny. Red faced and sulky, he slouched back onto his bench and stared at the table.

"I don't know what Cuddy means, Father." Her voice sounded shaky, and she cleared her throat. "Perhaps this is another of his imaginary friends. You know he—"

Cuddy shook his head. "Harry's my friend, and he's real. You like him, too." He looked at her as if she betrayed him.

Cuthbert Carnaby flung down his knife and bellowed to his Steward, stationed at the hall door. "Send down to the old stable. Bring anyone you find here immediately." He glared around. "We'll soon see if any one threatens the hall tonight. I refuse to be surprised by raiders twice in the same week."

Alina touched her fingertips to her brow and found her hairline damp with sweat. Had Harry gone? Pray God that he had.

Everyone waited and cast anxious glances around the hall. People went on eating, for food was too hard bought to waste, but Alina surreptitiously fed the remains of her meal to the hounds.

Her mother noticed, and shook her head in rebuke. "Why, Alina, I thought you liked roast mutton?"

"It's only a lump of gristle, Mama."

She clutched her hands so hard the small bones rubbed together. They had exchanged farewells that morning, but he spoke of waiting till dark before leaving. A hurried glance at the window told her the sun was still in the western sky. She could hardly blame Father for taking no risks with their security. If only Aydon had not suffered a raid this week, if Harry's surname had been anything but Scott, and if these wretched Border lands would settle down into some kind of civilised life. Oh, dear Lord, she could hear footsteps pounding along the passageway, and every head in the hall turned in anticipation. Alina sat motionless, expecting the worst. The Steward appeared. Behind him two guards jostled a tall man into the hall.

Harry looked bedraggled, but courage spoke through the tilt of his head and the way he carried himself. The white of his shirt showed through the tears in his doublet and his face and throat were patchily pink. They must have struck him. She supposed he would have resisted them, for she did not think he was the kind of man to give up easily.

His black hair hung over his brow and as they pushed him forward into the hall, she saw that his wrists were tied together behind his back.

Oh, Harry. Alina felt sick, yet filled with pride in him. Lance sat white-faced and still. Cuddy, obviously frightened, ran to his mother, who held him in her arms and made soothing noises.

The sentries marched Harry to the east end of the hall, towards the high table. He did not look for her, but stared grimly ahead. No doubt he thought she had betrayed him.

Father got up, walked the few steps around the table to confront Harry. They were of the same height. Her father carried more bulk, and the rich red of his doublet proved a strong contrast with the dull browns of Harry's garb.

The silence stretched on. Frightened but unable to look away, Alina watched Harry lift his chin and survey the lord of Aydon with a gaze neither cowed nor unsteady. The tendons of his throat stood clear in the flickering candlelight and the shadows around his collarbones swelled and died with his breathing. Her stomach quivered in response and she feared for him. Father might be lenient, if Harry looked frightened or begged for clemency, but this display of courage would only aggravate him.

She looked again at Harry's expression. A spasm of alarm ran through her. *For goodness sake, Harry, don't stare at him as if he is nothing more than a field hand.*

Cuthbert Carnaby obviously felt the same. The silence in the hall seemed ominous as he contemplated his prisoner through half closed eyes. His hand, heavy with rings, lashed out and caught Harry across the cheekbone.

Several feet away, Alina jolted on her bench as the blow struck. She gasped aloud, and her fingers clenched on the table.

Harry took an inadvertent step sideways. Dark hair tumbled over his brow. He steadied himself, tossed his hair back and faced his tormentor. He ought to be wary, but the tilt of his head was insolent.

"Who are you?" Carnaby demanded.

A thread of blood trickled towards Harry's mouth. A surge of heat and anxiety ran through Alina. She sat taut and rigid with her teeth clamped in her lower lip, unable to think of a single thing to say that might help.

"My name is Harry Scott." He inclined his head. "My home is in Carlisle."

Oh Harry! Why did you not lie? You know that name will enrage Father.

"What are you doing on my lands?"

"A fall from my horse meant I needed a day or two's rest." The wide shoulders lifted an inch. "I intended to move on as soon as I was able."

"A likely story!" Hot with excitement, Carnaby leered at the prisoner. "Rode here with the rest of your thieving relatives, did you? What a pity you got left behind. How inept of you!"

He thinks he's found one of the raiders, and he's pleased.

Harry glared at him. "Unhappily we can't all be fortunate as the man who talked an earl out of leaving his goods to his sons."

Oh God! Harry, no! He referred to Uncle Reynold, who talked the Earl of Northumberland into leaving estates to Reynold rather than the true Percy heirs. Blood rushed into her father's face and his fists clenched.

"Father, he was unhorsed and unconscious." Alina cried. She could not let Harry face this alone.

Carnaby swung round and glared at her. A cold shiver ran down her spine. *She had spoiled his pleasure and he did not like it.*

Harry's glance followed her father, and meshed with hers. His mouth tightened and he gave a tiny shake his head as if to say she should stay silent. His chin lifted. *Let me deal with this*, his eyes commanded.

"You know this man, daughter?"

"Only that I found him unconscious in the meadow, sir. He had suffered a blow to the head."

Carnaby turned from Alina. He grasped Harry's jaw in one large fist, tilted his head up towards the candlelight to search for bruises. "There is a mark, I grant you."

"He rode into a tree branch, sir."

Carnaby stared into Harry's face, and laughed. The sentries at either side smirked. Harry scowled. Alina guessed he hated to be made to look a fool. "It was dark!" she cried. "Any one could ride into a low bough in strange country in the dark."

The laughter slowed and stopped. The sentries looked at her father. She realised she had made things worse when Carnaby swung around and grinned at her.

"He was riding the night we were raided? Alina, are your wits addled?" He turned back to Harry. "It's a damned clumsy raider who gets knocked off his horse," he snarled. "But the Scotts are ill-bred to the last snivelling bastard, so why am I surprised?"

"I am no raider, sir. The fact that my name is Scott is pure chance. I bear no relation to any of the Scottish family of that name. My home is Carlisle."

"Anything to save your skin, eh?" Carnaby jerked his head. "Fling him in the dungeon. He can take the Leap tomorrow."

"Father! No!" Horrified, Alina sprang to her feet, unaware and uncaring that every eye in the room swung to her. "He is not a raider! You can't do this! I beg you!"

Lance was on his feet as well, his eyes wide and frightened. Cuddy buried his face in his mother's skirt.

The sentries hustled Harry towards the door. Alina ran to her father and grasped his arm. "Please, Father. He is innocent of any crime. He is not a reiver."

Surprised, Cuthbert Carnaby detached her hand. He stared at the three men heading for the door and shook his head. "Don't be a fool, Alina. The man's guilty as the devil. Now go back to your seat and eat your dinner."

She stood there, unmoving. "Father..." She backed away from him. "Father, I...please don't send Harry over the Leap tomorrow. He is innocent, and speaks truly."

"Are you listening to me, girl? What is this Scott fellow to you? Where did he come from?"

Alina seized her chance. He was listening, at least. "I met him in Corbrige when Mama and I went to market." She wheeled round. "You remember him, Mama? The young man buying needles for his sister?"

Her mother's expression remained guarded, but she nodded slowly.

Her father snorted in derision. "Probably means he was looking the place over for the rest of those rogues."

"He saved my life, Father!"

"Oh, get away with your wild ideas, girl! How could he save your life in Corbrige market?" He laughed at her. "Go and finish your meal. Stop mooning about him, and get yourself ready to meet Errington tomorrow. I won't hear another word on the matter. Either eat or get yourself to your bed."

"Then I'll go!" Alina ran from the hall without a backward glance. She tore through the solar, stamped up the rickety stairs to her tiny chamber in the attic and flung herself onto her narrow bed. Full of temper and frustration, she pounded her fists against the pillow and spared not a thought for John Errington. Her whole mind was focussed on Harry and his impending doom.

Chapter Seven

Harry lay flat on the damp, cold stone shelf and pondered the weight of the tower above him. Not so far above him, either, for if he lifted his arm his fingertips grazed the rough edges of the curved stones that made up the ceiling. A runnel of moisture oozed through the stones on his left, which made him think it formed part of the curtain wall that surrounded Aydon Hall.

He breathed cold, dank air. Too long in here and he would stiffen into a lump of lead. Wind gusted through the iron grill that closed off the entry and brought with it the damp smell of woods and leaves. At least the wind scoured the cell of noisome prison odours. Pity any poor sod thrown in here during the winter months. At least it was summer, and he was to be here only one night. He would not die of cold, though the stone shelf was far from comfortable.

It would be this infamous Leap of Carnaby's that would kill him.

Tomorrow.

He turned his head. Beyond the square bars, moonlight silvered the stones and grass of the outer courtyard and lit the dark bulk of the inner courtyard wall. Trees rooted in the ravine threw shadows that swayed and danced across the grass. The sound of the wind in the leaves came faintly to him in his isolation. Now and then a man's voice spoke a sentence or two, and someone replied, but they were too far away for Harry to hear their conversation.

The anger and shock of imprisonment had worn off after the first hour. The chill dark silence lulled him into contemplation, almost into acceptance of his fate. His mind moved idly over things past, and he smiled now and then. It was such a pity it was all to end so soon, and for such a stupid cause.

End it? Harry clenched his jaw. He wasn't ready to leave the world yet, not with so much still to do. The mission to complete, the rich bride to find, and a whole life yet to live. One fist banged into the other. How to get out?

Closer, so close he guessed they were only a yard or two from him, he heard the swift patter of scurrying mice. Very large, well-fed mice. He chose not to pursue the thought. Time enough to worry if they sought to join him on his rocky shelf.

Human voices caught his attention. He levered himself up on one elbow.

A woman's voice. A few broken words came into his cell on a gust of wind, and he swung his feet to the floor. Somewhere in the dark the pad of footsteps came closer. On his feet in a heartbeat, he clutched the cold iron grill in both hands.

"Harry? Harry?"

She came from the west side, where the main gate stood. Moonlight hit one side of the dark cloak that covered her from neck to ankles, and her hair, drawn back in a long plait, swung out behind her.

"Alina." Warmth flowed through him even as he worried for the risk she ran.

"Oh, Harry, I don't have long." A gust of wind belled her cloak. She shivered and dragged the edges together. "Matho is on duty tonight, and he's agreed to let me talk to you, but only for a brief while."

"Good for Matho, whoever he is. He should have been on duty the other night when the raiders attacked." He grinned like an idiot. She wanted to see him badly enough to risk sneaking out of the hall and across the courtyard in the dark.

"Father reamed them out for carelessness and now they're all extra vigilant. But Matho's my friend. We grew up together. Harry, I am so sorry! I had no idea Father could be so ruthless and I couldn't think of anything to say that would—"

"Don't apologise." Her hand flattened against the bars. Harry clasped her fingers, drew her hand through the gap and cradled it close against his chest. "You tried to help, and we knew it was always a risk." He kissed her cold fingers. "Another hour and I'd've been away. I should have gone in daylight, while I had the chance," he added with a rueful smile.

"But if I had been clever—"

"Shush, my darling. It is not your fault." He heard the endearment leave his tongue with vague surprise. Whether it was the privacy of darkness or the thought that after tomorrow nothing would matter, the words slipped easily off his tongue. He didn't dwell on it, for it hardly mattered.

"Tell me," he said, before he forgot all practical things in the delight of her presence. "Your father threatens me with something called the Leap. What is it?"

She dipped her head. He heard her sharp intake of breath, and the moonlight showed him the shadows of her puckered brow. "It's the ravine, Harry." She pointed towards the dark bulk of the hall. "On the other side is a ravine. It is deep, with the Ay burn at the bottom. Father...he makes prisoners jump from the precipice outside the hall."

"Ah." He raised her knuckles to his mouth, and kissed them to dispel the shadowy presence of Death looming in the darkness behind him. He remembered looking into the ravine the night he rode up here. His tongue probed the cleft between her fingers. She gasped. Harry's blood sang through his body, and he kissed her knuckles again. "How deep, do you think?"

"Twenty times the height of a man, they say." She shivered and frowned as she watched him nuzzle her fingers. "There are rocks and trees..."

"And no one ever survives?"

Her face crumpled. "Oh, Harry, sometimes they do, but they are broken, twisted creatures—"

A deep voice sounded from above, and Alina flung up her head. "Matho, please!"

Matho must have agreed, for she turned back to Harry. Her hand was warm in his and when he kissed it once more, her other hand came snaking through the bars and stroked his face, crept to the back of his neck.

"Ah, Alina," he murmured. "Would that we had no iron bars between us."

His flesh hardened. If this was his last night on earth, he wanted some pleasure to beguile his thoughts. He reached both hands through the grill. Obeying some deep instinct he drew her close against the iron bars and in truth she was not reluctant, even when his hand roamed beneath her cloak, caught a ribbon and her nightgown gaped from neck to waist. His palm found the firm weight and curve of her breast and nestled around it.

Warm, silky flesh and the sound of her gasp in his ear as his fingers closed on her.

Alina choked, pulled back and met the firm resistance of his palm on her spine. Murmuring her name, he continued to caress the miracle of smooth naked flesh. Elation flashed through him as the hard stub of desire unfurled and grew beneath his fingertips. She turned easily under his hand and her breath came faster.

"Oh, Harry! I cannot bear it…"

His fingers stopped instantly.

"Not that," she said. Her gaze raked the air above them both. Perhaps the invisible Matho lurked on the wall-walk above.

Without conscious thought, his fingers moved once more. She quivered in his hands, and her head went back, rolling from side to side. Her eyes were closed. Moonlight silvered the tear that rolled down her cheek. Something closed hard and painful in Harry. He let go her spine, moved his hand up and caught the back of her head in his palm. "Alina, kiss me," he whispered.

Her eyes opened. She released him and caught hold of the bars in both hands, pulled her body hard against the iron and angled her face to meet his. Harry licked the salty tear from her skin.

"Thank the Lord that the blacksmith made the grill squares so large," he muttered. She uttered a small, indistinct sound. He found her lips, explored them. She trembled, and he could feel the echo of her heartbeat in the soft, sweet flesh of her breast, still cupped in the palm of his hand.

She shuffled sideways, giving him better access to her between the bars. His mouth, light as a feather, brushed against hers over and over until she moaned in the back of her throat. The small sound opened her mouth, gave him access. His tongue rimmed the soft cushion of her lower lip, grazed her teeth, retreated before she could back away.

"Harry…"

She pressed against the grill. He looked down. The mound of her breast, outlined by the dark square of the grill, drew him. He caught her spine in both hands, pulled her closer and used his tongue and lips on her in a frenzy of need.

"Harry…" Her voice was a moan in the darkness.

Her hand sought his shoulder, found his neck, clung. "I cannot bear to lose you tomorrow."

Harry breathed deep and held the air in his chest. He pulled her against him as if the grill was not an iron barrier between them. His fingers began their task again, and he listened to the sound of her swift, shallow breathing.

A large black shape loomed up out of the shadows behind her. "Get away, man!" Harry swore. "Leave us be!"

He heard an inarticulate sound from Alina before she jerked back from him, yanking her cloak fast around her.

"Canna dee that, sir. The Master'll be around soon to check that all's well."

"Oh, Matho!" Her soft voice held not shame, but concern. "Really?"

Matho nodded. His face remained in shadow, but Harry felt the intensity of the man's long hard stare. It didn't matter what he thought. Harry's only concern was for the girl.

"You must go," he said to Alina. "Make yourself useful," he snapped at the man called Matho. "See her safe home."

She backed away, her cloak clutched tight about her. "I love you, Harry."

She turned and disappeared into the darkness. His last sight of her was a pair of slender white ankles beneath the dark cloak before the shadows swallowed her.

***

Alone once more, he lay on the hard stone. Already his blood slowed and cooled. Without his leather jack he had little protection against the cold. He smiled in the darkness. If he caught a chill, it would not matter now, since he was to die tomorrow. The stark fact sank into his mind and chilled him more quickly than the cold.

Accept it, my lad. Be calm. No good getting into a froth about it.

No, but it was damned unfair. He should have tried to argue his way out of it. He could have said that he'd saved Alina's life and then surely the man would have set him free.

But Carnaby was an odd man. Unlike his brother Reynold, who seemed able to charm the breeches off most of the nobility, a reputation for raw belligerence hung about the younger brother. Snippets of his father's conversation came back to him. Hints about a ruthless streak in the Carnaby family, that their wealth came not from honest toil but from the dissolution of the monasteries. Such rumours did not make them well liked, nor did the fact that they virtually owned Hexham, Corbrige and snippets of Langley. The younger Percys' hatred of Sir Reynold was legend in the Borderlands. Speculation on the topic of exactly how Reynold obtained such a hold over the Earl of Northumberland still flourished after twenty years.

The Tynedale men, the biggest parcel of rogues on the English side of the Border, banded together to oust him, yet with Cromwell's help, Sir Reynold hung on to his lands. Cuthbert Carnaby seemed imbued with the idea that he could get away with anything. Even down to executing someone because his name was Scott.

Harry frowned. There was a distant connection between the Carnabys and the Wharton family. Perhaps he could have used that as a lever. He sighed. Too late now. Harry wondered what his father might do on discovering his son had been executed, and realised his family might never what had happened to him.

He toyed with the idea of asking for paper to write a note but a moment's reflection told him nothing would ever be delivered.

How in damnation had he ever got into such a predicament? It all started with the mission. That was the reason he'd not given his real name.

He groaned. It was the worst day's work he had ever done.

Harry sat up abruptly on his stone bench and clasped his arms about his knees to stop himself shivering. Reviving anger threatened to overtake him. He wasn't ready to die. He'd met a wonderful girl and he felt more alive now than at any time in his life. The memory of her, warm and ready in his hand, made his heart beat faster.

Had he missed a way out of this? It might have been better if he'd not remembered who he was, for if he'd still been in a grey fog of lost identity, he would have been ignorant of his mission to suborn Scots into helping Henry of England gain control of their baby Queen. He might have been convincing enough to wriggle out of the snare. As it was, he'd been all too focused on not allowing his mission be traced back to his father.

A chink of sound at the entry made him look up.

"Harry?"

He recognised the deep, gruff voice. It was the man she had called Matho. Alina was not with him. He got up and walked over to the grill. "What is it?"

"The Master's bin and gone, thinkin' all's weel."

Harry waited. The man cleared his throat. "The lady Alina isna anybody's fool, and she claims ye're innocent o'any crime."

"That is true."

There was a long silence.

Harry shifted restlessly.

It spurred Matho into speech. "They say ye name's Scott. Will ye be deein' anything to hurt the folks o'Aydon?"

Harry gripped the bars of the grill. It was time for honesty. "I swear," he said, his voice strong and steady, "that I have done nothing and will do nothing that will bring hurt or harm to the people of Aydon."

Matho shifted, trying to get a good look at Harry in the shaft of moonlight that struck one side of the stone entry. Harry moved further into the moonlight. He sensed that something good might come of this exchange.

The slow, deliberate voice cut in. "Aye, well. Tomorrow. There's nowt as'll change Carnaby's mind once it's made up. He hates the family Scott to the last wee de'il in it, and since ye were daft enough to say ye name was Scott, he'll have ye tossed off the crag, ne doubt aboot it. But there's summat…"

"What? What, man?" Hope rose in Harry's chest like bubbles of air through water. He thumped his chest to be rid of the pressure they caused.

"A wee chance, maybe, if ye're a lad wi ye wits about ye. The Master hasn't noticed yet, but a tree came down a day or two back, an' it lies fair across the gully below the crag. If ye were to hop onto it, like as not ye'd be able to shimmy down and get clean away."

"How far down is it?"

"Ten feet, maybe." A grin slid over the solid Northumberland features. "Figurin's no my strong suit, y'knaw."

"And below that?"

Matho looked him straight in the eye. "Nowt but the Ay burn."

***

Alina walked cautiously through the cold hall, eased the door shut and tiptoed by the heavy curtain that ensured privacy for her parents in the room off the east side of the solar. She groped her way to the wooden staircase and, afraid of waking her brothers, crept up one step at a time.

Once in the safety of her bed, hot tears trickled into her feather pillow. One of the less vigilant men might never have spotted her, but Matho pounced on her the moment she ran through the door to the outer courtyard. Convincing him to let her speak to Harry had not been easy and he'd stood out of earshot but within sight of her the whole time.

Frustration burned because she had not been able find the key that would have freed Harry. Perhaps the boys knew where the keys to the tower were kept. Lance might have helped, but it was too late to think of that now.

She touched her lips, and remembered the gentleness of his mouth, how strong his grasp had been when he pulled her in against the cold iron grill. Her fingers sought the gap in her nightgown, and traced the curves as Harry had earlier. A dart of mingled pain and pleasure followed.

What might have happened if there had been no grill between them? She shivered all over again. It wasn't a shiver of fear, or cold, but excitement. This man was special. Her skin warmed. He meant more than her first kiss, more than her girlish dreams of a knight of old come to claim her. Harry was real, and fine, more than handsome and she hated her father for his harsh treatment.

Harry must not die.

She planned speeches in her head, visualised how she would throw herself at Father in the morning and plead with him to let Harry go. Mother could—

Alina shook her head. That would not do. Mother had been in the church gossiping with Lady Alice and she would not lie for Alina. Joseph had been with her mother, so there was no one to verify her story. She would have to convince Father all on her own.

Full daylight came early in the summer. Alina left her bed quietly, shuffled her blue gown over her chemise, combed her hair, plaited it neatly and hauled a plain white coif from her clothes chest. She hated wearing them, but a demure appearance might help her persuade Father to let Harry ride away. With the same thought in mind, she rummaged deeper in the chest and dragged out a lace partlet she usually wore in winter to provide an extra layer of warmth around her shoulders and throat. She wriggled into it and secured it with a silver brooch.

Carrying her soft leather shoes, she crept downstairs to the area outside her parents' chamber. Her father usually slept on well beyond dawn, but this way he could not leave his chamber without her knowledge. Too agitated to sit, she walked over to the window.

The sky was a soft, clear blue from horizon to horizon. Sunshine burned away the light haze rising from the trees and birds flew busily about feeding their fledglings. Supporting life, as nature directed. She watched them, and thought it was not a day to die. The sound of her father's muted snores came from beyond the curtain behind her, and her fingers tightened their grip on the stone sill.

Alina waited for a long time, shifting her weight from foot to foot. At long last she heard her father's low tones and her mother's lighter response. As if on cue, a maid climbed the stairs with a can of warm water. The girl bobbed a brief curtsey to Alina and took the water to her parents.

The sounds of splashing water and heavy footsteps seemed to last forever. When Alina thought she could stand the waiting no more, Father, dressed in a crumpled shirt hanging over his breeches and hose, yanked back the curtain and stepped into the solar. Alina turned. Her shadow stretched across the floorboards to his feet. He frowned and looked up.

Alina ran forward and blocked his path to the hall. "Father, please let me speak. I must speak to you."

He stopped, but so grudgingly she had to take two steps back to prevent him walking into her. Shaking out his jerkin, he shrugged into it and fastened a couple of buttons as he stared down at her. "Well?"

Her heart rattled against her ribs. "I was in Corbrige market, sir—the day before the reivers came—I nearly lost my life to a runaway bull."

He stared her up and down. "You seem to be in good health, so I must conclude you came to no harm. Must you waylay me on my way to eat?"

"The man you plan to punish saved me, Father. He risked his own life—"

Carnaby frowned. "You mean that wretched Scott? The man in the dungeon?"

Alina nodded. "He saved me—"

"The man was currying favour, no doubt trying to worm his way into my good graces."

Carnaby waved her aside and moved on.

Alina grabbed at his arm to stop him. "Do you place such a low value on my life that you will not listen, sir? Harry—"

"Alina, I warn you, do not pester me. I will not have it." Carnaby's brows lowered. "Your mother said nothing of any escaped animal threatening you."

Alina sank to her knees. "Mama did not see it, Father. She was in St Andrews talking to Lady Alice. Joseph was with her, or he could have told you how Harry threw a cloak over the bull's head. Wait!" Alina cried as her father nudged her aside and walked towards the doorway. She grasped his sleeve and hung on. "Master Rutherford saw it. He tried to make Harry pay for the cloak and I told Joseph to pay him."

Her father stopped. "You paid? What gentleman allows a woman pay his way for him? The man is a rogue and your story confirms it. No, daughter, leave me be."

He evaded her clinging hands and strode through into the hall. The door banged against the wall and remained open. "A good slice of ham," he snarled to a servant she could not see. "Be quick about it."

Chapter Eight

Harry forced himself to rest through the dark hours of the night. Thanks to Matho, he had something to hope for, something to focus on and now his mind raced through the many ways the scene might be played out in the morning. Stupid and foolhardy Matho's plan might be, but when there were no other options, foolhardy and stupid must be the road he would take.

They came for him when the sun was halfway to the midday point of the sky, and it was a relief to be out in the warm sunshine and fresh air after the oppressive closeness of the tower cellar. By stretching his muscles at regular intervals from daybreak on, he had kept himself toned and ready, anxious that he should not miss his one chance because he was stiff and cold.

Carnaby stood in the centre of the outer courtyard, a powerful, menacing figure in a fully buttoned crimson doublet, brown hose and riding boots. The eldest son stood at his side, a tall youth with a hint of the same heavy shoulders as his father. Lionel looked up at the battlements and lifted his shoulders in a small, helpless shrug.

Harry followed his glance. He recognised two brown heads leaning through the crenels, but there was no sign of Alina though he searched the length of the parapet.

He waved, and Cuddy waved back. Lance ducked out of sight.

Matho stood at Carnaby's other side. In daylight, his red hair shone like a beacon in the sun. A short, loose leather jerkin covered a heavy brown shirt, and not by a flicker of a glance did he betray his midnight conversation with Harry. At Carnaby's gesture he approached, spear held upright in one hand, short sword hanging at his thigh, and grasped Harry's arm. He pushed him across the outer yard toward the smaller middle courtyard, and from there through the shadows of a collapsed building to small doorway in the south curtain wall.

Once through the door, the sun slapped into his eyes and the sharp smell of grass and greenery hit his nose. Squinting against the brightness, he looked around. Hollyhocks and roses clung to the side of the building and clouded the air with their perfume, but on the far side of the narrow strand of the pathway the land dipped away at angle too steep to walk. Harry's guts clutched tight for a moment. That must be the dreaded ravine. The slopes were so deeply wooded he could not see much.

Matho took his arm, urged him forward to a patch of grass. He stopped where a small spur of land stretched ten paces out towards the sun.

"Take him to the edge, Matho." Carnaby's voice held a purr of pleasure. "Let him see what is in store for him and then bring him to me."

Harry looked sideways at Matho. The man's reddish brows jutted over a Roman nose, and he kept his gaze forward, making no effort to speak. Anything he said would be overheard by Carnaby, of course. As they reached the edge of the ravine, Matho's brows lifted and with a subtle indication of the head and a significant flicker of his eyes, Harry understood that he ought to look to his right.

"What do you think now, Harry Scott?" Carnaby's voice gloated behind him.

Harry stepped to the edge, peered over. The drop was dizzying. He looked down on the rustling canopy of leaves, the sharp spikes of conifers and after a moment turned to confront his enemy. Twelve men plus Carnaby faced him, blocking off all hope of escape.

"You have no right to do this."

Carnaby's hands opened in an expansive gesture.

Harry imagined Carnaby would try and prolong the moment and make his victim squirm, beg for release.

"Who, do you think, is going to prevent me?" Carnaby laughed. "Who will know what has happened to you?"

Harry looked at Matho and then along the line of twelve guards. They were not professional soldiers. They were field hands and grooms, still on duty because of the reivers. They would not go against their lord because he held their lives and the lives of their families in the palm of his hand.

"Your conscience. Your children know, your wife knows. These people—"

"And you think women and children are going to save you?" Carnaby laughed aloud, his fine teeth startlingly white against his swarthy skin.

Harry thought of Alina's desperate voice in the darkness, the touch of her lips and the sweet bold way she had responded to his desperation. She was not going to forget him, any more than he would forget her. Except, he thought wryly, she might have longer than he to remember those moments at the iron grill in the moonlight.

"Matho? Bring him back!"

Harry committed a picture of the drop to memory. An uprooted pine lay across the slope, just as Matho had described. The pine's root base was out of sight beneath the overhanging crag on which they stood, but the trunk sloped gently down to rest in the cleft of another tree. From there, it was thirty feet to the ground and a precipitous slope. If he could manage the tree, he could certainly manage the slope afterwards.

Harry looked at the slender trunk and then at Matho. "You were right, Matho. Figuring is hardly your strong point."

Matho's mouth pulled to the left in a swift grin.

"Bring him back, Matho." Carnaby's bellow gave them no time to converse.

"Dang it, but he loves this," Matho muttered before they turned. "Ye're supposed to be nowt but a quiverin' heap o' shite now, lad. I'll 'ave nowt te dee wi it." Matho's rough hand jostled Harry around, and pushed him towards his tormentor.

Harry stiffened his shoulders. The warm grey of the stone walls rose behind Carnaby and towered above them all. A flash of blue behind one of the windows caught Harry's eye and he wondered if it might be Alina. Perhaps it had only been a reflection of the sun on the glass.

Matho moved unobtrusively to the back of the troop, leaving Harry isolated.

Carnaby moved forward, smiling. "Ready to meet your maker? I can have Father John brought here if you want him. I'll not be accused of sending a man unshriven to his death."

Harry resisted the urge to land a punch on the dark-skinned, grinning face. He gritted his teeth until his jaw ached, determined not to let fear rule him. He flexed and relaxed his muscles, preparing as best he could for what would be the leap of his life. He pictured the scene behind him and gave Carnaby only a fraction of his interest.

"My conscience is clear," he said quietly. "Remember me to your boys, and Alina. I hope they live long and happy lives."

Carnaby leered. "They will soon forget you." He gestured to the men forward to grasp Harry. "Take him to the edge. Throw him off, and be damned to the entire family Scott."

"I hope you rot in hell," Harry said. He gave himself no time to worry. Before the guards reached him, he swung round, ran for the crag and jumped. Once launched, he could not change direction. The silver-beige trunk rushed up to meet him. One foot landed square on the trunk and the other hit the rounded side and slid off in a scatter of loose bark.

The tree sank, groaned and rebounded under his weight. Debris rattled over the spear shaped leaves of the bluebells and garlic clinging to the slope below. Harry bit his bottom lip clear through as he teetered. He threw himself forward, grasped the trunk with both arms and legs and hung on until the juddering ceased.

He lifted his head. The fallen pine presented a narrow pathway towards the tall beech. He sucked in a huge breath, kept his body close to the wood and clambered along the trunk. Patches of bark fell away. Branches loomed up, sharp spikes that gouged his flesh and no doubt ruined his boots and hose. Some smaller stuff he forced aside, or wriggled over.

Panting, spitting bloody froth into the empty space below, he swarmed down towards the sturdy beech, anxious to reach it and be away before Carnaby entertained thoughts of checking for a body.

The beech was old, massive and many-branched. Harry climbed down, jumped the last few feet to the ground and sank between the huge roots. He looked up, expecting an audience peering over the crag. Leaves obscured his view. If he could not see them, he doubted they could see him. No sounds of a chase reached him.

He glanced around. The slope was steep and the soil damp beneath the ground cover, but there was no time to waste. Picking his route with care, he skipped, hopped and jumped down to the stream at the bottom of the ravine and dropped over the muddy bank into the stream bed.

Harry doubled over, hands splayed on his thighs until he caught his breath. Raising his head, he looked back the way he had come. No trail of bruised greenery betrayed his passage. They wouldn't find a body, either. He snorted with faint laughter.

Scratches burned across his face. His body ached and he tasted blood from his bitten lip. He thrust his fist into the sky in a victory punch. Bruises would fade. He was alive. And Carnaby would be flummoxed when they found no body.

Harry weaved his way downstream between the trees, then struck at an angle up the slope towards the fields to find his horse. Once mounted, with his sword in his fist, no one would stop him.

Jubilant bird song echoed around the leaf canopy as he moved silently through the woods, resting a palm now and then on a rough-barked pine or the smooth-trunk of a beech. Treading delicately through a patch of last autumn's dry leaves towards sunlight and open space, he slowed and parted the foliage warily. Bessie grazed not too far away. Alina's pony kept her company, and though he scanned the fields in every direction, there was no one about to hinder his progress.

It was the work of moments to run to the old stable, collect his gear, saddle up and ride away. He took the field route towards Dere Street, shook himself and settled down to a gentle ride north to the old Port Gate and beyond.

A passing carter gave him a curious look. Harry ran his hands over his hair and face, and knew why. Bits of twig and leaf drifted out of his hair, and his fingertips found several scratches across his face. He stopped at the horse-trough on a gentle bend, no doubt intended for carters and their beasts. Bessie nuzzled the water, and Harry soaked a handkerchief, bathed his face and beat the dust and debris out of his clothes.

If he'd made this journey three days ago, he would not be in this bedraggled state. His wits must have been addled the night he rode out of Corbrige. Sheer nosiness had certainly played a part in his reason for riding by Aydon in the dead of night, but there had been something else, something to do with the attraction of a pretty face, a lithe figure and impertinent manners.

If he was honest, if he had the courage to admit it…In short, he had been following her lure.

An image of Alina's face appeared in his thoughts. He remembered the flash of blue cloth at the window. Did she see him jump? Would she think he was dead? She seemed sure that no one survived such a leap.

Ha! Delight ran through him because he had succeeded at something others believed impossible. There was always a first time, though without Matho's help he would surely have been nothing but a crumpled heap at the bottom of the ravine by now.

Unable to repress a shudder, he groaned. Bessie snorted and flicked her ears.

Alina would soon find that he was not dead. If nothing else, she would see that Bessie had gone, along with all his gear. But before then, he imagined her father would be gnashing his teeth at the thought of a Scott escaped. Harry laughed quietly. Carnaby's rage would be a thing to behold.

He was well out of it, and it would be the maddest folly to ride back into Aydon in the hope of seeing Alina again. For the moment he would concentrate on Edinburgh, and it was likely that after a day or two of strenuous activity, he would forget all about Alina. Then he could go back to his original plan and focus on finding a rich heiress.

Definitely a much safer plan.

***

Alina saw Harry jump. She had stood a pace behind her brothers, unwilling to show herself, unable to meet the accusing look she imagined must be in his eyes as he was led from the dungeon. The dark scab on his cheekbone looked sore. Some dreadful fascination made her run inside as the men marched Harry around outside the building. She flung herself at the hall window in time to see him look over the edge of the precipice. He spoke to Matho.

Strangely, he did not seem afraid.

His head held high, he stood tall and straight, a good few inches taller than Matho. But surely he must be afraid? Grasping the small gold cross at her throat, she drank in every detail of his intent profile and wound the chain tighter and tighter until it bit into her skin.

Father stood in the sunshine, smiling. Lionel, at his side, looked rather pale. She did not think Lionel had seen anyone pushed over the crag, but they had both heard the stories. Watching in fascinated horror, she saw Matho leave Harry and push to the back of the row of guards. His red hair flashed in the sun as he looked up towards her window. Perhaps he guessed she was there. Matho always looked dour, but now he looked grim.

Matho believed it was going ahead.

Alina's hand flew to her mouth and with a dreadful sickness rising in her stomach she whirled on her mother. "Mama, there must be something we can say that will save Harry!"

With an unexpectedly gentle look in her eyes, her mother hurried to the window. Their hands met and clung together. "Come away, Alina. You should not watch." Mama grasped her arm, drew her forcibly from the window. "I spoke to your father last night, but he was adamant the execution must go ahead."

"Harry has done nothing. What Father is doing is not lawful...." The pain in her throat made her voice sound shrill. "How can I face him after this?"

A hoarse, deep throated cry went up outside.

Alina broke from her mother's grasp and rushed to the window. There was no sign of Harry. Every man, including her father, stared at the ravine where branches trembled as if a heavy body had hurtled through them. Sickness rose into her throat. Hand clapped over her mouth, Alina pushed her mother aside and rushed to the outside steps.

"Alina!" Her mother's cries grew fainter behind her as Alina blundered down the wooden staircase.

Halfway down, she fell to her knees and vomited.

When the retching ceased, Alina huddled against the cold grey stone and buried her face in her arms.

"My dear, are you....Alina? Please come back inside." Mama's voice came from the door at the head of the steps.

Alina dried her tears on her skirt and scrambled to her feet. "No. I cannot stay." She shook her head at Mama's outstretched hand. "I cannot face Father. I will walk until I am calm. Then, perhaps...." Moving down the stairs, away from her mother, she added, "I shall walk to Grandfather's house."

Alina walked swiftly across the inner yard and through the second gate. She stared straight ahead, barely aware of the few barns and cottages tucked around the gates. Concentrating on the wisp of blue smoke that signalled Halton Tower, Alina wondered if she would ever have a normal conversation with her father again.

How could she speak to the man who had order Harry's death? Mama had been correct when she said Alina should not watch what happened. At least she did not have a visual memory of her father pushing Harry off the crag. How could Mama live with such deeds?

But a small, neat picture formed in her mind's eye. A an image of Harry tumbling through the air, hitting trees, falling at the last onto the sharp edged slabs and squares of dark, moss covered rock through which the burn ran down to Corbrige.

The stream she had played beside so often as a child.

Eyes closed against hot, stinging tears, she walked across the boggy patch in the valley bottom and up the slope and only slowed as the lane grew steeper. Her breath rasped in an aching throat as she turned into the churchyard, hurried by the church door and burst into the Halton Tower.

Squat, stone built and crenellated, the original tower had been built to withstand siege and fire more than two hundred years ago. When danger threatened, the family abandoned the modern, comfortable living accommodation built onto one wall and barricaded themselves in the Tower.

Alina headed to the open outer door in the two storey house and thrust the heavy inner door open. Grandfather sat in a large carved chair between the fire and the latticed window, where sunlight fell across the pages of a leather-bound book in his hand. He looked up in alarm and winced as the heavy door rebounded off the wall.

Alina ran to him, leather soles slapping on the flagstones.

He rose stiffly to his feet as she reached him, threw herself against his chest and sobbed as if the world had come to an end.

He held her close and tight against him. "Alina! What is it, girl?"

When he received no answer, Sir William grasped her by both arms and shook her so hard her teeth rattled.

"Stop this caterwauling, do you hear me? I have no time for female hysterics, young lady. If you can't talk to me sensibly, you can turn around and go back to Aydon."

Gripped between his gnarled but surprisingly strong hands, Alina stared up into his dark eyes and found alarm rather than sympathy there. She tried to breathe, snuffled, and hiccupped. Tears dripped off her chin and plopped onto her dress. Her cheeks smarted where salt tears had run.

Grandfather pushed her into the chair he had vacated. "Sit down and compose yourself. Then tell me what's wrong. Is it Reynold?"

A stab of guilt shot through her misery. Of course Grandfather would think of his son, so ill these last few weeks. "No, oh no. I'm sorry. I should have remembered…"

Beneath the silver hair and eyebrows, his brown eyes studied her. "H'mm. I trust your mother and father are well? Your brothers? Then, if no one has died, we will—"

She moaned covered her face with her hands. Harry would be dead by now, or so badly maimed that death would be preferable.

Grandfather sighed. "I take it someone has died. I'm sorry, Alina, but you are going to have to talk to me before I can help. Talk to me. Must I shake you again?"

He turned from her and fumbled in a dark oak cupboard. He shoved a square of clean white linen into her hands. "Blow your nose and sit up. I mean it, Alina. Stop this snivelling at once."

She blew her nose several times, and eyed him over the linen as she did so. His blunt approach restored her more quickly than sympathy would have done. She had always considered him an older, heavier, more wrinkled version of her father, but now she was glad of the subtle differences.

He held out a small pewter mug. "Drink this."

She drank a mouthful of the tawny liquid he offered. She opened her eyes wide as it burned down to her stomach.

"Now," he said, brown eyes warming at last. "The brandy will settle you. What is it? Don't you dare start weeping again. Reynold is still alive?"

Alina bit her lip. "Sir Reynold is as he was when you saw him last. No worse, but no better. Oh, Grandfather, I'm so sorry. I did not think. Of course you would assume the worst…"

Sunlight peered through the lattice window, laid a pattern of diamond shapes across the old man's face and turned his hair to snow as he nodded. He put his hands behind his back, paced a step or two in front of the dark oak table and turned away, but not before Alina caught the resignation in his eyes.

"So, it must be something Cuthbert has done."

She nodded. "He pushed a man over the ravine this morning." She bit her lip to stop it wobbling. "A man called Harry Scott."

"Ah." Sir William sighed. "Headstrong as ever. Cuthbert was ever thus, even as a child. I tried to beat it out of him, but to no avail. He has done this before, and not been called to account for it because of our position in the country. Was there a reason?"

"No reason at all," Alina declared. "Harry saved my life in Corbrige last week. It is all because his name is Scott. You know how

Father feels about that family." She cocked her head. "You must hate them too, of course. I forgot about the Stagshaw Fair Day."

He regarded her over his shoulder. His eyes were clear in the rubble of his face. Inhaling, he studied her as he tugged his crumpled doublet into position. "I cannot say I admire the family, my dear. Their handling of me at Stagshaw was uncouth, to say the least. I take it this Harry Scott was a young man? You liked him?"

Alina considered the soggy linen in her hands. "Yes." To force speech made her throat ache. "I liked him very much indeed. I would marry him in a moment if he asked me. He says he comes from Carlisle. I don't know how I can face Father again."

Grandfather paced before her, his leather shoes squeaking in the silence. His hair straggled onto the collar of his worn velvet doublet and his hands, once more clasped behind his back, were veined with thick, gnarled blue cords.

"Did you see him thrown over?"

She shook her head. "No."

"That is something, then. If the deed has taken place you will have to make the best of it, for there is nothing to be done. But there is always the possibility Cuthbert may have changed his mind at the last moment.

"There was no change of heart. I know it." Tears brimmed again and her mouth twisted unbecomingly. "Grandfather, how can I make the best of it?"

"You must. Go to church and say a prayer for his soul. What else can you do?"

There was a long silence. If she were a man, she could avenge Harry, ride off and never have to speak to her father again. As a woman, the only way she could leave home was to marry, and that would bring its own troubles. How could she stand a man in her bed who was not Harry?

Grandfather did not speak. After a long time she looked up and offered a tentative, wobbly smile. "You are right, Grandfather."

The old man nodded. "I heard he was hoping to match you with Errington's lad. You should marry soon and move away from home. You will not need to see your father very often."

So grandfather had reached the same conclusion. "I shall be glad of it." She sighed. If that was all marriage offered, it might be worth it, even if there was nothing but friendship between her and her prospective bridegroom. She hoped there would at least be friendship.

The old man considered her. "You must have liked this young man a great deal. Who was he?"

Alina blew her nose and thought about the question. "He....What do you mean?"

"His father? Family? Home?"

"He came from Carlisle and that is all I know. He was going to Edinburgh. But he was honourable, I'm sure of it."

"A stranger, then, of whom you know nothing." He shook his head, and reached out to grasp her chin between blunt fingers. "We must be careful in these times. There's more to look for in a suitor than having a pretty turn of phrase or a handsome face, Alina. Come. You must go back to Aydon and it is time I visited Reynold. I will tell Henry to bring the horses round."

Chapter Nine

Alina rode without speaking beside her grandfather, her gaze on the grey stone battlements of Aydon peeking above the rim of encircling trees. Her tears had dried, leaving her with a dull headache and a heavy feeling she thought might be with her for the rest of her life.

Grandfather turned in the saddle. "Did you trust this young man?"

There was no need to stop and think of whom Grandfather spoke. She met his sharp glance with little enthusiasm. "Yes, absolutely."

"Why?"

She frowned and looked out across the fields. "Because..." Grandfather would scoff if she told him she believed in Harry because he was tall, handsome and so attractive that she could not envisage him as anything but a gentleman. "Because he did not boast or brag. He lost his memory for a while, but he told me the moment he remembered who he was." With some hesitation, she recounted the entire tale of how and where they had met.

Grandfather listened, but did not seem overly impressed. "An exciting interlude in your quiet life, was it? I suspect you will get over it in a day or two. By Yuletide you'll have trouble remembering him."

Alina doubted it, but supposed Grandfather had no reason to think otherwise. He had not met Harry, nor felt the force of his personality. He had no idea of Harry's quality, or how she had reacted to him. A swift, fleeting memory of his hand on her breast at the dungeon gate made her shiver.

"Grandfather, if you think I was won over by some handsome gallant showering me with compliments, you are quite wrong. Harry never offered me a single compliment."

"Aye, well. Just remember this, lass. All that glisters is not gold."

With that, he left her to her thoughts. She pondered his statement, and refuted it. In this case, what glistered *was* gold. She was sure of it. As they drew closer to Aydon, she recognised the small figure dancing up and down on the wallwalk and frowned. What did Lance have to celebrate? He'd liked Harry as much as she did. How could he be so excited? She caught a glimpse of him racing along the alure to the kitchen door at the end of the parapet. It wasn't long before he hurtled through the main gate and tore along the lane towards them. Puffs of dust rose under his feet. Her horse shied as Lance skidded to a halt and grabbed at her leg.

"He's gone, Alina! He's not there!" His cheeks were scarlet, and he looked about to brim over with delight.

Grandfather reined in and held onto his snorting horse. "Speak plainly, boy. What do you mean? And for the Lord's sake, stand still!"

Lance stiffened, greeted his grandfather courteously as he had been taught, and looked back at Alina.

"Harry. He did the Leap and we can't find him!"

She stared down into her brother's face. His hazel eyes, full of mixed wonder and hope, gazed back. Slowly the sense of what he was saying sank into her mind. Her mouth curved in a hesitant smile before she bit it back. She did not dare to hope yet.

Grandfather snapped the question she dared not ask. "You mean there's no body?"

"The men are still searching," Lance said. "But no, they haven't found anything."

"Oh, Lance, is that true?"

Grandfather grunted. "Don't get your hopes up, girl. He could be hidden in a crevice or such like."

This was hardly the time to remind Grandfather that he had suggested her father may have changed his mind at the last minute. But Lance said Harry had made the leap. Puzzled, she looked at her brother.

Lance stepped up close, so that Alina's horse hid him from his grandfather's eye. He beckoned with one grimy hand, and nodded in the direction of the stables.

Lance was not stupid. If he wanted her to go to the stables, he would have a very good reason for it. And he looked fit to burst, so whatever it was excited him.

She smiled at Sir William. "Lance will take your horse to the stable, Grandfather, if you wish to go straight in and see Sir Reynold. Lead me to the mounting block, Lance, and I'll help you take the horses to Auld John."

They watched grandfather stride away. In the stables, Lance hopped from foot to foot while Auld John lectured them on the proper way to care for a horse that worked hard for its rider. He glanced at them both from under bushy grey brows. "Thoo's taking nee notice." He flung down the rubber he had been using on Grandfather's chestnut, and stamped towards the door. "Ah divven't knaws why ah bother."

Lance giggled. Alina shushed him. "Don't let him hear you. He's a good man, and he loves his horses. Lance!"

She could not understand his levity after what had happened to Harry such a short time ago. Still on edge, she cuffed him lightly, and knocked his cap to the floor. "Be serious, Lance and stop giggling. He's gone now. Tell me what happened. I know there's something you haven't told me yet."

He picked up his cap, shook it and clapped it back on his head. "Ay, that I 'ave."

"And don't mimic Auld John. If he should hear you, he'd be hurt."

Lance sighed. "Harry didn't wait to be pushed. He ran at it and jumped off to the right."

"What? He *jumped?*" Shock ran through her. "You little liar!" She grabbed at him.

Lance ducked out of reach. "It's true." He watched her dubiously from the far side of a barrel almost as big as himself. "He ran at it before they could get hold of him, and jumped off at an angle. He didn't scream or shout. There was an awful silence, and then a thud and the sound of branches cracking. Matho wouldn't let any one look over. He said if everyone crowded onto the crag it would give way like it did two years ago. So nobody saw what happened to Harry for absolutely ages."

For a moment she did not see the dark shadowy stable, but an image of Harry leaping off the crag. The picture made her heart thud in her chest. She swallowed down the impossible lump in her throat and clenched her fists. "What did Father do?"

Lance leaned both forearms on the top of the barrel and rubbed his chin against his sleeve. "He ordered Matho away and stalked out to the edge. I don't know what he saw, but he went red, swore and ordered all the men down into the woods. Then he called them back again, and said it was hopeless. He'd let the reiver go."

Her knees wobbled, so she sat down on a hay bale. She could not make sense of it all. "Are you sure? You seem to be saying that Harry jumped over the edge, but he escaped, that he isn't dead. I don't want to build up hope and then…"

"Of course I'm sure." Lance's teeth flashed in a swift grin. "I wouldn't lie to you. I know you're sweet on Harry."

She bridled, thought of denying it and then let it go. "Well, it doesn't matter a docken, does it? We'll probably never see him again." It occurred to her that she had a way of checking. "Oh, I should see if his horse…can you do that, Lance? Please? If I disappear again, mother'll have a fit."

She told him exactly where Harry's chestnut would be found, and Lance nodded and sauntered towards the door. He hesitated, fingers grasping the doorframe. "I think Matho could tell you more. He won't talk to me, I've asked him. But he might talk to you." He grinned. "He's sweet on you, like you're sweet on Harry."

"Oh!" Alina swung around on him, but he vanished before she reached the door. His laughter drifted back to her as she sat back rather suddenly on the hay bale.

It seemed that Harry had escaped after all. She ought to be smiling. Instead her eyes leaked as she sat there in the gloom, hugged herself and listened to the horses moving on the cobbles. Was it possible? Had he really escaped?

Slowly everything sank into place. Harry had not waited to be pushed, and more than that; he had jumped in a particular direction as if he had known a route to safety. Only one person could have helped him.

Perhaps she could begin to believe in Harry's escape after all. She leapt up from the hay bale. Matho Spirston would help her. Matho had always treated her with condescension because she was a girl, yet she knew, in some instinctive way, that Matho was fond of her. She smiled, remembering the times he had taken her side in an argument against Lionel.

Why had she not thought of it before? If she confided in Matho, he would help. And when Matho decided to do something, it got done. Alina knew that if Matho told Gilbert Richardson and Robert Cooper and the others to keep an eye out for Harry's return, then they would.

If Harry chose to return. Her high hopes died and her steps slowed to a halt as she reached the stable door. Many a man would think himself well out of a dangerous situation and never look back.

***

That afternoon Alina changed to her brown and russet gown and sat in the sunny southern half of the solar with her mother and hemmed a lawn shirt for Cuddy, wishing she had found Matho this morning and received news that would let her rest peacefully in the knowledge that Harry was alive.

The men were out searching for Harry.

The news that no body had been found below the ravine had raced around Aydon and surprised everyone. Father stamped about with a frown cut deep into his brow. For the moment she must be content to know that Harry had somehow escaped The Leap.

Her fingers moved at a steady pace. She took pride in her small neat stitches. Such precision helped keep her thoughts from Harry and saved her from having to respond to Mama's glowing account of John Errington.

Alina's last glimpse of the Errington boys had been across the church during Easter Week three or four years ago. Thomas, already a man, had been tall and handsome, John the tall, thin boy of fifteen with pimples and skinny shanks in wrinkled knitted hose. The year before that, she and Lionel had been amused when John's voice ricocheted up and down the scale without warning. Lionel, his voice safely broken, ought to have been more sympathetic. Instead he'd sniggered behind John's back.

This morning Grandfather had made it plain he thought the marriage a sensible arrangement between two families of rising importance. He expected her to be a dutiful granddaughter, lift her head, smile and march willingly off to make a success of the match in the hope of advancing her family's fortunes.

If she had not lost her heart to a stranger, it would have been easier to bear. But now she knew a man and dreamed of marrying him. A romantic dream, no doubt, but one that was deeply part of her. What if she objected? Fled to Grey House? It should be possible to hide there for a while. Father would search, but so many nooks and crannies existed around the old farmhouse and many more in the stables and barns. She could hide out there forever if needs be.

She shook her head. It was impossible. Why was she thinking of running away? It was the kind of reaction expected from someone of Lance's age rather than a mature young lady. Parents always arranged marriages and it was a daughter's duty to smile and accept it.

Her dream of Harry was doomed. Even if he cared, which was doubtful, he would never know she was to be married in the next few weeks. She did not know where he lived, could not contact him. She didn't want to risk involving Lionel, for now he considered himself a man he would feel obliged to reveal her secret to Father. Lance was too young. All she could do was pray that Harry would return.

If she were wise, she would give up all thoughts of him, bow her head and be nice to John Errington when he came calling.

It was difficult to know how she felt about John.

Lance poked his head into the solar. "This might be him. He's so tall he needs to duck under the gate. Auld John's taken his horse to the stables. He'll be here in a moment."

Alina stared at her brother. "Who will be here?" For a moment she thought of Harry.

Lance stared back at her as if she was stupid. "Isn't it today Father said John Errington would call? I think it's him talking to Lionel in the inner yard."

Alina stabbed her needle into her sewing, disregarded her mother's protests and hurried to the window at the north end of the solar. Lance got there before her.

Staying well back against the wall, she peeped out into the yard. A tall, well dressed young man stood in conversation with her brother Lionel. "Yes. It is indeed John Errington." Would he make her a happy bride? She felt no rush of emotion at the sight of him. Would she make *him* a happy bridegroom?

Lance regarded her with an impish grin. "Do you like him?" He lowered his voice. "As much as Harry?"

"Come and sit, Alina." Her mother's voice came faintly from the far end of the solar. "I wish I had remembered his visit. You should have dressed your hair more becomingly."

Alina patted the skin beneath her eyes and hoped the signs of weeping had disappeared. "I wish he had not come today."

Lance grinned. "If he's to be your husband you'll have to defer to him in everything."

Glaring at her brother, she walked back to the south end of the solar.

"Can I come?" Lance remained at the window, but his whisper followed her.

"Small brothers are not welcome when one—" She stopped and turned back, her thoughts racing. Lance would make a useful buffer in the first uncomfortable moments of meeting her intended bridegroom.

"Alina! Hurry!"

"Coming, Mama." Alina hesitated, regarding her brother with a speculative gaze.

Lance approached her warily. "It makes me nervous when you squint at me like that, Ally. What are you thinking?"

She beckoned. "Go downstairs and wait in the courtyard. If John and I come outside, stay with me and don't let him chase you away. If I tell you to go, pretend you think I don't mean it."

He looked puzzled. A moment later his eyes widened beneath the thatch of brown hair. "You want him to think you're telling me to leave, but really you want me to stay?"

Alina smiled and patted his shoulder. "Exactly. I'll go and sit with mother. After the first few pleasantries we shall most likely be sent out to stroll in the orchard. That's when I shall need your help."

"I bet he's not a patch on H—"

Alina whirled, a finger to her lips. "Don't mention that name, Lance, please."

She returned to the sunny part of the solar while Lance scuttled down the old stairs to the kitchen.

"Where would you like me to sit, Mama?"

Margery Carnaby had already packed her spindle away and sat bolt upright with her hands clasped in her lap. "Where you usually sit, Alina. I don't think we should put ourselves out for a younger son of the Erringtons, do you?" She ran a considering gaze over her daughter. "Your hair is neat and that gown suits you. I expect he will not stay above an hour."

Alina seized a cushion, hesitated and looked at her mother. "Do you dislike the Erringtons, Mama?" She banged the cushion against the wall, placed it on the higher ledge of the window seat, stepped up and sat on it.

"Of course—Not there, Alina!" Her mother looked scandalised. "You know perfectly well the higher seat is not acceptable today. Here, girl, in the chair beside—"

She broke off at the sound of footsteps. Alina stayed where she was as the Steward tapped and bowed at the doorway. "John Errington, ma'am."

Mama beamed at the young man in the stone archway. "Ah, good afternoon, sir. Please, be welcome."

John Errington advanced into the flood of sunshine pouring through the lancet windows and bowed over her mother's hand. Alina, knowing the bright sunlight behind her would prevent him seeing her as little more than a silhouette, felt free to study him. If he had retained the slender build of his youth the padded sleeves and shoulders of the sober, well cut and expensive doublet disguised the fact. He was very much taller than she remembered. A small sparkling ruff hid his throat and neck, and a scant brown beard disguised his chin. Leather riding boots covered a good deal of his legs. He held a pair of leather gauntlets in one hand, and their silver embroidery glinted as he moved. Lace ruffles hung below his doublet cuffs and concealed much of his unadorned hands.

Alina considered him carefully. Most fashionable men wore rings on each hand. Rakish young men sported earrings. Lionel had bored them for weeks debating the purchase of an earring. Errington didn't even have a jewel in the band of his cap. It crossed her mind that she ought to be insulted he did not care enough to dazzle her with the quality of his jewels. Did he expect the splendid doublet and the depth of his lace cuffs enough to win her?

He rose from an unhurried and perfectly executed bow and made the required responses to her mother's greeting. His voice boomed around the room. Alina started at the sound. Such a deep, rich voice proclaimed him man rather than boy. She realised she did not know him at all and yet in a month or less she might be sharing his bed.

The thought unnerved her. Twisting her fingers together in her lap to still their trembling, she studied him. The only signs of the once despised pimples lay in a scattering of small craters across his forehead. His face had somehow grown to accommodate the nose Lionel once described as beaky.

"You remember my daughter Alina?"

He turned in her direction. His hazel eyes narrowed against the light. "Of course. I trust I find her in good health?"

Alina bowed her head in acknowledgement. "You do, sir. You have—" She stopped. She could hardly say he had grown up and lost his gangly looks. "You look well, sir."

The expensive tawny velvet was not a shade she would have chosen to match his fresh complexion, but his hazel eyes glowed with friendliness and his mouth curved in a smile. At least they had chosen the same coloured outfit today. Perhaps it meant something.

She found herself returning his smile and then a twinge of guilt touched her. John had come in good faith. He was not to know that her heart had been stolen by another. Guilt seemed always with her these days, but she pushed it to one side and decided to try a more informal approach. "Hello, John. How are you?"

The white feather in his rakish cap almost touched his prominent cheekbone as he nodded. "I do very well, Mistress Alina."

The deepness of his voice surprised her again. His eyes flashed, and she wondered if he too remembered the way his voice had mortified him by sliding up and down the scale last time they had met. He turned to her mother and conveyed his parents' warmest greetings and esteem. He remembered to ask after the health of the family and Sir Reynold in particular.

It was well done of him and Alina approved. She studied him as he added a sentence or two about the weather and wondered how long his visit would last.

"It is a fine day, ma'am, as I mentioned. Perhaps you might allow your daughter to walk with me and enjoy the sunshine?"

Her mother was unlikely to refuse permission requested so politely. Alina ducked her head and decided to take it as a compliment that he wanted to be alone with her, that he wanted no eavesdroppers to any conversation they might have.

"I see no reason why not." Prepared to be generous on his first appearance at Aydon, Margery Carnaby smiled. "I shall stay here and leave you two young people to renew your acquaintance. Alina, I know you will not go too far. Perhaps the orchard? It is sunny and sheltered there."

Some things were so predictable. Alina suppressed a smile. The young man stepped closer and held out his hand. "May I help you down from your perch?"

Hearing amusement in his tone, she looked at him warily and saw nothing but kindness in his expression. She placed her fingers across his waiting palm and his curled about hers. If they had still been children, he'd have expected her to get down on her own. She flicked a glance at her mother, knowing Mama would be nervous in case Alina chose to jump down and spoil the illusion of a gently reared young lady.

She stepped daintily to the floor, revealing one slender ankle for a moment, and kept on walking. John, with a swift inclination of the head to her mother, followed her towards the door.

Alina glanced over her shoulder. Mama, smiling, sank back in her chair.

Chapter Ten

John held her hand high between them as if he led her into the dance. Alina kept her gaze on the stiffened front edge of her russet skirt as she advanced across the floorboards. They walked silently and steadily through the hall. At the door, a deafening cacophony of sound met them. Alina stole a glance at John's profile, and saw him grimace and survey the stonemasons who tapped and chiselled stone into shape.

His colour seemed less florid out here in the shadow of the building, and that rendered the tawny velvet more attractive. His lace cuffs tickled her fingers as he led her down to the cobbled yard. She caught a glimpse of Lance goggling from the orchard wall.

Alina bit her lip. This might be the antidote she needed after the morning's high drama. She would have to think of something to say, and that would keep her mind from Harry. Against all logic and reason, a tiny kernel somewhere deep inside her had begun to believe Harry would return, but she must squash it down out of sight, keep it hidden. So she smiled, tilted her glance to John's face and spoke teasingly. "You could hardly look more serious if you escorted me to meet King Henry and his Queen, sir."

One eyebrow lifted as he considered his reply. "If I remember correctly, King Henry no longer has a Queen."

Alina shivered. Could he not have accepted her comment in a more light-hearted way? "Aye. Queen Katherine Howard met the headsman last February, sir. I spoke loosely. I apologise." *He* could offer the next conversational opening, for *she* would say nothing more.

He lifted her hand to his mouth and deposited a light, chaste kiss on her knuckles. Surprised, impressed more than she cared to admit by his confidence, she watched him and noted how the chased silver aiglets of his shirt cords glinted. Almost jewellery, then; but discreet rather than showy. It spoke volumes about his character.

"The King seeks to marry yet another lady." His mouth relaxed in a smile. "Romance is in the air again."

Alina shuddered. "I am glad he does not glance in my direction."

John looked down from his vast height. "Is it too cold for you? May I get you a shawl?"

"It was merely the thought of meeting the headsman that made me shiver...Oh, look, here's Lance." Fluttering her lashes, she smiled. "Perhaps you have not met my younger brother?"

"Once, I believe, but he was little more than knee-high. You've grown, Lance. How old are you now?"

Lance removed his shoulder from the wall. "Fourteen, sir."

"Almost fourteen," Alina interposed. "We are to walk in the orchard, Lance."

Lance's mouth turned down. "You can be all around it inside five minutes."

"I know, sweetheart. But we can go round it several times, can we not?"

"You'll get your gown wet. The grass is long and still bedewed."

"Any one would think you did not want us to walk in the orchard, Lance."

"I don't."

Before Alina could demand why, her suitor interrupted. "I'm sure a lad like you has more exciting things to do. We won't mind if you leave us to our own company."

"Of course not." She shook her head at Lance as she spoke.

Lance frowned. "I think I'll stay." His gaze shifted from her to John. "I could ask John about horses."

"Master Errington to you," Alina rebuked.

John linked her arm through his and patted her hand. "I think we must resign ourselves to a juvenile chaperone."

He saw through her little ploy and yet he did not seem annoyed. John Errington went up a notch in her estimation. "We could sit in the sun and talk. Father never tells me what's going on in the neighbourhood, much less in the country. He believes women should have no interest in such topics."

They approached the wooden seat in the sunniest corner between the two high stone walls. John stared down at it dubiously. "Are you sure it is sturdy enough?"

"It's really, really old," Lance said from behind them. "It was made before the raids started. Auld John told me."

"Which raids? You don't mean the ones that started with Edward's death in 1307?"

Lance nodded.

"But that would make it...two hundred and thirty-six years old." John looked at the seat with new respect.

"The oak is older," Lance said. "Auld John says it was a young sprig when the Romans lived up on the hill."

Alina walked forward and sat down. "See? It is quite safe."

John laughed. "Is everything here as old as this bench?" He looked around. "I noticed a roof that could do with some attention." He nodded at the sagging roofline on the kitchen block. "You've moved here recently, I think? We thought Aydon was a ruin and wondered why Sir Reynold bought it."

Alina blessed him for his thoughtfulness. It was far easier to talk of mundane things. "The de Raymes family exchanged Aydon for lands near Shortflatt. Aydon was dilapidated but Uncle Reynold started repairs. Now it is a staircase they renew, and after that the new roof goes on the kitchen block. I shall probably be deaf by then," she added with feeling. "We used to live at the Grey House and it was much nicer than this. I think—no, I shouldn't say that."

Father liked the idea of living in a castle and had been swift to leave the comfortable farmhouse, but she could not be disloyal and say so to a stranger. John waited, but Alina shook her head.

John Errington cleared his throat. "You will like the house at Sandhoe. All our modifications are complete and there is a splendid view down to the Tyne. But perhaps you have seen all it has to offer and remain unimpressed?"

The deepness of his voice still surprised her. She twitched on her seat at his courteous reminder that he wished to be considered as more than a visitor. If she married him, she would live at Sandhoe, midway between Corbrige and Hexham. She sensed his approval and glanced down at her hands.

If only Harry stood over her rather than Errington she would not have begged Lance to stand guard. She remembered the swift exchange of kisses in the windswept darkness and glanced at John Errington. His mouth was narrower than Harry's, with more sharply incised curves. The thought of kissing him did not make her heart beat faster, but he would expect kisses and much more once they were married.

Unless Harry returned in time.

She would think about that later. "Tell me about Sandhoe." She would be polite and pleasant but that was all. Let some other girl snare John Errington.

"Surely you've been?" He laughed with hardly a sound, his teeth small and white in his sunburned face. He leaned closer, reached out and ran a strand of her chestnut hair through his fingers.

"I don't think so." Alina flicked her hair away from him, pushed it back under her coif and glanced up at Lance. He leaned against the wall, his sturdy young arms folded across his chest. "Have we been, Lance? Do you remember?"

"I went with Father one day. It still has the tower but there's a new house to one side, bigger than this, with a walled garden and a pond stocked with fish. You were not at home that day," he added, looking at John.

John's hazel eyes regarded Alina. "Would you like to ride over and visit? With your mother's permission, of course…"

Alina shook her head. There was no point in seeing the house, or building up his hopes of marriage. "Perhaps another day."

***

Lionel dropped his spoon into the empty bowl, shoved it out of his way and placed his forearms on the table. "Errington is the sort of brother-in-law a man would like as a friend. A gentleman born and bred, one who'll be loyal to the last drop of blood."

Alina wound her spoon through the pool of honey on her porridge and did not answer. John Errington's daily visits took up so much of her time she did not know if she enjoyed them or not.

Certainly they removed her from the daily tasks of spinning and sewing for a little while, but everyone's calm acceptance of John as her bridegroom unsettled her. After a week of visits even the workmen in the yard stopped chiselling long enough to greet him, the servants welcomed him by name and her mother seemed charmed by him.

She wrinkled her nose at her brother. "I'll choose a bride for you, shall I? Or better yet, *you* marry him."

Lionel laughed and flipped the lace flounces at his wrist into place. "I'll do my own choosing, thank you. Father and Mama like him well enough."

Alina blew air through her nose. "You mean Father values the connection with the Erringtons."

Lance frowned at them both. "He'd be my brother in law too, and I'd rather have Harry Scott."

Lionel heaved a sigh and pushed to his feet. "You'd better get used to it, both of you. Scott has gone, he won't be back and the bridegroom will be Errington."

Lionel snatched his bonnet from the table and left the hall. Alina spooned up porridge. She liked John, and she hated misleading him. Yet until she knew Harry had returned, there was no point in making a fuss. She got up and wandered to the south window seat. When Lance trailed behind her, she tucked her feet out of the way to make room for him on the opposite ledge. The seat was big enough for two, the sunshine warmed them and they had the hall to themselves.

"Is Harry going to come back?" Lance whispered.

"I hope so." Alina strove to be positive. "I know it's been a whole week, but he'll come, I know he will."

"But Father tried to kill him. He'll try again if Harry returns."

Alina looked out of the window. Lance was right. Father would be furious if Harry sought her out. But if Harry felt anything for her, he would surely come. After all, a week had not lessened his appearance in her thoughts, nor his importance to her happiness.

"I wouldn't go back to a place where they'd tried to kill me," Lance said. "Would you? Honestly?"

"I don't know, Lance. I've never had to think about such things before. I don't suppose I would, unless I had very good reason." She had to hope Harry considered her reason enough.

"Well, he can't come back unless you've made Father accept him."

"And how do you propose I do that?"

Lance shrugged.

Alina clasped her hands about her knees and rocked back and forth on the stone seat. She could almost feel the strands of the net tighten about her as the day for her marriage to John crept closer. The Errington family were pleased with the arrangements, her parents were delighted and messengers scurried between the two houses on a daily basis.

Her gaze lifted to the delicate tracery of vines, a soft translucent green against the promised coat of lime-wash that shone white as fresh snow in the sunlight. The hall had been washed and limed in two days, but the artisan needed a further three days to paint the vine across the full width of the wall behind her father's chair. Her mother admired the work, but the artist might as well have painted the word Marriage in bold red letters for all that it meant to Alina.

Lance's nose pressed up against the glass and he peered down into the ravine below. Did he remember how Harry chose to jump rather than be pushed? She knew Lance wished for Harry's return almost as much as she did herself.

Madcap ideas of how she might evade the marriage with John flowed through her mind. She considered telling Lance her plans, looked at him and remembered his youth. Her fingers tightened around her knees. The temptation to confide gained in the battle with good sense. She reminded herself that the fewer people who knew where she planned to hide would mean she was less likely to be found. On the other hand, she needed someone to tell Harry where to look for her. If he returned…

"Lance…"

She recalled how the boys had tried and failed to cover their tracks when Cuddy blurted out Harry's name at the dinner table. *Discretion, Alina, discretion! Don't overburden your brother because you need to talk.*

"Oh, nothing," she said aloud.

It was too much to ask such a young boy to keep silence. She would wait a while longer. The wedding was still three weeks away. If Harry failed to return, she might as well marry John. It would be the more sensible option. Father would see that she married someone, and rather John than some corpulent fifty-year old with acres of land and a ready-made family older than her.

***

Two weeks went by with no word of Harry. At the beginning of the third week, Alina lay in bed as dawn crept in through the small round window above her head and watched the darkness turn to grey. The murmur of doves and the sharper song of the blackbird and finch blended together and told her it was time to rise.

Privacy was hard to come by at Aydon. Once she dressed and went downstairs there would be her parents, three brothers, the servants, maids and farm hinds bustling about. Staying where she was, Alina's gaze roved the patterns in the wattle wall between her and the boys, examined the knot holes in the wooden planks around the door, and settled on the stone wall to her right.

How long before Harry returned?

She lay still, folded her hands together and closed her eyes. Using words like an incantation, she focussed her mind on Harry's blue eyes and urged him home. *Come, Harry, come to me!* Over and over the words whispered through her mind. Wherever he was, she must reach him. He must come, for time was slipping away like sand in the hourglass. If he did not come soon, she would be John's wife, and that would be that. She would be trapped. Within months, or perhaps within weeks, she would be pregnant.

She opened her eyes. The effort of sending her message out into the ether made her warm and the day had moved on. Now a beam of sunlight flooded into her room and hit the opposite wall. Small sounds told her the boys were stirring next door, and that meant the peace would soon give way to mutters and grumbles and the thud of feet on the floorboards. With a sigh she prepared to get up and meet the coming day.

After breaking her fast, Alina held the reins of the little cart and drove down the hill and through the ford into Corbrige. Confident of her skill, she tipped her face to the sunshine and enjoyed the rush of air as the pony whisked the cart towards St Andrews grey tower. Joseph sat at her shoulder, one foot braced against the footboard and a wary eye on the way she handled the pony.

"Not so gentle, Miss Alina. He needs to know who's master."

"Mistress, you mean." Alina pursed her mouth to hide a smile. Auld John had taught her to drive when she was ten years old, but Joseph always thought she needed more instruction. She flicked the reins and the pony obligingly picked up speed on the flat stretch. She glanced at Joseph. "He does everything I ask, so why should I treat him as if he's naughty?"

Joseph sighed. "He refused at the ford back there."

"No, he didn't. He hesitated to make sure of his footing. It's a mossy bottom."

"Aye, it's no good arguing with you now you're grown, Miss Alina. You know everything."

"Dear Joseph, I drive the cart well and you know it." She leaned sideways towards him and smiled. "Auld John taught me, so how could I do anything else?"

He grinned but didn't answer. His mild gaze surveyed the market place ahead of them. "There's a spot, over there by the church wall. D'ye see it?"

She drove into the space at the end of a line of farm carts and shaggy horses and drew her pony to a halt with his nose a hand span from the church wall. "There we are. He'll be comfortable here in the shade. We won't be long, after all."

She waited for Joseph's hand to assist her down from the cart, and while he looped the reins and tied the cart to a ring in the wall she removed the woollen shawl from her shoulders and bundled it beneath a piece of sacking. The air was warm enough now. She slid her palms down the sleek sides of her green gown, checked for creases and decided she would do. Tossing her thick chestnut plait behind her shoulders, she walked forward a few paces. It would not take long to make their purchases in a swift progress around the market stalls and then a steady journey up the hill and back home in time for the midday meal.

Joseph seized the big wicker basket from the back of the cart and caught up to her. "It's crowded, even for market day, Miss Alina. You stay close by me." He set off through the crowd. He'd barely gone a few yards when he slowed and turned. His expression hardened and Alina saw the glint in his eyes as he gestured over his shoulder.

"There're a few wild types here, so don't you be traipsing about on wee jaunts of your own, Miss Alina. That's Footless Will Dodd over there and Dandie's Hob next to him. They're known reivers from up Otterburn way."

Alina stared across the market place. "Which one's which?"

Joseph regarded her with pity. "Don't be daft," he said, with all the warmth of a man who had watched her grow from childhood. "Why would a whole man be called Footless Will Dodd?"

Alina suppressed a grin and looked again. "Ah, I see. It's obvious when he moves, for he drags that leg and his boot looks rather odd."

She swung around and glanced at the pair of bog trotters waiting patiently alongside their cart "That's why those ponies looked so rough and unkempt. They belong to those two, don't they?"

"Aye, no doubt they do." Fascinated, she stared across the market place at the reivers. Both wore sleeveless jacks, a thick wool scarf, fustian doublets, leather breeches and thigh-high riding boots with cruel looking spurs. She eyed their beards and moustaches with distaste.

"They don't look very clean."

Joseph grunted. "Neither would you, Miss Alina, if you lived like they do." He steered her through the crowds to the market stalls. "Never mind them. Let's get on with the job in hand."

"It's not often I see reivers, Joseph." She smiled at him and could not resist another swift glance over her shoulder. "Regard it as part of my education."

"Education?" Joseph shot her a glance that said she was being foolish. "You'd regret it if they got a hold of you and no mistake."

"I have no intention of being got a hold of," she grinned.

Joseph scowled. "Get on with you," he muttered.

Alina consulted her mother's carefully written list. "What does that say?" She pointed to a word on the paper. "Mother's written it so small and crabbed I cannot make it out."

Joseph, proud of his ability to read a few basic words, peered over her shoulder, frowning. "It's lucky it's not been written over three times already. I think it says salt. Aye, salt."

Alina stared at the scrap of paper in her hand. "Joseph, you clever man. Salt it is." She carefully folded the scrap and shoved it in her belt purse. "Now, where first? Fish, fowl or vegetables?"

They assembled what they needed inside half an hour. Joseph hauled the heavy wicker basket back to the cart, anxious to be off. A gentle tap on Alina's shoulder made her turn. The woman from the silk and thread stall stood behind her.

"Why, Mary, how are you? I haven't seen you since…" Alina's voice faltered, for Mary's plump, homely face reminded her of the day she had seen Harry and chided him for knowing nothing about needles.

"Ah, Miss Alina, I do well, thank ye for askin'." She glanced at Joseph and lowered her voice. "I have a message for ye but ye might not want Joseph to hear it." She stepped back a pace or two and drew Alina out of range of Joseph's sharp ears. "There's a bonny lad a-waiting under the church tower if ye've a mind to speak wi 'im."

Alina stared into the rosy, smiling face and suddenly found it a struggle to breathe. Could it be…could it be Harry? She could not frame the words to ask the question.

Mary nodded as if she understood. "Aye, it's him. Off wi ye. I'll keep Joseph company."

Alina half-turned, casting about for an excuse that would pacify Joseph. "Mary reminds me I ought to say a prayer in church for Sir Reynold before we leave. I believe I shall."

Suspicion clouded Joseph's brows but before he had chance to complain, she was away, her skirts bunched in one hand as she winnowed through the crowd towards the church.

Chapter Eleven

Harry! It must be! Who else would Mary send Alina to meet? It had to be Harry. These last two weeks had proved the longest of her life.

She reached the gate, flung it open and sped along the flagged stone path. Excitement lent speed to her heels.

The heavy wooden door of St Andrew's church stood open. She stopped abruptly on the threshold, panting lightly from the run, her palms flat against the stone door jamb to either side, and peered into the dim interior. Cool air flowed out of the building, bringing with it an overpowering smell of stone, wood and perfume from a huge bunch of meadow flowers someone had dumped in a wooden bucket by the stone font.

Her eyes ached. She blinked, then scanned the gloomy interior for any sign of Harry. The rapid hammering of her heart reverberated in her ears, through the bones of her skull, and pattered against the stiff buckram of her bodice. She inhaled, and listened to the silence.

Where was he?

She took a step over the threshold and pushed the door shut. The wood scraped across the flags and she had to put her shoulder to it before it finally closed. If he was here she wanted no witnesses to their meeting. She turned to face the tall Roman arch beneath the tower and her skin prickled in the cool, shadowy air. Was it her imagination, or could she hear her heart thudding like a child's drum in the stone cavern of the church? Even her shallow breaths sounded loud in the deep silence

A shadow moved in the space behind the stone font. A tall, well built man stood there, naught but a silhouette against the sunlight pouring in through the paned window behind him. With her back to the empty nave, dazzled and unsure, Alina remained still.

"Alina? How are you?"

It was the exact timbre of his voice. He spoke softly, perhaps remembering he was in church, but he was real, he had returned. Her prayers were answered at last. She launched forward, her steps light across the smooth grey flagstones.

"Harry! It *is* you!" Her fingers clutched at his leather sleeve, tightened on the hard flesh beneath. He caught her in his arms, lowered his head and sought her lips.

Then she remembered that nothing had been decided between them. She ought to behave with propriety.

She drew back.

He chuckled. She had a fleeting glimpse of his dense blue eyes before he reached for her again, gathered her in and folded her tight against his chest. Her feet left the floor and all the air fled her lungs on a squeak of protest. She hesitated only a moment and then flung her arms around his neck and buried her face against the soft collar of his linen shirt. "Oh, Harry. *Harry!*"

Unaccountably, her throat swelled and she couldn't breathe. She buried her face in his shoulder to hide her ugly grimace.

His palm pressed her against him. "Alina, what...?"

"I thought you were dead!"

His murmur of laughter sounded against her ear. "Oh, is that it? Didn't you know I was safe? Surely you knew?"

She snuggled her face to his throat and breathed in the warm, dizzying scent of him. Then she pushed back in his arms and regarded every feature of his face. With one finger she traced the line of his cheek, found it led to his mouth. He kissed the finger.

"You look well," she whispered. "And happy. Matho told me how you escaped—by landing as light as a squirrel on that fallen tree. But Harry—"

He laughed and swung her to and fro in his arms. "I assure you it was hardly that easy."

"Put me down." He lowered her but did not let go of her. With her feet firmly on the cold flags, Alina wrenched her head back to see him better.

"I looked over one day afterwards, when I knew you were safe, and I saw the tree, stretching across the ravine." She shuddered and shut her eyes. "If you'd missed it..."

Harry shrugged. "I didn't have much choice, did I? I slammed into that tree trunk like a sack of corn hitting the threshing floor and all but bounced right off again."

Her hand flew to her mouth. He drew it slowly away. "Once I shuffled along to the beech tree it wasn't so bad. The last six feet to the ground was easy."

Suddenly aware that she was in his arms, she wriggled out of his grasp. Face flaming, she patted her hair smooth and stepped back. "I'm glad. Father should never have done it. He had no right at all." She pulled a face. "He's had the fallen tree taken down and chopped up for firewood, swears no one else will escape him in such a manner."

"I'd never have got away without Matho's help."

"You'd never have known about the fallen tree, that's true. But Harry, why did he go against my father to help you?"

"I owe him a great deal. Matho isn't in trouble, is he?"

She shook her head.

He stepped towards her, his eyes alight. "I told you I would come back. Did you not believe me?"

His eyes taunted her, and the problems of Matho and her father faded away. Nothing mattered as long as Harry was alive and well and at her side. "I don't remember you saying anything like that. In fact, I'm perfectly sure you said nothing of the kind."

"I thought I did. I certainly intended to do so."

"Oh, Harry." She shook her head at him. "Don't tease me. Your nose is sunburnt. And your hair is curling over your collar. You've been away ages."

"Did you miss me?" He grinned and checked her from her toes to her crown. "I think you did, for you are thinner than when I saw you last. And I remembered you in your pretty green dress."

Alina glanced down and realised it was the gown she had worn the day she met Harry. "Do you wonder I'm thinner? Ever since the day Father discovered you I've been afraid for you."

"Ah, yes. A memorable day, certainly. And the one following wasn't easily forgotten, either." He sobered. "But do you know what I remember most of all? What brought me back here?"

She shook her head. Surely he had come back for her? Words stuck in her throat.

"I remembered that you came to see me in my dungeon. How I held you through the iron bars…"

Heat swirled into her skin, crept into her cheeks. She steadied herself against rising hope.

"…how delightful you felt beneath my fingers. I couldn't forget you, Alina, no matter how hard I tried."

Her body remembered, too. The skin he had fondled that night rose and tingled in anticipation. She drew her lower lip between her teeth and saw his eyes darken.

"Alina, I have to find a way around your father."

Was that a declaration? It might be. "What do you mean, Harry?"

He paced towards the nave. "How do you feel about me? Would you marry me?"

"I might, if you ever asked me." Her eyes wide, she waited, and it seemed that the stones of the old church stretched out in the tingling silence. There was nothing she would like better than to marry him, but already she was promised to another. When he did not reply, she cried out. "Oh, Harry…Father insists I marry John Errington."

The hint of laughter vanished from his eyes.

The sunlight crawled across the floor of the tower as they stared at each other. The shadow of the window leads bisected his face and gave her the odd sensation that there were two Harrys; one she knew and one she did not.

Of course, she did not know him well. Their bodies may match, and she might adore him, but what did she really know of him?

He walked out into the nave and gripped the rim of the stone font so hard his knuckles shone white. "Then I must find a way to face your father, and quickly. Perhaps with an army at my back, heh?"

She spread her fingers on the opposite side of the font. "Don't joke, Harry." The mockery in his blue gaze frightened her.

"Do you want to marry this...Errington?"

He bit the name off with a snap of his teeth. Alina did not know what she had expected, but this did not seem right. "It isn't John's fault. I should have married nearly three years ago, but John—he was called John, too—died suddenly before he came of age. Father was...took it as a personal insult, and for a long time refused to do anything about seeking another match for me. I think he received several refusals, which didn't help. Now he has settled on Errington, and I have no say in the matter. Neither does John. Given my age and the absence of other offers, I suppose it was inevitable. They are our neighbours."

She spoke stiffly, staring at him. Could he not say what she wanted to hear? What she needed to hear? Exasperation burst through. "Did you not miss me *at all?*"

Her words resonated through the hollow church. His expression softened. "Oh, of course I did." His hand lifted from the stone, but she backed away from him. "I missed you so much it brought me straight back here instead of presenting my report in Carlisle as I should have done." He offered a small smile. "You see, much as I dislike it, already you have come between me and my duty."

She eyed him speculatively. "What do you mean, you dislike it?"

"Oh, because I had planned to seek out and marry a rich heiress. I'm not a rich man, Alina. But it seems I am drawn to you like no other."

"That's something, I suppose."

He chuckled. "I don't suppose I told you why I was riding so close to Aydon that night?"

She shook her head. "The night you rode into the tree?"

He glanced at his feet, a smile curving his mouth. "Now, being of sound mind and whole memory, I can tell you. I ran into the raiders that night. One of them pursued me, hurled his dagger at me. Bessie saw it flash in the moonlight, flung away so violently I flew straight on and crashed into the tree."

"You *saw* the raiders?"

He nodded. "I not only saw them but rode right into them outside your gates. I ran for my life. Did your farm hind never complain about hoof prints across his vegetable patch? One of them chased me back to the meadows and I'm dammed lucky he didn't stop and slit my throat. So you see it's your fault."

Wide-eyed, she stared. "Me?"

"The route I had planned did not go anywhere near Aydon Hall. It must have been you."

"And that's supposed to impress me?"

"But don't you see? It means I was drawn to you in spite of everything—the hatred of the name, my duty, everything."

Alina thought about it. "I think it means you came in spite of your better judgement, which is hardly flattering. I know nothing about you, but I suspect Scott is hardly your real name and you come and go like a thief in the night. Why should I trust you?"

He let go of the font and looked down his nose at her. "If you knew—" He stopped, silenced perhaps by the way she stared at him. "I jeopardised my mission because of you—"

"Your mission?" Alina let scorn flavour her voice. "Now you are going to tell me you dabble in state secrets, and scurry around at the King's behest?"

Harry hesitated, his eyes wary. The silence stretched out around them.

Alina blinked. "That's what you do? Harry, tell me!"

"In a way, yes."

She opened her mouth and then closed it again. He meant it.

"You may believe what you like but I must go and make my report. Then I will be free to do what I wish." He took two swift strides around the font, and caught her face between his cupped palms. She flinched away from him but he held on. "I swear that I will return before you have had time to miss me."

She slapped his hands away. "Harry, that's no answer. How long will you be? What if I'm forced to marry before you get back?"

"Where has that pretty smile gone, sweetheart?"

"Tell me when you expect to be back here in Corbrige. You could ride out of here and vanish and I wouldn't know where to find you."

"Um." His brows rose high as he considered her.

She waited, but he said nothing more. Rattled, she clung to some semblance of dignity. "I don't want to know what you were doing in Edinburgh, but I would like some home truths. *Is* Scott your real name?"

"No."

"I knew it! You've lied to me from the beginning!"

"You needn't scowl so. I know they say never trust a man who says trust me, but….Trust me, Alina. I need time, perhaps as much as a week and I shall return and make everything plain."

"I am to marry on the third Friday of the month. You have exactly four days to ride to Carlisle, make your report and return. Otherwise I shall be married to John Errington. Do you promise?" She looked up into his face. "If you do plan to disappear, then please, say so, Harry. Do not tease me in this."

He seized her hands in his, raised them to his lips and kissed them. "I shall return on the fourth day. I swear it on my honour as a gentleman."

His next kiss was swift and hard on the lips.

She made a small, incoherent sound, heard it as if it came from someone else's throat, felt the hardness of his teeth against her mouth and flinched away from him. Harry softened his grip. "I'm sorry, I'm sorry."

He lowered his head once more, slowly this time, and hovered over her, waiting.

She wanted his mouth. Stretching up on tiptoe, she found and played with the touch of his lips. Enjoyed the softness, the warmth, the moisture. Breathing deep, she let the scent of him flow into her, and felt the leap and bound of her blood, heard it in her head, felt the pulse beat in her throat. Her knees tingled and she realised how dangerous a kiss could be.

His strength surrounded her, held her in a grip as strong as steel, but she was not afraid. Had she not dreamt, in the privacy of her bed, of such kisses, believed she knew what might be in store for her when they met once more? Her body glowed, places that she had barely registered before today now tingled and itched. A most indecent urge to rub against the hardness of him took over her senses.

"Oh, my!" She drew back, shaken by her responses, wanting more, much more and yet wary at the same time. When he would have pulled her closer, she pushed against him.

His gaze, bright and eager, swept over her. "If I forgot earlier, then this time, I tell you to your face—I must have you."

The pulse in his neck hammered, and she wondered if her heartbeat galloped at matching speed. Light-headed, she clung to him. "Ah, but what shall you do about it?"

He dragged a hand through his thick dark hair. "Oh, Alina." The groan became a low murmur of laughter. "I have returned from Edinburgh, where I achieved…" He frowned as if trying to remember all he had done. "Let's say much of my business there is done. Now I am on my way to meet with…the Deputy Lord Warden, and offer a report. I should have gone straight to Carlisle, but….Once my report is made, I will be free to travel back here."

Alina looked up at him, her eyes pleading. "Must you go now?"

"I must, Alina. I have that report to make." He smiled. "But first, I think another kiss would not be too much to ask?"

He caught her arm, pulled her towards him and dropped a swift kiss on her puckered lips. "It won't be too long. I promise you that."

One hand swept her close, pinioned her hips against him while the other slid up between them and found the curve of her breast. He groaned, and a tingle of excitement shot through her. His hand lifted, but his fingertips caressed her flesh so lightly she arched against him, anxious for more.

"And when you do return? Father will still hate you. Also, I might be married."

The church door opened with a squeal of timber across stone. The heavy wood stuck halfway, and Harry used the moment of delay to push Alina behind him.

Chapter Twelve

Harry's broad back cut off Alina's view of the church door, but she heard the crash as the solid wood hit the wall and the smothered expletive that followed it. She peered around Harry and saw John Errington stepping into the gloom of the church.

John was hardly going to be pleased to find her alone with Harry. Something of her trepidation must have shown in her face, for Harry glanced at her and then turned to face the newcomer in such a way that he shielded her from view.

John's deep voice rolled across the stone church. "I was told Miss Carnaby was here. Ah, is that Alina behind you?"

Of course, he would be able to see her green skirts behind Harry's boots. She must face him; it was silly to think that she could avoid him.

"It is," she said, moving to Harry's side.

Alina flashed a taut smile at Harry. "This is John Errington."

Harry's mouth flattened. "Harry Scott, sir." The slight inclination of Harry's head did duty as a bow.

John ignored him. "What are you doing here, Alina?"

"I came to say a prayer for my uncle." She summoned a smile. "Were you looking for me?" John returned her smile and ignored

Harry. Alina walked slowly towards him. "I did not know you were to be in Corbrige today."

"Your father is outside, waiting for us. Come, Alina."

Oh, Dear Lord! Her father! She threw an agonised look Harry's way. John moved forward, one arm outstretched to sweep her out of the church. The difference in the two men stuck her in that moment. Harry's muscular build and rough riding clothes contrasted sharply with John's velvets and plumed hat. In her bones she knew the difference went deeper and saw it confirmed when Harry stepped forward ready to do battle.

Behind his head dust motes danced across the single ray of sunshine from a high window. A thread of noise from the market place drifted through the half-open door.

Alina shook her head. "Forgive me, Harry, but I must go. There is a lot to do before next week."

She smiled up at John and his facial muscles relaxed. Anxious to part the two men, Alina hurried towards the door. Errington followed, placed his hand on the latch and then stopped. He looked back at Harry.

Alina glanced from one man to the other and sensed a confrontation looming. She placed her hand on Errington's sleeve. "Come, sir, it is time to collect Joseph and drive home."

John shrugged, smiled and followed her out of the church. Relieved that no voices had been raised, no blows struck, Alina held onto his arm. Anxious to distract him from thinking about Harry, she gestured towards the gate. "There's Joseph, waiting for me. And Father, too."

John frowned suddenly as if he had remembered something. "That name seemed familiar, Alina. Was Scott not the man your father wished to execute a little while ago? The reiver?"

"No, of course not—a different Scott." Alina prayed that the Lord would forgive her for the lie. She smiled brightly. "There are so many of the creatures. Harry saved my life when a bull ran wild in the market, and I wished to exchange a few words, thank him—Heavens, how he would hate it if I told him you thought he looked like a reiver—"

"I trust you have given him your thanks today. He has mine also." Errington smiled down at Alina, but she noticed the frown still held his brows together. As if that wasn't worry enough, she knew that if her father saw Harry, there would be blood spilt on the cobbles. She glanced back over her shoulder. There was no sign of Harry.

She kept her hand on John's velvet-covered arm and hurried to keep up with his long stride. If Father accompanied them back to

Aydon, it would leave the coast clear and Harry could depart in safety.

At the gate, John paused, his free hand resting on the ancient grey wood. "A church gate should always be open." He tucked her arm close against his side and patted her hand as it lay on his sleeve. "Soon we shall do this in earnest," he remarked, hazel eyes gleaming down on her.

It took Alina a moment to realise he thought of them walking into and out of church together on their wedding day. She offered a weak smile, murmured assent, ducked her head as if shy and stole a glance over her shoulder.

Harry padded across the churchyard towards the sycamore tree, the place where they talked the day they first met. In a way it was a good thing John Errington had come into the church and announced that her father was outside. Without that warning, Harry might have walked straight into him. As it was, he should be able to slip over the wall at the far end of the market and remain safe.

Lionel grinned at her and Joseph waited quietly at the church gate. Father greeted her briefly and found something of interest at the far side of the marketplace. Alina looked back over the churchyard, but Harry had vanished. He must be over the wall and in the marketplace by now.

"By God, look who it is!" Her father grabbed Lionel by the arm and pointed. Alina's muscles clenched.

In disbelief she watched her father break into a lumbering run across the cobbled square. After the briefest hesitation, Lionel followed, one hand holding his sword in place against his thigh.

Alina stood on tiptoe but could not see what was happening. "John, what is it? What's the matter?"

"There seems to be some kind of altercation going on," he said, peering over the heads of those flocking across the marketplace. "Your friend Harry and two ugly-looking brutes—"

"Footless Will Dodd and Dandie's Hob," Joseph murmured for Alina's benefit.

"Oh, no!" Her hand went to her throat. "What shall we do?"

John gave her a strange look, then swung round on the Aydon servant. "And they are…?"

"Border reivers, sir. Tynedale men. They've had a running argument with the Carnabys for a while now."

Alina did not wait for John. She ran after her father and elbowed her way to the front of the cheerful crowd. Full of fear for her father, her brother and Harry, she got there in time to see Harry race to his horse, unhitch the reins and vault onto its back. The two reivers laughed and let him go.

Harry disappeared between the cottages that led to Carelgate and the river track towards Hexham. Alina whirled back and found Errington behind her, protecting her from the jostling crowd. She watched open-mouthed as her father pushed his way through the crowd.

"Get out of my way, you useless swine!" Carnaby roared. "He's getting away!"

Footless Will and Dandie's Hob moved again and again to block any pursuit of Harry. Alina, hand to mouth, watched Footless Will draw his sword and brandish the steel a finger's length from her father's nose. Lionel, full of bravado but uncertain of his father's intentions, faced a chortling Dandie's Hob.

"Now, now, let's no' be hasty," Footless Will chided. "Yon lad's a stranger here, right enough, but that's no reason to cut up rough wi 'im."

"Dodd, that man's a Scott. Let me after him! He deserves punishment for reiving my cattle!"

Footless Will looked unimpressed. He was hardly likely to aid her father against one of his own. The sword tip waved in a circle that was never far from her father's face and she shivered at the thought of cold steel slicing through warm flesh. Behind her, the stallholders and the good folk of Corbrige muttered and chortled amongst themselves in anticipation of some fun.

A stentorian bellow came out of the crowd. "He's no reiver, Carnaby. He's the brave lad who saved your daughter. Did she no' tell ye?" Alina recognised Master Rutherford's round face at the back of the ring of onlookers. *Thank you, Master Rutherford. I wish you had told Father two weeks ago.*

Father wasn't listening. His gauntleted hand swept Fingerless Will's sword point to one side. "Get out of my way!" he snarled. Red faced and furious, he prepared to try and shove his way after Harry.

Alina couldn't help a stab of pride at her father's courage even though she had no wish for him to chase Harry. If Footless Will did not stop her father, she would have to do whatever she could to bring the confrontation to a peaceful end. Wrenching her shoulder out of John's grasp, she flew straight to her father's side, grasped his arm and hung on.

"What's wrong, Father? Why is that man holding a sword against you?"

Carnaby turned purple and shoved her to one side. "Errington, take the girl away!"

A cackle of amusement split Footless Will's whiskers and revealed a surprisingly even row of teeth. "Well, dang me if this'n ain't a pretty young thing. Will ye look at this, Dandie?" Footless Will's wicked black eyes gleamed in his dirty face as he surveyed Alina from head to foot. "How do, missus. Wud ye no' fancy a wee trip back to my tower to meet wi ma bairns? They'll be reet glad to knaw a leddy such a yer'sel."

Carnaby snorted. "Errington!" His hand dived towards his sword.

Alina reached her father, clutched his sleeve and hung on grimly with both hands. "Father! No fighting! You have no cause here. Mama would not wish you to fight! You will be hurt! Lionel, help me!"

Her brother shouldered Dandie's Hob aside and hastened to join her. John Errington moved up to join in the affray. Dandie stuck a boot in John's path. John lurched forward, arms windmilling. Dandie skipped after him, got the sole of his boot against John's backside and shoved.

The crowd roared in appreciation. John's palms scraped the cobbles.

With a roar of rage, Carnaby propelled his daughter to one side. She rolled into Lionel, knocked him off his feet and followed him down.

Dandie's Hob emitted a squawk of laughter and buried it behind a grubby hand. Alina, trapped beneath her brother's legs, saw her father, sword in hand, attacking Footless Will, and shrieked. "No, don't let him fight!"

Lionel swore, hampered by his sister's skirts as he struggled to his feet. Alina got her arms around his knees and hung on. Her brother teetered, arms waving. "Alina! What in damnation are you doing? Let me go!"

She buried her face against his knees and hung on desperately. "You'll be killed," she moaned. From the corner of her eye she watched the two reivers face her father, and prayed he would see sense and give up. Even he could not fight two much younger men. John, having got to his feet, stood off to one side, watching the scene as if unable to believe his eyes.

The crowd roared with good humoured advice and laughter as Footless Will backed off before the furious onslaught of her father's sword.

"The lad's well away beyond Red burn, Carnaby, and your lad's all tied up there wi his sister hangin' off his knees. Time to gi'e up."

Carnaby roared in wordless rage, and lunged towards Footless Will.

Dandie studied the situation, leaned in and with a precise flourish of his weapon, pierced the velvet doublet and drew blood from Carnaby's burly chest. "Ye won't last out," he remarked with chilling confidence. "Will's a clumsy bugger wi only one foot, but the two of us can best ye any time we want. He is'na fightin' serious like. It's only a bit o'fun."

"Fun!" Carnaby's howl rang round the square and bounced off the stones of the church tower. Alina hung on desperately as her brother, almost puce in the face, tried to prise her off his knees without hurting her.

"He's right, sir."

Alina squinted through a tangle of hair. Lionel stopped struggling and looked around. The calm voice came from Joseph, stolid on the sidelines. "I cannot help," he said, arms held wide to indicate his lack of weapons. "Best to withdraw, sir, and fight another day."

Alina let out a long breath and sank back on her heels. Thank the Lord for a man of sense. Her movement tipped Lionel over the point of balance and with a growl Lionel struck the cobbles. The Corbrige stallholders let out a bray of laughter.

Slowly Cuthbert Carnaby lowered his sword and looked around. Lionel sprawled full length on the ground, and Alina sat on his chest. She looked up and caught her father's eye. "You must stop, Father, for I will not let him up to help you."

She caught a glimpse of John Errington's face. He had retreated, red-faced, to the sidelines. His expression suggested he thought they had all gone mad, that he didn't know if it would be wiser to laugh or be furious with her. Oh, dear. She might have to soothe him later, but at least Harry had got away, and both Father and Lionel were safe.

Her father glared at the two reivers. Lionel, furious, tossed Alina to one side and punched her arm for making him look a fool in public.

"Ow! That hurt, you beast!" Alina cried, clutched her arm and then thumped her brother's chest with her fist, much to the amusement of the onlookers. Her father rammed his sword back in its sheath and stalked off without a word. The crowd, hiding their smiles, parted to let him through and then flowed back again to watch the rest of the action.

Lionel grabbed her arm and yanked her against his side. "You're a fool to have annoyed Father so," he muttered for her ears alone. "He'll make you pay for it. You know what he's like these days. He looks to be in a furious temper."

Cuthbert Carnaby rode off alone, and left Joseph and Lionel to follow with Alina. They chose not to hurry home in the hope that Carnaby's temper would have cooled by the time they returned. John Errington took his leave also and set out for Sandhoe. Alina bit her lip and gazed after his retreating figure. She had the feeling he regretted being anywhere near Corbrige this afternoon.

Alina drove the pony cart with half her mind on the task and let the other half wander. Was she right to trust Harry Scott? He was handsome, charming and plausible, but she knew very little about him. Secret business in Edinburgh, if she believed him. He lived in Carlisle, that city noted for its endurance under siege, the veritable hub of the Borderland. She had visited only once, and been amazed at the huge red castle, cathedral and grammar school. Lawless men tended to avoid the city, no doubt disliking the brooding presence of the gallows on Harraby Hill.

It was possible Harry was one of the West March Warden's men. He certainly did not have the look of a tradesman or a farmer. She frowned. Perhaps she had been unwise to give her heart so precipitately. Yet given it was, and she would prove herself a coward if she settled so easily for marriage to John Errington.

"You like John," she called to her brother, riding alongside the cart. "Why? Why do you like him?"

Lionel's shoulders lifted briefly. "There's nothing to dislike about him. He's quiet and considerate and he'll listen to you." He glanced at Alina from the side of his eye. "He's not as flash as Harry Scott, but he has many of the same qualities, I think."

His remark surprised her. "What do you mean?"

Lionel sighed. "Think of the best horse you've ever seen. Now think of the pony that pulls your cart every day of the year. They both do their best for you but you will always favour the horse over the humble pony."

Alina stared at him. "You think I'm so horrid? I love my pony almost as much as I love Dragon!"

"Don't be so literal," Lionel snapped. "Think about it and maybe you'll grasp what I mean." He nudged his horse and cantered on, heading out across the fields where the cart could not venture.

Alina glanced sideways at Joseph, who stared straight ahead as if suddenly struck deaf and dumb. He had heard everything her brother said and he was so much older than either of them. Perhaps he understood.

"Joseph? Do you know what he means?"

Joseph looked down at his blunt-fingered hands and twisted them in his lap. "Aye, I know what the lad means, but I'm not sure I can explain it any better than he did."

Alina sighed. She focussed on the pony's ears. "Do try, Joseph. I need to know. Does he mean that I only care for expensive things?"

Joseph shook his head. "No, Miss Alina. I think he means that the pony is worth as much as the horse though they do different things and the horse will always catch your eye first. Anyone's eye, that is."

"So, he thinks John is worth as much as Harry."

Joseph nodded.

Alina rolled her eyes, but refrained from staring at the man at her side. "But Harry is so much…so much better than John."

"Only in your mind, Miss Alina. To anyone else, they are much the same."

She frowned. "Really?"

"As peas in a pod. Both gentry, both young, both handsome. Both care for you."

"But…" She shook her head. "I cannot agree with you."

"That's because you think yourself in love with one of them, and not wi t'other. That's what makes the difference."

"Oh." She could feel warmth creeping into her cheeks. It seemed even Joseph could tell she was in love with Harry.

"Keep thinking of horses," Joseph said. "It makes life that much easier."

***

When Alina walked into the solar, the atmosphere was heavy with disquiet. Her steps faltered as she glanced around the room. Her mother's restrained greeting and blank expression told its own tale. Alina looked beyond her mother to where her father stared out over the ravine. Alina hovered uncertainly by the table. Her spindle lay there next to the carding basket. She reached for it and then froze.

"If you ever disgrace me again, in public or out of it, I shall take the leather strap to you as I did for the boys when they sheltered Scott." The cold fury in her father's voice stunned her. He stared out of the window, his words pitched to carry no further than the solar. "Do not think that because you are a girl, you will escape."

She stared at him. The boys never mentioned a beating. Had she escaped the leather strap simply because she was female? "No, Father. I'm sorry, but I thought only to save you—"

Carnaby swung round and took a step towards her. "I do not need you to save me, you interfering little bitch!"

"Husband!" Margery Carnaby jerked upright in her chair.

"It is all right, Mama. I did not mean to annoy Father, but if I have, I must apologise." The look in her father's eye caused a shiver to run down Alina's spine but she gritted her teeth and forced herself to meet his gaze.

"I don't want your apologies," he growled. "Nor your half-baked excuses. I am tired of arranging matches for you that come to naught. The sooner you marry Errington, the better I'll like it. Go to your room and stay there until I say you may leave."

Alina turned, her back stiff, and walked to the stairway. Her father's voice followed her as he vented his spleen on his wife. "That girl is full of her own importance. I give her the best of everything, and she repays me by favouring that snivelling whelp Scott. She made me look a fool in front of the entire marketplace today."

With one foot on the lowest stair, Alina halted and looked back. He was watching her. "Ungrateful girl," he snarled. "Don't think to come down to the next meal. Dry bread and water is all you may expect."

She opened her mouth to apologise once more. His hand flashed out. "No. Don't speak. Go."

Alina went slowly upstairs and lifted the latch of her door. As far as she knew, he had arranged only one match for her with the young Woodrington who died. She supposed he had tried to make other matches, and failed. He would hate being refused, take it as a slight and probably never speak of it. How many families had he approached, trying to marry her off? It was a chilling thought, made even colder by the thought that they had all refused.

Her small room under the rafters of the sloping ceiling was on southern side of the building with only a small round hole to let in a little light. Sometimes a sparrow perched there, or a pigeon. It was a room fit only for servants. But at least it offered privacy, of a kind. She could hear the boys' conversations next door. She sat on the edge of the wooden bed frame and covered her face with her hands.

It was no good crying.

Why should she cry? She had saved her father from injury. It was fortunate she had learned of her father's visit to Corbrige before Harry and he met. When she compared Harry's health and strength against her father's age and bulk, she shuddered to think of the outcome of a swordfight between them. To have Harry kill her father would be the last straw. She had done the only thing possible, though her brother and her father's pride had suffered. Probably put herself in a bad light in John Errington's eyes as well, but that could not be helped.

Well, she would endure her punishment. Surely Mama would see she did not starve? Lance and Cuddy would creep in and talk to her. She had a book to read. With a sigh, she realised she had only the stub of a candle and no means of lighting it.

Her stomach growled. Everyone seemed to have forgotten food but it must be time for the evening meal. Would anyone remember her? She lay back on her bed and waited.

Her room at Grey House had been so much better.

Chapter Thirteen

Alina opened her eyes, heard the birdsong outside and discovered the kitten curled into a soft grey ball on her throat. Disentangling herself, she remembered how tedious the last week had been. Today was the day Harry was due to appear. Warmth rolled through her at the thought of him, swiftly followed by worries that made her stomach churn. If Harry should appear, her father was likely to froth at the mouth and attack him with a sword.

She sighed. Father allowed her to speak with John Errington when he called, or to sit and sew with her mother; but the rest of the long, dreary week had been spent in her small, cramped room. There was every chance her punishment might continue. If so, she might never see Harry.

She had endured it all without complaint, for there was no point. Her father's word was law. But now the week was at an end, Harry was due to return and everything must change.

She grieved for John, who would be hurt if the marriage ceremony scheduled for the morrow did not take place. It was something she could not avoid. Mulling over Joseph and Lionel's impressions of John, she had treated the young man more kindly and in doing so had discovered his quiet charm. John visited every afternoon, but of course, she spent the bulk of the endless, depressing week dreaming of herself and Harry as man and wife.

She closed her eyes. Harry would stand close behind her, one hand on her shoulder, the other at her waist. Because he was so tall, his chin would touch the top of her head. She wore her best gown, the one with the dark green stomacher and the gold embroidery, and her hair was braided in a coronet around her head. Harry wore...she frowned. She had only seen him in drab brown, no doubt selected to make him as unnoticeable as possible. In her imagination she promptly changed the brown to crimson, and found he suited the rich colour. When she clothed him in tawny velvet, he looked better still.

A sudden clamour erupted in the solar below. Hurried footsteps rattled across the floorboards and a maid shrieked and called for Mistress Carnaby. Alina sat up and pushed her blanket aside. Some urgent matter was afoot.

She stole to the landing with a blanket clutched about her shoulders and peered down the rickety stairs to the solar. The boys' door opened and Lance padded barefoot across to join her. "What's happening?"

"No idea," she muttered, hearing the muffled sound of sobs. "But I think I'll get dressed and go down."

She retreated, but Lance, clad only in his long linen nightshirt, skipped down the narrow stairs.

By the time she splashed her face in her basin of cold water, combed her hair, pulled on her clothes and persuaded the kitten it really didn't want to hook its claws into her skirt, Lance thudded back up the wooden stairs. "Ally!"

She yanked open her door. "What is it? What's happened?"

"It's Uncle Reynold," he said. "They think he's going to die."

She stared at her brother. She wondered if her eyes had rounded, like his, and if he felt the same mixture of sadness and horror. "Of course," she said slowly. "He has been ill for so long…I am ashamed to say I had forgotten him. Oh, how awful of me."

Stricken by guilt, she tied off the end of her plait and forced her feet into soft, round-toed shoes. The kitten pounced and she put the creature back on the old blanket.

"Are we to see him?" she murmured, waiting outside her brothers' door. Lance, fully dressed, joined her there.

"Don't know. Mother's with him now. Father's getting up." He looked back into the room he shared with his brother. "Cuddy, get dressed!" His troubled hazel eyes regarded her sadly. "I've never seen a dead person."

"Oh, Lance, neither have I. We'll see him together, shall we? And I expect Mama will be there, too. Father will miss him."

She couldn't guarantee what her father would do. Cuthbert had always deferred to his elder, more successful brother, but there was no obvious sign of love between the two men. None that she had been allowed to see, certainly.

"I'm not sure I want to see a dead…um…body." Lance went back into the room he shared with Cuddy, shut the door and left Alina standing on the dark landing.

Slowly, she went to the ground floor, the oldest part of the hall. The low ceiling, the bare grey stone walls and the small windows made the long room gloomy. A few candles burned beside the stone sink and a fire glowed in the vast stone hearth. Servants tiptoed about with cloths and pans of water. A maid sat and peeled potatoes. Alina retreated to the fireplace in the corner of the long room, and waited for her mother.

The door to Sir Reynold's room was shut, but a rim of light shone under the door. She glanced at the window. They must have lit candles against the gloom of grey and overcast skies.

Someone descended the narrow wooden staircase from the solar. Alina saw her father's hand drift uncertainly over the handrail until he came to a halt facing the doorway into Sir Reynold's room.

Cuthbert Carnaby hesitated on the bottom step. His hand closed on the handrail so hard his knuckles turned white. Three deep, rasping breaths followed before he squared his shoulders and lifted his head as though a battle awaited him in the silent, candlelit room his brother had occupied most of the summer.

Alina rose from her stool by the fireplace, but he did not notice her. She watched him walk slowly forward to say goodbye to his dying brother. His hand hovered over the door latch as if he was reluctant to enter and his shoulders lifted as he drew in a deep, mournful breath of air. It came to her that she knew the cause of her father's irascibility this summer, the hot temper that had marked him out from the man she had known all her life. Tears welled, and she was hard pressed to stay them as her father finally entered the room.

Once, she supposed, he and Reynold had played together as boys, and been friends, just as she and Lance—

One hand to her mouth, she turned away, and walked to the window overlooking the orchard. To her, Sir Reynold Carnaby was a small, well-dressed man who spent his life moving between his many residences. He bestowed liberal gifts and then vanished once more on his eternal business with local gentlemen. She realised she hardly knew him. Her visits to him had been infrequent over the last few weeks as he grew weaker, and now it was too late.

For her father, of course, he meant so much more. An older brother who would have been part of Father's life from the day he was born, someone who was always there, always a reassuring presence through the precarious days of childhood adventures and mishaps.

Lance and Cuddy clattered down the wooden stairs to join her. Alina met them, shushed them and bade them sit by the fireplace. Almost immediately their mother beckoned them into the room where their uncle lay. Alina hesitated, but the boys moved forward, half curious, half in awe. Her mother put a calm hand on each boy's shoulder and gave a reassuring squeeze.

"Say your goodbyes now," she whispered. "Bid him Godspeed, for he will not last long."

Alina's throat tightened. She wondered if she would be able to speak at all.

The rest of the day passed in quiet prayer and contemplation, and time grew heavy. The household crept about, all visitors refused except Sir William, who arrived from Halton and marched into his son's room with barely a word for any one.

Alina caught a glimpse of her grandfather's ravaged face and took the boys into the orchard, where they sat in the sunshine and played with Midge and Fly, the herder's dogs. Against the tragedy of death, her own problems concerning her coming wedding and Harry Scott seemed of little consequence. Yet as the morning wore on she wondered how Harry would reach them if all visitors were refused, as they had been today.

"I didn't like that." Cuddy's small voice broke into her thoughts.

"You didn't like what?" Alina asked. Cuddy's face was pinched and white. Lance stared fixedly at Fly, who waited for him to pick up the ball once more.

"Uncle looked like the tharecrow in the Eath Field."

"Oh, Cuddy!" She gave him a swift, one-armed hug, privately thinking that his description was accurate.

Lance stuck out his bottom lip. "It's true. He did, you know he did."

"I never said he didn't," she replied. "He got so thin of late, I know. But can you not remember him as he was at Christmas? Or last year, when he was happy and healthy? That would be a better memory."

"Will we look like that one day?"

She looked down at Cuddy's small, white face and hugged him again. "No, of course not. Uncle was ill, has been ill for a long time. Since May, I think."

"Is that why he was so thin? I've never seen any body that thin, not even Alice." Lance was too old for cuddles, but he sat beside her and allowed Midge to jump onto his lap. Alina noticed how he clutched the bitch close beneath his arm and allowed her to lick his cheek. Nor did he object when she pushed her smooth head beneath his chin.

Alina nodded. "Alice isn't ill, Lance. She doesn't have much to eat, and she's growing so tall. She is thin, though, I grant you that."

"We could take her thom bramble fool," Cuddy said.

"Not till the brambles ripen we can't," Lance muttered. He looked up. "Hello, Matho. Have you heard? Uncle's dying, so everyone's got to be quiet."

Matho's red head gleamed in the sunshine like autumn bracken. "Aye, I know." His burly shoulders and thickset body dwarfed Lance and Cuddy as both boys ran towards him. Midge went, too, in that silent, slinking way of dogs trained to herding.

Matho sombre gaze met Alina's over the boys' heads. "You know I've orders not to let any one in for the next few days?"

Her eyes widened in horror. That meant Harry would not be able to enter. "Has any one I know approached the gate, Matho?"

"Only t'local folk, and they made no fuss. Ah was wonderin' if any one else was expected, so ah could warn them like."

Alina relaxed and smiled as she realised what Matho wanted. "Matho, what would I do without you?" She walked across to join him and laid a hand on each of her brothers' shoulders. "Boys, I must speak to Matho. Play with the dogs. I'll be over there by the gate."

When she stepped out onto the narrow path winding along between the rim of the ravine and the south front of the hall, Matho strode behind her. She did not need to go any further. She could have stayed in the orchard, but walking the little distance gave her time to collect her thoughts and decide what she wanted to say.

The sun heated the vast grey stones of the hall that were comfortingly warm on her back when she leant against them. She looked at Matho. "Harry said he would come back, and he's due today, but I don't know if he'll ride up to the front gate. I have no idea what he plans to do."

Matho nodded. "He'd be daft to dee that, right enough. Better t'slide in by the back door." He stared out across the treetops. "I wus thinkin' that he'd be on the look-out for a handy lad who'll tak a message to ye like. He might think I'd dee it."

"You would, wouldn't you, Matho?" Alina laid a tentative palm against the rough linen of his shirtsleeve and let her eyes plead for her.

His grin was fleeting. "Aye, I suppose so. There's summat aboot that lad." He shook his head. "He went off that bloody cliff like he was sure of soft landing in a pile o'—er, in a haystook." He met her glance, and nodded. "Oh, aye. Nae doot aboot that. It's not knawin' where or when 'e'll come, that's the problem."

"You know I'm supposed to marry John Errington?"

He nodded.

"Well, if Harry hasn't arrived by midnight, I shall leave. I'll go back home, to Grey House. If Harry comes, send him there."

She saw Matho's brows lift and matched his look with a steadfast one of her own. "I've had many hours alone in my room this week, Matho. Before you ask, yes, I've thought about it."

Her father's punishment had given her ample time to consider her future. Dreams of Harry had given way to a more sober consideration of the probability of happiness within marriage to John Errington and she had reluctantly drawn the conclusion that she might come to hate him. His pleasant and comfortable presence would always be a reminder of what she had lost, may even become the symbol of all that forced her to give up Harry.

Added to that was the plain fact that whereas John might always be her friend, he would never be her lover. There was no small shock to her system when he appeared, no jolt when he touched her hand, no sense of something missing when he was not with her. She knew she could live without John in her life, but she was not sure she wanted to live in a world without Harry.

"That's a bit daft, 'ent it? 'ave ye really thought aboot this?"

The rough sentiments brought her back to Matho's worried face. His heavy brows almost met across his nose, and he shook his head.

"I can't marry John."

Matho glanced about as if they might be overheard and Alina realised that they were not far from the window to Sir Reynold's room. She crossed her arms and shivered.

"'as Harry ever spoken to ye aboot marriage? Will he wed ye? Ye name will be good for nowt if ye run out on Errington and Harry doesna want ye. Errington's not a bad lad, when all's said and done."

"John Errington is a fine man," Alina said fiercely, "and if I'd never met Harry I'd have gone to my wedding without a qualm. But I love Harry Scott. Oh, Matho, do you know what it feels like to be in love?"

She'd said the words without thinking, and as soon as they were out expected nothing but ridicule. Matho was not a man to speak of insubstantial things like love. He had been looking out over the ravine, but at her words his head came slowly round and his gaze locked with hers. "Aye," he said slowly. "Ah reckon ah do."

Her relief was enormous. "Then you'll help Harry when he comes? You'll send him on to Grey House?"

He nodded.

Alina was so pleased she failed to see the shadow in his eyes.

***

When Harry walked into his father's comfortable rooms in Carlisle Castle, Sir Thomas Wharton was busy. He waved Harry towards the wine table and went on calmly dictating to the black garbed clerk who spent his life writing letters and reports for the Deputy Lord Warden.

Harry swung off his short cloak, dropped it on a stool and poured a glass of sherry sack. He swallowed a generous measure. Since Sir Thomas and his secretary occupied the only chairs, Harry crossed the floorboards to the small leaded window, leaned his shoulder against the panelled walls and looked out on the dour grey streets of Carlisle. Today the cobbles, slick with damp, were empty but for the crows stalking the rubbish for edible titbits.

Harry looked across the small room.

Father never changed. Even in his late forties, he was still the hard, spare-bodied man Harry remembered from childhood. Life as Deputy Warden of the West March kept him fit, and his victory at Solway Moss last November was characteristic of his ability to take advantage of an opportune moment.

Father avoided the enormous furred cloaks and intricately slashed doublets of the courtier. He preferred instead a plain shirt, sober breeches and leather tunic with a wide belt. A thick woollen riding cloak hung by the door, and even now, at rest in his office he wore riding boots of good leather. The ensemble of a busy and practical man.

His father's voice, chill and precise, continued. The scratch of the secretary's quill across the parchment seemed loud against the small sounds of the hearth fire. Harry listened with half an ear. Every village, township and parish must fetch its animals from their grazing into the streets at night. Both ends of the street or village, whichever was more appropriate, were to be watched and guarded. A hue and cry should be raised if thieves approached.

Sir Thomas's steady instructions paused. Harry glanced over his shoulder. His father consulted lists of crabbed writing, ran his finger down and across the page and barked out names of those to be appointed as setters of watches. Harry smiled as he heard the command that a second tier be set up to ascertain that men turned up and performed their appointed duty. Defaulters were to be reported, and fined.

"Alexander Heron and Alexander Baxter shall set watches for the areas of Alnewyke, Corbrige, Halton....The overseers shall be Cuthbert Carnaby and Thomas Weldon."

Harry's shoulder came off the wall.

"What's the matter, boy?" Sir Thomas's cold gaze lifted at Harry's sudden movement.

Harry shrugged. "I know Carnaby, that's all."

"Allow me time for another page, and this matter will be ended. Then we may talk."

Harry nodded and turned back to the window. His father went on at great speed, leaving Harry to stare at his own reflection in the glass. His thoughts turned to his last sight of Alina in Corbrige market. The reflection shuddered, reformed and a pair of great brown eyes surrounded by glossy chestnut hair stared back at him.

He stirred restlessly, remembering their stolen kisses beneath the Roman arch of the old stone church. She crept into his thoughts at the most inopportune moments, had done so most of the way to Edinburgh. She invaded his dreams, hovered at his shoulder while he persuaded desperate men to accept the English king's silver. He shook his head, unaware that he smiled.

She was not the bride he wanted, not the bride he dreamed of marrying. She possessed no title, no estates and no prospect of such things. He leaned his brow against the cool glass. He'd be a fool to tie himself to her. And yet, she haunted him.

The scrape of chairs drew him back into the room. The business of the day was complete and the black-garbed secretary rose and bowed himself out of the room.

"Now, Harry. How are you?" barked his father. "What news have you brought?"

Harry drained the last of his sherry sack, carried the glass to the table and dropped into the still warm chair vacated by the secretary. "My trip was an adventure from start to finish. Do you have time to hear it all?"

Wharton's stern features relaxed, though the grooves at each side of his mouth remained in place. "Are we likely to die of starvation before I hear it all?" he asked gruffly. "Should I call for food and wine before you begin?"

Harry nodded. While they waited for the meal, he heard how much King Henry's romantic inclinations daily interfered with his father's life. William, Lord Parr, appointed Lord Warden of the Western March in April, had recently shown an inclination to prove himself.

"Not yet thirty," his father scoffed. "Brother to Latimer's widow, the Lady Catherine Parr, knows nothing about the Borders. Got the post because the King showers favours on his latest lady love."

"She's to marry him, then?"

"She accepted him at Greenwich mid-June. I hear she's for Reform in England."

"That could be dangerous." Harry stared into the flames. "I hope she's as sensible as they say. He's vicious when he turns on someone. They say he never says farewell."

"Walls have ears," his father reminded him, shaking his head. "Leave it, leave it."

While they ate roast fowl, munched their way through apples and cheese and downed a cup or two of sherry sack, Harry got the Edinburgh business out of the way.

"I rode to Edinburgh and got through as if I had a charmed life. Not a hitch. It was easy enough to make the kind of contacts you wanted. Men are so desperate for coin that they would have promised to slit their grannie's throat for a small amount of silver. They vowed to hold themselves ready should we need them, and I have brought a good deal of silver coin back with me."

His father shook his head. "You'll not have heard yet of the Treaty of Greenwich, I suppose? King Henry made a deal with Edinburgh at the beginning of the month. According to that piece of diplomatic expertise the baby Queen of Scots, not yet eight months old, and Prince Edward, currently five years old, are sworn to marry in a few years. Then, so the story goes, our two countries may live in peace and security."

Harry banged his fist on the table. "Then my contacts are useless! Dear Lord, I went all that way for nothing." He slumped against the chair back. "That means…oh, hell and damnation."

He wanted to grab something large and smash it against the wall.

Chapter Fourteen

"So much for your plans of a rich heiress."

Harry looked across the hearth and met his father's sympathetic gaze, and if he wasn't mistaken, humour lurked at the back of the cool, considering eyes. Harry shrugged. "There'll be another chance, one day."

It wasn't quite all for nothing, a small voice whispered at the back of his mind. Think of Alina Carnaby. He frowned, groped inside his doublet and handed a slip of paper to his father. "Those are the names." He shrugged. "They may come in useful for something else."

"I'm sure they will." Wharton scanned the paper, folded it and slipped between the others on his desk. "Now, tell me the rest. I sense there is more to this exciting tale."

Harry poured another cup of sherry and settled down in his chair. "I met a man called Cuthbert Carnaby." He proceeded to recount the meeting in some detail.

Wharton swore violently at the story of the Leap. "Jesu, Harry! How in God's name did you escape? Tell me again."

"I had bruises for a couple of weeks but thanks to Matho, I'm alive. Without him, I don't know...." Harry ran a palm across his face. "I don't know how it would have ended. It still gives me nightmares."

"I'm not surprised. I must look out for Carnaby," Wharton said grimly. "You have been lucky in your friends. The girl helped you initially, then Matho. This man Carnaby," he said, and then paused, his head cocked to one side. With both elbows resting on the arms of his carved chair, he steepled his fingers and touched them to his moustache. "I think I may know him. He is the younger brother of Sir Reynold Carnaby, who still hangs on to life?"

Harry nodded. "The very same."

"His brother got more favours out of Percy than Percy's own family and he became Receiver for lands once belonging to Hexham monastery. He had Cromwell as his patron, until Cromwell vanished the way of Queen Anne Boleyn." Sir Thomas gazed at the fire. "His wife, you know, was connected to our family."

"You mean Sir Reynold's wife? But she's dead, isn't she?"

Wharton nodded. "And Sir Reynold, I hear, will not be long till he joins her. A timid man, I'm told, hated by the men of Tynedale."

"He acquired a good deal of life's riches, for a timid man," Harry said dryly.

Wharton chuckled behind his cup of sack. "He has the luck of the devil, for I know the Duke of Norfolk once wished him in Paradise, but Cromwell saved him. Sir John Heron negotiated Carnaby's release when the men of Tynedale kidnapped him back in '40. Believe it or not, he leaves three daughters in my wardship. You could do worse than marry one of them."

"What?" Harry caught back incautious words of refusal that leapt to his tongue. It was not time to mention Alina yet. "How do you know?—he isn't dead yet."

"No, but I have a copy of his will in safekeeping. A very careful man, Sir Reynold. He didn't want to leave anything to chance. He leaves Aydon Hall and his lease of Corbrige to this same Cuthbert Carnaby who damn near killed you, and the manor of Beaufront to his grandfather's second wife." He caught his son's glance, and chuckled. "What's the matter? Surprised?"

Harry grinned. "I learned long ago never to be surprised at anything you know, or what people do."

"What about marrying one of these daughters? They're young." Wharton grunted. "Probably far too young, now I think about it. I wouldn't like to see you waiting ten years for a wife."

Harry shifted about in the hard wooden chair then leaned forward and braced his elbows on his knees. "I'd rather not, sir. I've picked out a girl and offered to marry her. Her name's Alina—"

"Carnaby? Thought as much." Shadows moved on the lean, hollowed planes of Wharton's face as he loosed a brief guffaw.

"You're not against it?"

Harry watched his father pick up his glass and examine the colour of the wine against the glow of the fire. Harry emptied his own glass, held it nestled between his palms and waited. The political aspect of marriage was of vast importance in the border regions. He had no wish to put his father in a compromised position among the reiving families.

He wiped his palms against his hose.

"Have you thought about this carefully?" His father watched him from cool grey eyes. "Or are you head over heels and unable to think with anything but your balls?"

Harry stared. Father rarely descended into such common speech except on the battlefield. "Er, yes, I have managed to control my raging lust and consider the consequences of such a match. Alina is beautiful and intelligent. Her grandfather is Sir William Carnaby of Halton. The family as a whole own much of Corbrige and Hexham. Her mother is sister and heir to Roger of Horsley. You probably know more of the family history than I do, but remember she saved my neck at some risk to herself. If her father had found me the morning of the raid he wouldn't have stopped to ask questions. He'd have run me through and ridden off on his Hot Trod without a second thought. I don't like to think what he might have done to her for hiding me."

Wharton sipped his sack and stared into the fire. "The younger brother's a strange man, and one I know little of as yet." He looked up. "But then, you've lived in Cumbria long enough to know how people survive in this area. These damned feuds go on and on, and woe betide the man who gets between them. They know nothing but theft, arson, kidnapping, murder and extortion and all," he added, shaking his head, "pursued in peacetime. Anyone outside a man's kin is considered an enemy. It doesn't exactly surprise me to know that Carnaby considered you a reiver and treated you as such."

Harry's brows lifted. "So you condone what he did?"

Wharton shook his head. "No man should take the law into his own hands. But there is the King's Law, and there is Border Law. Borderers, they say, should be the judge of a Borderer and only he should assess his guilt and punishment. In a way I sympathise with them. Not that I'd let the devils know that." He dragged up a convenient stool, settled his heels on it and leaned back in his chair.

"It is easy to become a lawless man, living on reiving and a wild life in the woods, fields and fells. Very few can make a living without the backing of a rich man. In fact," Wharton added, "there's an old saying in Northumberland: 'where beggars increase and service decays.' It comes from the habit of dividing a deceased man's land equally among his sons."

"Each gets so little he cannot live on it?"

"Exactly. Yet these men make excellent soldiers. They are brave and hardy men." Wharton's expression held something close to resignation and Harry wondered what was coming next. "I have to warn you, Harry. To marry into such a family means you complicate your life unnecessarily."

"And yours, Father? Will it compromise your position as Warden?"

Wharton held out his glass for more wine. "I think you can allow me to plod my way through the complexities. But you," he added grimly, catching Harry's eye, "will find that all Carnaby's enemies become your enemies overnight if you marry this girl."

Harry stared into the fire. He had promised Alina he would return, and he intended to keep his promise. His dreams of an heiress had faded over the last few weeks. He didn't know how it had happened, hadn't been aware of it happening, but it had. It was as if he had pulled back a blanket and found a whole new landscape lying in wait for him.

Since he had reached his mid twenties without finding a girl who stirred his heart, then he would be a fool to let the blanket fall and hide such happiness now. Sitting by the fire Harry knew he could make all the wise decisions in the world, but half of his mind was already packing his saddle bag to ride out to her at the earliest opportunity. He looked up and encountered his father's steady grey eyes.

"If she has enemies, then I will protect her. I cannot give her up. And if I do not move at once, she will be married to John Errington."

Wharton sighed and shook his head. "Then we must think out a strategy that will at least keep you safe from Carnaby. The rest is up to you."

***

Alina crept downstairs one step at a time, her cloak bundled in her arms. The house was dark, and she took great care to avoid the creaky steps and the floorboard that rattled down onto the joist below every time someone stepped on it. By the time she reached the kitchen, her heart thudded as if she had been running.

It had been a trying day. Father, his face ashen, had retreated to his chamber without a word for anyone after Sir Reynold's death. Her mother tip-toed anxiously around the solar, shushing the boys and eventually sending them outside with instructions to walk quietly up and down the lane to Halton. Alina sat by the north window, hoping for a glimpse of Harry or Matho and as the day crawled by without their appearance, her doubts churned into anxiety.

At some point during the interminable day she had made the decision to leave Aydon. She had considered the idea in a flippant sort of way many times in the previous weeks but it had always been a last resort, something she'd never truly expected to act upon. Yet here she was, creeping out of her family home in the middle of the night.

Some things were in her favour. She had the key to Grey House safe in her pocket, and there was a moon tonight. The servants retired early to their beds, so bundling a loaf and hunk of cheese in her warmest shawl had been easy enough. The servant who snored on his truckle bed by the kitchen hearth never stirred and the guards, extra vigilant after the recent raid, were all at their posts on the wall-walk. Matho was in charge tonight, and they would not dare scuttle into the kitchen while he oversaw the watch.

She rolled and tied the shawl around her shoulders and flung her heavy wool cloak over the top. It would make her look like a hunchbacked witch, but maybe that was not a bad thing tonight. Trailing her fingertips along the stone walls so as not to lose her way, she ventured downstairs towards the storerooms beneath the kitchen where the blackness seemed thicker than ever.

Harry had promised he would come on the fourth day. Something must have delayed him. Tomorrow she must marry John and there had been no sign that Sir Reynold's death would delay the ceremony. If she did not go now, she would be married to John tomorrow, and should Harry ride through the gate five minutes after she'd said her vows, it would be too late. At least this way she would gain a day or two's respite. She could not hide out at Grey House for ever, she knew that. But surely those two precious days would bring Harry to Aydon.

Everyone would be horrified when they found she had disappeared. Her stomach quaked at the thought of her father's rage, her mother's recriminations and the displeasure of the Errington family. An image of John flashed into her mind. Her palms flattened against the wall, and she hesitated between one step and the next. He would be hurt and for that she was truly sorry.

She reached the last step and breathed a sigh of relief. The stone floor of the lower levels would not betray her. Warm air met her, and the stink of beasts penned inside for the night. What if the cowman had left them to blunder around in the dark? Edging towards the opposite wall, one hand against the stone and the other held out in front of her, she moved towards the side door and prayed that she would not walk into a cow in the darkness. Beasts moved restlessly, sensing her presence even if they could not see her. A cow bellowed, and Alina's heart leapt to her throat as the sound reverberated around the stone byre.

The old wooden door creaked as it turned on the socket pins. She cringed, for it too sounded overloud in the stillness of the night. Opening the main door of the hall would have woken countless servants, but no one slept within hearing distance of the byre. She stepped over the stone sill and turned to bar the door.

And realised she could not do it. Faced with a blank wooden door, she could not heave the wooden drawbar into its socket on the inside.

It was a cardinal sin to leave a door unlocked. Was she leaving a way open for marauders to gain entry to the house and murder everyone in their beds? She laid her forehead against the old oak and closed her eyes.

A horse shifted in the stable not far away. She sent up a quick prayer for the safety of the house and glanced around. The old lodging house had once received guests to Aydon but after years of neglect the thatched roof had collapsed and fallen in upon rooms below. She picked her way through the broken joists, rafters and rotted thatch that littered the floor and soon stepped beyond the broken walls onto the beaten earth of the courtyard. A dark pool of shadow surrounded the well and then the gate loomed in the curtain wall not far ahead.

She took a deep breath. A dark figure stood above the exit arch in the curtain wall. It would be Matho, watching out for her. The massive wooden doors stood ajar and he would secure it behind her.

The huge drawbar that secured the main doors was seven inches square and far too heavy for her to lift.

Matho would probably check the door into the storeroom, too, and she felt better for the thought. She slipped through the narrow gap between the doors and gasped as cold wind blustered around her ankles and slapped her cheek. For a moment she stood there, undecided. This was madness.

The lane to Halton showed as a lighter ribbon through the shadows before it disappeared beneath the trees. The squat, cosy hind's cottage stood in darkness on her left, and the bushes before the door shook and rattled in the wind.

Madness or not, she had to go. Pulling her cloak tight against her throat, she hurried to the crossroads. The undulating land rose towards Grey House, snug and protected below the old Roman Wall. Open fields all the way, with only the odd scattered tree to give shade to the beasts in summer. Fields she had run, walked and skipped across all through childhood; yet the thought of striking out on her own, in the middle of the night, made her stomach curl into a tiny ball of fear.

With Lance and Cuddy at her side, she would have thought nothing of it, would have comforted Cuddy if he did not like the rustling darkness. *If you could do it with them at your side, you can do it alone.*

The sharp wind tugged her cloak and frisked her skirt about her ankles. Well, now she had better get on with it or admit defeat and return to her bed and an unwanted marriage. She glanced back at the gate, but the solitary figure of Matho had vanished.

She really was on her own.

A vicious gust of wind left her gasping.

Alina set her teeth, clawed her cloak tight around her and thought of Harry. She wanted to be free when he came back for her. *If he came back.* The words curled out of her innermost thoughts without warning. Her heart plunged. What if he never came? What if he had only amused himself with her? What would she do? Her father's wrath would boil over and everyone would condemn her as a...jilt and a harlot.

The voice of doubt was relentless. *What do you really know of Harry Scott? He is nothing more than a kiss in St Andrew's church and a promise made in the heat of the moment.*

The wind mocked her as it hissed through the long grass by her feet. If she called out, Matho would let her back in.

It wasn't too late. If she could creep out, she could creep back in. No one would know, except Matho.

She turned and looked back at the gate. It represented safety, security and family warmth. She bit her lip. It also represented marriage to John, a lifetime of regrets if Harry came riding up tomorrow and found her married to another. It was nothing but cowardice that made her think of returning. *Admit it Alina, you are afraid of the dark, afraid of venturing alone across fields you've known all your life.*

Or was she afraid to admit that Harry might not arrive and claim her?

She gritted her teeth. If she returned to Aydon now it would be tantamount to believing Harry was nothing more than an untrustworthy knave, a liar and worse.

Pride came to her rescue; pride, and from somewhere deep within, a warm, stubborn, deep belief in Harry. Fists clenched, she ducked her head and struck out in the full force of the wind, heading northeast for Grey House.

The wind and darkness ruled the meadows. Her glance leapt from undergrowth to hedgerow as shadows danced, trees rustled, branches creaked and groaned. Her cloak thrummed in the wind and tore at her throat. Panting and struggling over the uneven tufts of grass, she struggled uphill and the effort kept her warm.

She clawed her hair away from her face, turned and faced into the wind. *So much for summer nights in the Borders.* Caught in a strange region somewhere between fear and laughter, she clambered over the last stile, unsure of her footing in the shadows and saw the welcome sight of the long, low farmhouse straight ahead, breathed a sigh of relief and plunged towards it. Once inside, she would be safe. Soon she would snuggle up in front of a fire.

It would have to be a small fire. She wanted no keen eye spotting the glow across the dark countryside. If the local farm hind noticed, he would feel obliged to tell her father's hind that beggars had invaded Grey House and then men armed with pitchforks and spears would arrive to shift the unwelcome visitors.

She fumbled in her pocket for the large iron key and groped for the keyhole. The lock had always been stiff. Neither she nor her mother had ever wanted to move to Aydon. Grey House was comfortable and spacious. There were four bedrooms upstairs and hers caught the sun first thing on a morning. Tonight she would snuggle up in her old familiar bed.

Her hands felt bruised by the time the recalcitrant key finally clicked over.

Cold, still air met her on the kitchen threshold. Eager to be out of the wind, she stepped inside, shut the door and gazed across the dark kitchen. The brooding silence of the old house enclosed her. Somewhere close at hand a beam creaked. Her skin prickled as she stared into the blackness. The house had been empty since May, when Sir Reynold fell ill.

It smelled peculiar. When she lived here, the warm, appetising smell of freshly made bread permeated the kitchen, but now only a faint acrid tang of wood smoke lingered.

Her skin prickled and the hair rose on the back of her neck. Perhaps this had not been such a good idea.

Don't be such a coward. This is Grey House and you have always loved it.

She groped her way to the kitchen table and on towards the fireplace. Mama always insisted that the tinderbox must stay in the square recess on the left of the vast stone hearth and that the box should hold flint, steel and tinder.

Alina found the recess and groaned. No box, no tinder. That meant no fire. Her fingertips traced the rough edges of stone back to the farthest corner. At last, her fingers encountered wood. Shivering, she grasped the box and sank to the hearthstone.

Her mother believed that a good tinderbox should hold both char cloth and dry, powdered bark from birch trees as the combination of the two worked best. Countless times Alina had watched mother heat the fuel until it was ready to burn, and then scoop it out into the tinderbox and snap the lid down.

The basket of kindling, still half full, sat at the side of the hearth. Ignoring the thought of the spiders and mice that might have set up residence in the family's absence, she delved into it for small sticks and twigs.

The wind whined and sent cold air swirling down the chimney, found the gap where her cloak met her neck. The darkness behind her held a sinister quality. A swift glance over her shoulder was hardly enough and not at all reassuring.

Oh, if only Harry were here. With the comforting warmth of his solid body at her side, she would have no worries about the darkness, or the cold.

He will be here soon.

She placed the tinderbox on the hearthstone, arranged the char cloth and kindling and picked up the flint. She struck it against the steel. The sparks fell on the fuel, and a tiny flame curled into life. She hovered over it, fed it and did not dare leave it.

Only when she was certain the fire was well and truly alight did she get to her feet. Her knees cracked after crouching so long on the cold stones.

The flickering firelight picked out the big kitchen table, a dulled copper kettle and a few odd bits of pewter sitting on the shelves. Almost everything had gone to Aydon.

She unfastened her cloak and shawl, put her bread and cheese to one side and then slung the shawl round her shoulders again. Her face was warm from the fire, but the creeping cold had her shivering three paces from the hearth. She went to the stone cupboard and took out a handful of tallow candles, looked at them and then put them back. Somehow she could not face the reek of tallow tonight. Reaching further in, she extracted one tall beeswax candle, took it to the fire and lit it.

She added another handful of sticks to the flames, moved to the door in the corner and lifted the sneck. The wooden stairs, deep inside the house, seemed colder and darker than the kitchen. The candle flickered. She shielded the flame until it steadied and then went up. A damp cold enveloped her, made her shiver. Perhaps she would sleep downstairs after all. A blanket from her bed would keep her cosy in the big wooden chair pulled close to the kitchen fire, and she could sleep there till daylight.

At the top of the stairs a small window shed pale ghostly light across the boards. The silence stretched out around her, so thick and heavy the air vibrated in her ears. Her eyes darted from shadow to shadow, her heart thudded very fast and she lifted the candle higher. *This is your home, the house you lived in all through your childhood.*

Once there had been the sound and scent of people and laughter. Now there was naught but the creak of a floorboard beneath her feet and the wind gusting around the eaves.

She longed for the sound of Lance and Cuddy galloping up the stairs behind her, the thud of footfalls as one of the maids rushed from room to room with armfuls of clean linen. Even the sound of her mother's voice remonstrating with the cook over one of her receipts in the kitchen would have been welcome.

Or Harry.

If he were here at her side, his warm hand on her waist, then all would seem different. The darkness would be an ally rather than an enemy, the threatening shadows soon forgotten in the warmth of his embrace. Would she feel nervous or strange, taking Harry into her bedroom? She was not ignorant of what happened between a man and woman once they were wed, but the thought of sharing a bed with him roused shudders of anticipation, a tingling excitement and a tiny frisson of fear.

She walked to her bedroom door, lifted the latch and gazed around in shocked dismay. It was empty. The weak light of her candle shuddered across the bare, dusty boards and at first she thought she'd walked into the wrong room. Then she remembered, with a pang of disappointment. Her featherbed, bolster and blankets were at Aydon now.

All she had to keep her warm was her cloak.

And her memories of Harry.

Chapter Fifteen

Harry crossed the River Eden on Thursday morning and rode alongside the old Roman Wall towards Walton, happy in the thought that he would soon see Alina. His brief time masquerading as Harry Scott was over, and he was pleased to let the deception go. It had proved an adventure that almost cost his life.

It was fortunate he caught sight of the austere red stones of Lanercost Priory nestled among the trees in the valley bottom not long before his horse cast a shoe. He dismounted and walked Bessie down the hill, certain that Thomas Dacre, who owned the place along with nearby Naworth, would have a resident blacksmith. Like Sir Reynold Carnaby and many others up and down the land, Dacre had profited from the Dissolution in 1536.

Harry glanced around. The three hundred year old Priory church of Lanercost was shut and bolted, but work had already begun on its adjacent buildings. A handsome residence might please Dacre, but it would cause the local people to mutter and scowl. On the whole, they wanted the comfort of their old religion but dared not openly defy their lords.

Harry, like his father, was a practical man. He had no argument with Dacre or anyone who benefited from the Dissolution. In some ways he missed the old religion, but thought it was a good thing to be able to read the Bible in English should he ever wish to do so. He didn't feel strongly about it, as some did. So he left his horse at the smithy, had himself announced, shared an excellent dinner with Dacre and his family and headed east next morning after an excellent breakfast.

Riding back up to the ridge where the going was dry and firm, Harry whistled happily and tunelessly as he followed the old Roman Stanegate across Haltwhistle Common. The day was bright and calm, with little wind. Stone farmhouses squatted in hollows and clefts beside streams, cannily out of the wind that swept down from the ridge in winter. Over to his right rose the Westmorland Fells and the

North Pennine Hills and Harry knew that notorious reiving families lived among those wild slopes. Families whose names ran like a litany through his mind: Charltons, Bells, Forsters, Grahams, Musgraves and Storeys.

All through his Cumbrian childhood the riding families, the names to watch, had been dinned into him. They remained with him still, though his years in the south of England had dulled his appreciation of the code and culture of the Borderland. His meeting with Carnaby had reminded him how troublesome the place could be.

To speak of a family being *on the road* was to tell your neighbour a raid was in progress. A whisper that *the Armstrongs were riding* and everyone rushed their animals into the bastle or byre with enough food and water to last a few days until the raid was over. Dour farmers up and down the Borders knew the families that were said to be *ever riding* since they spent so little time by their own hearths.

Harry shifted in the saddle and looked to the north where the land rolled away in green and brown swathes, dipping and rising towards the blue arch of the sky. Tufts of bog cotton waved miniature banners on the breeze. Brown sedge vied with emerald moss and endless small streams wound through the heather hags. Stunted hazel and alder clustered the slopes and leaned with the prevailing wind.

The land rose over the hump of the Pennines and then sloped down to the east and the North Sea. By the time he approached the junction of the North and South Tyne, it occurred to him that it would be good to have a wife from the area, one who knew the ways of the Borderlands. Any girl born and raised in the soft south would hate the harshness of life in this part of the world and most likely live in constant fear of a raid. He headed towards the ford, happy in the knowledge that he would soon see Alina Carnaby and whisk her away from the threatened marriage to staid John Errington.

He rode wearily into Corbrige that evening, fought his way through the crowded tavern and demanded ale. The chubby landlord thumped a brimming tankard before him and watched Harry drain half of it.

"The place is busy tonight," Harry remarked, gazing around the small room.

"Oh, aye, it is that, right enough."

"Something special today?"

The landlord grabbed empty tankards from nearby tables and clutched them against his soiled linen shirt. "Special? Aye, you could say that, lad. Sir Reynold Carnaby died yesterday morn, it's his niece's wedding day and the lassie's upped and vanished."

"Oh." Harry's thumb gestured at the happy faces around them. "At a guess, I'd say Sir Reynold will not be missed, then?"

The inn-keeper's gaze switched to someone behind Harry before he turned and went back to his duties.

"Ah've been lookin' for ye all bloody day, man."

Harry recognised the voice before he swung round. Sure enough, a stocky, red-haired man stood at his elbow and glared at him.

"Matho. You look fit to burst. What's been happening?"

"Carnaby arranged to marry the lass off to John Errington from Sandhoe. T'was to be today, but she took off in the dead o' night, awaitin' on ye, and I'm to tak ye to 'er. If'n ye've got the time." Matho cocked one challenging eyebrow.

"Jesu! Matho, my horse cast a shoe but I'm only a day late!"

Matho gave him a sour look. "Ay, well, it was no' a good time to be late."

Harry downed his ale in one long swallow, abandoned the tankard and got to his feet in the same movement. "Well?" He gestured to the door. "Let's talk outside."

They strolled to the pant on the opposite side of the rutted lane where the soothing gurgle of water reached their ears. Harry seized the handle and pumped hard, cupped his palms beneath the torrent of cold water and splashed his face. Shaking his hands dry, he turned to Matho. "Well, where is she now?"

"She's up at Grey House, where they used to live. So far, Carnaby's not twigged where she's at, but it won't tak him ower long to guess."

"How long has she been there?"

"Most o' last night and today. I haven't been in case someone trailed me. I've got food to tak wi ye. She won't have much left by now."

Matho's directions proved good. Harry walked through the gathering dusk into the farmyard at the back of Grey House and whistled the tune Greensleeves as plaintively as he could manage. It had been Matho's final instruction. "Mak sure ye dinna forgettin', either, or like as not she'll skewer ye wi an arra. That's if she's got her bow wi 'er."

His surprise must have registered, because Matho added a few terse words. "She may look a leddy, but she's northern born n' bred. Like me, she knaws how to use a bow, all reet, an' no' just for show, either."

Harry increased the volume of his whistle. He did not want to be skewered.

A face appeared at the small, deep-set window at the back of the house. He waved. The face vanished, the door opened and Alina flew across the yard towards him. "Harry! Oh, Harry."

His horse snorted and backed away, yanking Harry off-balance. Somehow, he held onto the animal and pulled Alina towards him. She thrust her face into the hollow between his shoulder and neck and the scent of wood smoke deluged him. The pressure against his chest could only be where her breasts pressed against him and the thought made him dizzy.

"I'm here," he murmured, as much to ground himself as reassure Alina. "Late, but I'm here."

An indistinct squawk came from somewhere around the level of his collarbone. "What is it? Are you crying?" He laughed and tightened his grip on the reins. "Bessie, come here, you—" The reins relaxed in his grip. He heard Bessie's pace forward, felt her whiskers on the back of his neck and concentrated on getting both arms around Alina and gathering her close. "Please don't cry. I'm sorry I was late, but….Alina, why are you crying?"

Her brow rolled against his collar bone. "I was afraid you would not come—it was the most miserable night of my life."

"My horse cast a shoe," he murmured against her ear. "I had to stop and get her re-shod and that cost me half a day and a night at Lanercost." He held her away from him, and ducked so he could see her face. "I couldn't help it, Alina. Surely you trusted me to come as I said I would?"

Eyes closed, she shook her head and covered her face with her hands. He wanted to pick her up, take her indoors and find a bed, comfort her, caress her…but he couldn't leave his horse standing here in plain view. Damnation. Why was there never a groom waiting when he wanted one?

Her head came up. She pushed away and glared at him. "Trust you? I've done nothing but trust you since the day I met you, Harry Sc—" She stopped short and sank her teeth in her lower lip. "I couldn't sit at home and wait for you to appear, Harry! By now I would have been married to John Errington."

"Matho told me it was today. I've been thinking as I rode up from Corbrige. I seem to have got my days muddled."

Alina shook her head. "The fourth day was yesterday. I told you, Harry, in those exact words." Her steady brown eyes skewered him much as an arrow might have done.

What had he put her through? "Oh, my God." Even without the problem of Bessie's shoe, he had been a day later than he thought. "My God, I am sorry, Alina." He raised her hand and kissed her palm. "So you…you came here? Alone? When?"

She wrenched her hand out of his grasp. "Late last night, after everyone had gone to sleep."

"Christ, Alina, you took a risk."

Her mouth flattened. "Don't lecture me," she spat at him. "It was bad enough without that."

"It was very brave of you, but I hate to think of you out here alone in the dark. I should have been with you." He hesitated, watching her. "Does your father know…will he guess where you are, do you think?"

"He will eventually. Then he'll come searching."

Harry glanced around. The house and outbuildings shielded the north and west sides of the yard, trees cut off the view to the east but open fields showed the glorious vista to the south. He squinted. "Is that Aydon down there in the hollow?" Abandoning Alina, he grasped his mare's reins. "Where shall I take her?" At the ensuing silence, he looked at her. "Alina?"

She gestured to the building behind him. "The stables are there."

Harry frowned. Obviously he'd said something she didn't like, but he forced down the sharp rejoinder that sprang to his lips. She'd left home, which was brave, and last night would have been…He couldn't imagine how she must have felt in the abandoned house wondering why he had not arrived.

Shoulders stiff, she led the way across the uneven yard and through the doorway of a low thatched building. Harry set off after her. Once he had the mare settled he would concentrate on Alina and make it up to her. It didn't usually take him long to lull girls into a sweeter mood. He hoped she wasn't the kind of person who held grudges for days and days.

He tugged on the reins. Bessie was tired, and paced slowly after him.

Alina stood to one side and pointed.

He paused as he led the mare to the stall she indicated. "Why are you so angry? Surely you wanted me to come?"

Inside the stable, the light was subdued and her eyes seemed very dark. "I was alone here last night."

"Ah." He looked at her as she stood there in her plain woollen gown and thought he understood. "I'm sorry you were frightened, but I'm here now, and—"

Her brows rose. "Who said I was frightened?"

Harry lifted his hands, palms open. "I thought that's what you meant." Bessie rubbed her head against his back, urging him towards the promise of warm straw and a good feed. Harry resisted. "According to Matho, you used to live here. Why be frightened of a place you've known most of your life?"

Alina stalked into the stable and halted by an empty stall. He sensed rather than saw her glaring at him. Tired and hungry, Harry tried to hide the impulse to yawn behind a gauntleted fist.

"There is straw there." She pointed to the loft above their heads. "And possibly oats in that barrel." She lifted the lid to check. "Yes, there are. You may draw water from the well with that bucket." She kicked it, bit back an exclamation and tucked her foot round her other ankle.

Harry looked at the heavy wooden bucket and then at her lightly shod feet. "That must have hurt."

"What do you care?" She flounced by him with her nose pointing at the loft.

"Where are you going?"

"Back to the house."

"You'll do no such thing." Harry spoke quietly, but grasped her arm and dragged her back to him. He put both hands on her small waist, lifted her and set her on the wooden barrel. "You can sit there and talk to me until I've bedded down my horse."

"I shall not!"

He looked at her. It was a big barrel. Perched on top of it she was at eye level with him. He stepped close and wagged a finger under her nose. "You are behaving like a child, Alina. I made an honest mistake, for which I've apologised, and may do so again if you change your tune. Now tell me what's really annoying you. I can't believe you were afraid of the dark."

She attempted to slip down. Harry caught and held her in place. "Get off that barrel and I'll put you over my knee and spank you."

"You wouldn't dare."

Nose to nose with her, he glared back. "Who," he asked delicately, "will stop me?" He spread his arms to encompass the empty stable and smiled. "Certainly not you."

The mare whickered, nudged him so hard between the shoulder blades he took an inadvertent step forward.

"You'd better see to your horse before she sets about you." Alina's lips twitched. "Though you won't get any oats from this barrel."

"Why not?"

"Because I'm sitting on the lid." Suddenly cheerful, she folded her arms and crossed one leg over the other. She looked adorable.

Harry leant forward and gently pushed her knees apart. "Dream of what follows this, sweetheart." He kissed her lightly on the lips and drew back before she could complain.

Her mouth dropped open in surprise.

Satisfied that her mood had changed, Harry stepped back. With a lingering glance that promised her all kinds of things, he smiled. "My horse will be munching oats before she knows what's hit her, I promise you."

He jumped, grasped the rim of the loft, got his feet on the stall and hauled himself up in three easy movements.

"There are stairs over there, you know."

She sounded unimpressed, but he'd heard her startled gasp as he swung himself up and saw how she craned to keep him in view. Feeling smug, he kicked down enough straw to make a decent bed for his mare, and dropped back down into the stall.

Harry raked the straw into a rough bed, led the horse in and unsaddled her. Grabbing a discarded sack, he rubbed her down, well aware that Alina watched his every move. Returning from the yard with a bucket of water, he dumped it beside the manger, grabbed a wooden scoop and approached the barrel.

Alina gripped the rim with both hands and braced herself as he approached. The antagonism had gone and now that his sight had adjusted to the dim light, he saw the anticipation in her face. This was to be a challenge and she was ready to defend her position. Harry hesitated, studying the situation.

The barrel stood in the corner where two walls met. Hiding his grin, he strode toward her, leaned hard against her and pushed sideways. Her weight transferred to the wall and allowed him to tilt the lid sufficiently to sweep the scoop into the oats. He withdrew it, let the lid fall and tilted the scoop over the manager. Oats streamed down. He looked at her, laughing. "Told you so."

He patted Bessie affectionately as she snuffled among the oats, slung his saddlebag over his shoulder and made to walk out of the stall.

"Harry! What about me?"

He stopped, slapped his forehead and turned back. Halfway he stopped and folded his arms. "Shall we talk sensibly, or are you still at odds with me?"

Alina held out her arms. "I'll talk."

She smiled engagingly but he did not weaken. "Promise? You won't change your mind once you're on your feet?"

Shuffling forward on the barrel, Alina shook her head and waited for him.

"Do I have your promise?"

"I promise! Now lift me down!"

For a moment he assessed her then caught her beneath the arms and swung her to the floor. Holding her made him want to touch her again, anywhere, everywhere. He wanted to fill his hands with her, smother her with his mouth. He swept an arm under her knees and lifted her.

Alina gasped.

He walked to the door and looked down. "Tell me where to go?"

Wide-eyed, she pointed mutely to the kitchen door

Chapter Sixteen

Overwhelmed by his closeness and the easy strength with which he carried and set her down in the big stone-flagged kitchen, Alina remained where he placed her. The scent of burning pine logs and beeswax candles replaced the odour of horse and stable, and beneath it all and much closer, she breathed the subtle scent of Harry.

Her muscles lost their tightness.

"This is nice." The sound of his voice jerked her eyes open.

Alina tried to see the kitchen as a stranger might, and was not disheartened. Firelight shone on the dark wood of the vast carved dresser and gleamed on the few pewter dishes and the copper jug she had polished to keep herself busy. Everything was clean because she had scrubbed and swept to keep her mind occupied, and found that scrubbing didn't occupy her mind at all.

The only thing missing was food.

Under normal circumstances, Mama and the servants would have doled out of bowls of broth from the big cauldron hanging in the hooded fireplace, and her father would have carved whatever meat had been prepared for a guest. She had nothing to offer him and her stomach rumbled at the thought of food.

Harry heard it. Amused, he looked at her. "Hungry?"

"Yes, but there's nothing to eat. I thought Matho might have…I haven't seen him."

"Matho was in Corbrige. He told me where to find you, and to be sure and whistle otherwise you might shoot me. He gave me bread, bacon, and a couple of eggs." He walked to the table in the middle of the room and laid his saddlebag on it. "I suppose I was lucky you didn't let fly at me because I was so late."

"Eggs!" Her face lit up. "How—"

"He wrapped them in straw and then in a cloth." He shrugged. "If we have to, we'll pick out the bits of shell." He fiddled with the leather straps of one saddlebag. "How shall we cook?"

She rattled the iron frying pan off its hook at the side of the fireplace. "The eggs can fry in the bacon fat."

She took the unbroken eggs from his hands and sent a silent whisper of thanks to Matho. Soon the thick scent of frying bacon filled the kitchen. When the fat ran hot and smoking she cracked the eggs into the pan. Harry used his knife and offered slices of bread cut from the loaf. "Fry those, too. I love bread fried in bacon fat."

She put the pieces in the pan. It was odd to know he liked bread dipped and fried in bacon fat. There must be a thousand more little quirks she would learn about him now that he was here. But for the moment, they ate in a hungry silence filled with mumbled sounds of satisfaction and enjoyment. While Alina licked a fingertip and picked up crumbs from her platter, Harry used a piece of bread to soak up all the juices from the pan.

"Best meal I've eaten all day," he announced, sitting back from the table.

"It was good," she sighed. "And there will be enough for breakfast tomorrow."

Harry stretched his legs out towards the hearth. "We have a whole night ahead of us before we need to think of breakfast. Is this the master's chair?"

Alina nodded. "An old one. We left it for the shepherd and cowman." Sitting there, he looked in total control of the situation. He was far more confidant than she, but she put that down to education and travel. He had seen a good deal of the world. Edinburgh, at least, possibly London, while the furthest she had travelled was Tynemouth on the east coast.

All the doubts of the dark hours came flooding back. If he wasn't a Scott, who was he? The biggest question of all she could hardly bring herself to consider. Did he really want her?

At least he was here.

She had no idea what would happen next. Her thinking had not taken her beyond the point of his arrival and now a strange sensation of doubt, fear and longing roiled through her. Running from home may not have been the wisest thing she had ever done in her life.

They were alone here, and it struck her forcibly that she had put herself at some risk. If her instincts about him were wrong, she might get her throat slit in the middle of the night. He might take her to bed and then ride off next morning.

She shuddered. These dismal thoughts had to stop. That was Harry ensconced in the old oak chair, not some stray reiver wandered in out of the dark. Smiling at her own fears, she wondered what he would say when she told him all the beds had gone to Aydon.

Her heart beat faster. It wasn't that she objected, exactly, to the thought of going to bed with him. She knew she wanted to, eventually. But the thought of going to bed with him now loomed large in her mind. A question of how, and when and would she know what to do when the time came? She had got herself into this predicament. Her thoughts bobbed about like a rabbit in a meadow.

Harry seemed composed. He rested his head, eyes closed, on the carved chair back. Days of riding under clear Border skies had turned his skin so brown it almost matched his jack and hose. Only the white shirt at his throat relieved the drab shades. Firelight glittered on silver embroidery at the edge of the shirt collar, but no long lace cuffs like those John Errington favoured dangled beneath the sleeves of Harry's doublet.

An image of John, sitting disconsolate by the fireside, rose in her mind's eye. At least she had avoided that marriage. She could see how impossible it had been now that she looked at Harry. She thought of the ease with which Harry swung himself up into the loft, and a ripple of excitement rolled through her. And yet, she knew very little about him.

"Harry?"

His eyes opened and he squinted lazily at her before shoving one long, muscular leg towards the hearth. His riding boots, covered in mud and dust, reached above the knee and left very little hose on show between them and his breeches.

She shrugged, looked away. "I don't know anything about you."

"Of course you do. You know—"

"I still don't know what your real name is. I'll wager it's not Scott. In fact you've admitted that." Her hands struck the air in a gesture of helplessness. Rigid in her chair, she fixed him with a steady glare. "You could be anybody, Harry. Don't you think it's time you told me who you are? I need to know before I…before we…go any further."

He shuffled upright, leant his elbows on his knees and clasped his hands together. "Why do you think I'm *not* Harry Scott?"

"Of course you're not. Any fool can see that. Stop grinning at me, and tell me truth."

He did not answer immediately, but watched her, his blue eyes shining in the firelight. His skin clung close to the bones of his face, though no one would call him thin. Nervous and on edge, Alina got up and gathered their plates.

"Why did you choose to go through that ridiculous drama with my father? You nearly *died*, Harry." She carried their plates to the stone sink. "Why not tell him your real name?"

"Harry certainly is my name."

She glanced at him over her shoulder. The firelight struck one side of his face and threw shadows across the other half. She remembered she had once laughed at the fanciful thought that he was two people. Now she saw that she had been right without knowing why. She scoured the greasy plates with a handful of sand and rinsed them in the bucket of water. "But Scott isn't, is it?"

"No, it isn't. But how *the hell* did you know?"

"Ha! We get to the truth at last. Tell me." She put the plates into the wooden rack to drain and wondered if his real name would scare her any more than the fictitious one. If he was called Harry Elliot, she was definitely going home.

Elbows braced on the arms of the chair, Harry glanced down at his clasped fingers. Firelight washed over him and added a ruddy hue to his skin. She walked slowly to the fireplace and stared down. Firelight revealed every line of his face, gilded the curve of his eye, deepened the shadowed socket and lengthened his black lashes.

"Well?"

Firelight hit the dense blue of his eyes as he looked up. "My name is Harry Wharton."

Wharton. There were several families in the Borders with that name. There was nothing she could think of that would make him hide such a name. Unless…she inhaled rapidly. The name hung in the air between them.

"Wharton? Your father is…"

"Sir Thomas Wharton, Deputy Warden of the West March."

She sat down in the chair she had vacated so recently. He was still a puzzle. If he had flaunted his father's name instead of hiding it, she would have found it more natural. "Why should Sir Thomas's son hide his identity?" She tossed her head back. His gaze flickered away from her. Alarm rushed through her. "You weren't spying, were you?" She leaned forward and grasped one of his warm hands. "Harry, were you spying on my father?"

He shook his head. "I volunteered for a task in Edinburgh and my father did not want the name Wharton attached to it."

Relief rushed through her. His mission had nothing to do with her family. It was something, at least, but she had to know more. "What kind of a task in Edinburgh?"

"Must you know?" He flicked an assessing sideways glance at her.

Another rebuff. Alina swayed back in her chair and surveyed him while she gathered her thoughts. "I ran away from home for you, Harry. I have nowhere else in the world to go yet you still do not trust me." It was mortifying. She inhaled deeply, and lifted her head. "Yes, I think I must be told."

He stared into the flames. "It's nothing that's going to bring harm to anyone. In fact, it should be beneficial, both here and in Scotland."

She raised her brows and waited.

In brief, simple sentences he described how he bribed several Scots to bring the baby queen to England, at a date as yet unspecified, for a marriage with King Henry's son. "It will bring our two nations together and hopefully prevent more bloodshed," he finished.

"You mean they would kidnap her? A babe less than a year old?" Alina did not hide her shock.

Harry nodded.

"But you speak of a child barely a year old who may not survive rough handling! Her mother will be distraught! Did you think of that?"

Regret flitted across his face. "No, I didn't," he confessed. "My father wanted it done, and I wanted to do it. I did not think about it too much at all. Perhaps she will be older when—"

"You are no better than all the reivers who rape and steal!"

Harry jerked his feet under him and sprang from the chair. "It was done with the best of intentions."

"But with little thought, Harry." Her eyes followed him around the room. "What if it were your child?"

He wheeled round to retort, and then reconsidered. Tight-lipped, he returned to the fire, hunkered down and settled a new log on the fire. Sparks flew high and vanished up the chimney. "You may be right." He remained crouched before the hooded fireplace, frowning into the flames. "But there is no guarantee that it will ever happen. It was probably all a waste of time, for the Treaty of Greenwich took place while I was heading north. That's a formal agreement to marry the little queen to the prince in nine years time."

Alina relaxed. "Exactly what you wanted to happen! But it will happen properly, with the little queen's mother present."

He rose effortlessly to his feet, stared down at the flames adventuring around the new wood and shook his head. "All that effort for naught."

Alina eyed the slope of his shoulders. "Don't be despondent, Harry. I am sure your father appreciated your efforts."

"Hopefully, yes." He did not look around.

"And I appreciated it," she added softly. "For without it we would never have met."

He half-turned and regarded her. Flames turned his skin rosy, but his grim face made her unaccountably wary. "Are you glad, Alina? Here you are, run away from a marriage, outcast from your family and all because of me."

"All because of you? You have a good opinion of yourself, sir." She tried to smile, but her mouth quivered. Surely Harry was not regretting what she had done?

"It is a serious matter. I shall have to marry you."

The words reverberated through the quiet, firelit room. Swallowing the rising lump in her throat, she met his gaze steadily. "I thought that was what you wanted…what we wanted. I thought you…" Her hands crept together in her lap, twined around each other for comfort. She swallowed again, quickly. "Have you…have I done the wrong thing?"

He took a swift stride and knelt at her feet. "No, of course not. I *am* of the same mind. I'm tired, so I express myself badly. Forgive me. But I regret that you and your family are estranged. I wish it could have been done a different way." He cradled her interlocked hands within his own and dropped a kiss on her knuckles. "I do have a plan to present to your esteemed parent," he added with a wry smile. "Somehow we'll have to approach him and explain everything." He looked down at their intertwined hands. "If we marry, we can make everything good with your family. My father knows and he has no objections."

"You spoke of me to your father? To Sir Thomas Wharton?" Suddenly things did not seem so bad after all.

He nodded. "He was surprised, I must admit. He said he would ride over if he could and lend his support with…with your father. But meanwhile…" At last, his lashes lifted and his blue eyes spoke of matters that warmed her blood and caused a quiver of unease deep in her belly. "Meanwhile?"

"We are here, together, and alone."

There was no mistaking what he meant. *Oh, yes, Harry!* She wanted him, but her stomach knotted on the thought. "I want to know more about you. Tell me about your family. I want to be sure you are Harry *Wharton,* and not Harry Scott or Harry Jones."

Harry groaned. "Now who doesn't trust whom?"

"I haven't been traipsing around the countryside under a false name. You have."

"But—"

"You know exactly who I am and where I come from. You've met my parents, my brothers and our servants. I suspect that I am not what you wanted in a bride, but—"

"Where shall I start?" He cut in before she could voice her doubts.

"At the beginning," she said pertly, pleased with his capitulation. "How old are you?"

"I was born in '21." From kneeling beside her he slid back into the chair on the other side of the hearth without actually rising to his feet. His agility was a constant surprise to her.

So he was older by no more than a few months. "Do you have brothers? Sisters?"

Harry must have realised what she wanted, for he took her next question out of her mouth. "Look, let me give you the potted family history and save time, shall I? Edward knighted Gilbert de Querton in 1292 and seven generations brings us to my father. My mother was Eleanor Stapleton. She comes from Yorkshire. Wharton Hall is the family home on the banks of the river Eden in Cumbria. I have one older brother, George, and two younger sisters, Joan and Feorina. One son died in infancy. Yes, Father has been promised a barony for his work at Solway Moss last November, but who knows? Our king is an unpredictable man. Speaking of which, have you heard that he has another wife?"

"What? A sixth wife?" It took a moment to adjust to the new subject. "How do you know?"

Harry grinned. "Hearing things early is one of the better aspects of being the son of the Deputy Lord Warden of the West March. Messengers scurry about the countryside on a daily basis so my father is one of the most knowledgeable men in the country. She married him a week ago tomorrow."

Alina sank back in her chair. "It is not yet two years since he beheaded Queen Katherine." She shuddered, and crossed herself. "Marriage is such a shaky business these days. She must be a brave lady, whoever she is."

"Her name is Catherine, too. Catherine Parr, recently widowed by Lord Latimer. In March, I think. I doubt she dared refuse and I am sure her family will have urged her to take him. Already her thirty-year-old brother is Lord Warden, much to my father's chagrin."

She knew she stared, but couldn't help it, for he moved in circles she did not know. He must surely have hoped to marry a fine lady somewhere and take charge of her lands, whereas she could offer very little. This house, perhaps, if she was lucky.

Alina shook her head. "Women do not do well out of marriage on the whole. Look at me, sold to the Erringtons by my own father, the man who should care most for me…"

Tears pricked behind her eyes, and her throat tightened and made speech difficult. "I have been so foolish…I see now that I bring you nothing, Harry. You should aim so much higher than me. You should have a wife who can bring you property, and a title." Her throat ached and tears threatened. "You deserve that, I think. I must go back and make amends, beg to be accepted. I cannot do anything else."

Chapter Seventeen

Harry stared at her.

For the second time that night he slid off his chair and went to his knees before her. He did not speak, for he could think of nothing to say in the face of her distress. He pulled her down and into his arms and rocked her back and forth before the fire, crooning wordlessly against her cheek.

Her sudden changes of mood confused him. What had made her decide so suddenly that she should not marry him?

Her face was hot and wet against his throat. Laying his cheek against the top of her head, his gaze sightless on the bare stones of the kitchen floor, he held her until she calmed.

"What is it?" He asked when the sobs died away. "I know it is a stupid question, but why are you giving me up? And what makes you think I want to go jauntering off around the countryside looking for a rich and titled woman to wed?"

She hid her face against the already damp surface of his doublet. "You said that was what you wanted. Men *always* seek wives who bring lands and estates. Why should you be different?"

Her hair smelled of smoke, not the roses he remembered from the first day they met in Corbrige market. She hadn't been lighting or tending her own fires then as she was now. "But I don't want some rich heiress. I want you."

She stilled in his arms. A moment later he heard and felt the huge breath she took as if steadying herself to reject him again. He pulled a piece of linen from his doublet sleeve. "Here. I can hardly understand you."

Alina took the fabric, blew her nose, tossed her hair back and regarded him with eyes made pink by weeping.

"Ah," he said, "you've made your eyes sore." He leaned forward and dropped a kiss on her lips. She lurched away from him and scrambled back into the chair behind her.

"The day you escaped the Leap and disappeared," she said, with heavy emphasis on the last word, "was the very day Father told me John Errington would be my husband. John rode over to Aydon the next day, and came courting every day after that."

Harry remained on the flagstones at her knees. Had she grown fond of the man? Was she regretting running away from the marriage? "Do you like him?"

She shrugged. "He is a nice man. Our families have known each other a long time."

Harry ground his teeth together as she spoke. "But did you want to marry him?" His question sounded sharp in his own ears. A dark feeling he did not recognise twisted his innards in its grip.

"John is kind, considerate and I think he would have grown fond of me in time. What more could I have expected? Every woman expects to marry to her family's advantage." She flicked a wary glance in his direction.

"I expect a lot more than that from any wife I may take."

Her head lifted slowly. "I know. You want land, castles and riches before you'll accept her."

It occurred to him that he could give her nothing better than Old Lammerside. Perhaps she wanted a man richer than himself. "Errington would give you those, Alina. Can't you answer a simple question?"

Her eyes widened. "What answer? You haven't asked a question."

"Perhaps you should have married him." The words came without warning. He stared at her. Why had he said that? The words were exactly the opposite of what he intended. "*Christ!*"

"You want me to marry him? You really don't care about me?" She ground her hands together in her lap.

Harry shook his head. "No—"

"John won't want me now, so—"

Harry grasped her shoulders and shook her to silence. "Of course I don't want you to marry Errington. I want you to marry me." He groaned silently. There you go, Harry. Someone takes the pressure off and you fall headlong into the trap. Typical.

Her reaction was slow. Her eyes widened, chestnut and gold in the firelight, and her lips parted. Gazing at him, searching his face, she raised her brows.

Harry nodded.

"Do you mean it?"

"Of course I mean it. I love you." There it was. He'd said it, and he meant it. It hadn't been so hard after all.

Alina slid out of her chair, landed on her knees before him and grasped his arms. "Oh, Harry! What have we been arguing about?"

"Unhand me, woman." He growled at her, but could not repress the smile that wanted to burst through. "I didn't invite you to throw yourself all over me. Think of the scandal if someone walked in."

By the time he got the last word out, he was grinning like a boy and wrapped his arms around her.

"No one knows we're here, Harry."

Her soft lips tantalised him. He breathed deep, wondered if he breathed air that had been inside her body. Firelight flushed her pale skin to the colour of honey. Above the tight bodice, the drawstring neck of her linen drooped low enough to reveal the slender lines of her collar bones and the soft shadows where the bones met her throat. She breathed in fast, shallow gasps that made the shadows move and change.

Her lips met his, tentatively, a mere whisper of flesh against flesh. Harry's heart lurched as her lips touched him again, moved to the corner of his mouth. She laid her cheek against his and rolled her head against him, over and over, as she murmured his name.

He grasped her arms, and held her off. "Alina—"

She looked at him with such adoration his heart leapt up, knocked against his breastbone and he forgot what he had been about to say. A pulse jumped and fluttered in her throat. She leaned slowly towards him and pressed her lips to his.

He groaned. "Alina, should we…?"

He really ought to stop her. If he was wise, he would. If he didn't, there was no going back. What was he thinking? Already there was no going back. His old cynical reflexes kept getting in the way of this astonishing new direction in his life.

She went on kissing him, smothered his words with her mouth. Briefly, laughing, he pulled back. "If we must, then we must." On a surge of breathless laughter he added, "I'll say you forced me."

"We must." She ignored his attempt at humour. "But I don't know where."

He ran a line of kisses from her temple to her jaw. Slowly, as her words sank in, he paused. His brain didn't seem to be working properly. Even his words blurred together when he finally spoke. "Whaddyamean, where?"

She sat back. "There's little furniture here. It's all at Aydon."

"All we need is a bed. The house full of furniture can wait," he murmured, his mind concentrating on the information streaming through his fingertips. The sense of what she said coalesced all at once in his mind. He stopped caressing her and jerked back. "Are you telling me there's no bed upstairs?"

"No bed, no bolster, no blankets. My mother is a good housewife and she took everything we needed to Aydon. The house is nearly empty."

Harry stared at the stone flags of the kitchen floor. Impossible to make love there. The narrow wooden settle offered no safe refuge. Had they been practiced lovers, the chair or the table might have sufficed, but Alina was far from practiced. He groaned, ran a hand through his hair and met her amused glance.

"There's always the stable." Her smile was innocent. "They didn't take all the straw."

Their eyes met in mutual delight. "You have a wicked mind, Alina."

She grinned as if at a compliment, shuffled off his lap, and waited.

He did not move. "It will be cold, you know." Was she really suggesting they should go and make love in the stable?

"I have my cloak. We can make a nest in the straw. Did you never do that when you were a child? Or are you so old you cannot recall your childhood?"

She teased him, he knew. He wanted her so badly he ached for her but he tried not to appear too eager. "In daylight, yes. But never in the cold of night."

"It is summer, Harry. Jesu, what ails you that your blood runs so thin?"

He rose and grasped her before she could back away. "You have a bright, brave adventurous spirit, Alina Carnaby and I salute you. But you have changed your mind several times this night already. Remember, when you turn to an icicle in the straw, that this was your idea, not mine."

She laughed, and made for the door.

Harry threw a glance at the fire, decided it would burn for an hour unattended, and grinned as he strode after her. He got to the door, hurried back and pulled his cloak from his saddle bag.

His mare snuffled a welcome as they clattered into the stable.

"We should have brought a lantern," he muttered.

Alina guided him to the narrow set of rickety steps against the side wall and followed him up. Together they groped through the darkness. Harry used his knife to slit the twine binding a couple of straw bales and spread the fresh straw out on the loft floor.

"Imagine it makes a soft, golden bed." Alina's subdued whisper came out of the shadows and made his skin twitch.

"I suppose we'll be able to see something when our eyes adjust to the darkness. Where are you?"

"Here." She was a substantial form, warm between his two hands. Her wandering hand found his face, and the other joined it. "Let me spread my cloak and then—oh, Harry!"

The straw rustled and released the scent of summer fields about them.

"This is hardly what I imagined." Guilt, an emotion he rarely felt, flickered through him. "You should have a featherbed, Alina, and silks and jewels on your wedding day."

Her palm drew his face towards her. Their mouths met, joined and explored. Her hand clamped over his and held it still.

"You do love me, Harry? We will be together always?"

The age old plea. The one he had always avoided before. But this time, he must answer it, or she would be gone. And he must sound convincing. "I love you. I want to marry you."

"You could sound as if you meant it," she muttered and sank her teeth into his shoulder.

Heat pulsed through him. The darkness concealed his body's reaction to her touch. As a signal of his good intentions, he put his hands behind his back.

"I don't have a lot of practice at this declaration lark," he said. "I shall not touch you if you are not sure." He waited. An inner voice told him that he'd made a silly move. He should have kept hold of her. "Are you sure?"

"Aye, of myself." Her sharp voice came out of the shadows. "But what of you?"

He sighed. She was going to freeze him out again. "What can I say? I speak flippantly. Always have done. How can I convince you that I love you, that my heart is yours forever?"

He let himself fall full length in the straw. The rest was up to her.

After several long moments she came to rest beside him. In some ways it was a pity they had no light, for he would like to have seen her face and judge her expression. He wanted to see her unclothed but there were no guarantees and he must move very carefully. He risked losing her if he moved too fast.

"Let me tell you something," he said comfortably. "I told my father about you before I left, and he—"

The straw rustled as she sat up again.

"Be still." He pulled her down and resisted the urge to fondle anything more intimate than the curve of her shoulder. "Yes, I told him about you. He asked me much the same question you did, though not quite in the same terms, perhaps. I assured him that I wanted to marry the girl who had the misfortune to be Cuthbert Carnaby's daughter, and we—"

"Misfortune?"

He found he did not need light for she stiffened in outrage beneath his palms. "We hatched a plan whereby I should bring the Deputy Lord Warden's orders to Cuthbert Carnaby since his brother is ailing."

"He's dead," she said flatly.

"What?" He still could not see her. Not even a stray moonbeam found a way through the sturdy roof.

"Sir Reynold died yesterday morn. He's been ill since May, poor man."

He pulled her closer. She was slender, but her breasts were rounded mounds pressed against him and he longed to touch them. Later, he told himself sternly. Later. The innkeeper in Corbrige had told him Carnaby was dead. He ought to have remembered.

"I'm sorry. Were you close to him?"

"No, not really. He was always travelling from here to Halton, to Hexham, to Langley. Sometimes to Bearl, even Fallodon." She sounded subdued. "His wife is already dead, so his daughters will continue to live at Shortflatt with their maternal grandmother."

No wonder she'd shed a few tears earlier. Death was never easy and she'd had a lot of other things to contend with in the last few days. "Your lady mother will not accept the children?"

Alina sighed. "There's no room for them. Once the repairs are done, and extra chambers built, then perhaps they will come to us. But I interrupted. My mind is in such a whirl. Please go on with your plan."

"I've forgotten what I was saying…"

"Your father's orders for Aydon."

He settled more comfortably into the nest of straw and pulled the second cloak over them both. "Well, let's see. I've brought written orders from the Lord Warden to your father. That means he cannot attack me now. Or if he does, he'll have to face the Lord Warden, with three thousand soldiers at his back. Not a likely prospect, I think."

She said nothing. He hoped she was happy with what he told her. "Once I've given him the orders, I can then ask for your hand in marriage. I don't think he'll refuse, do you?"

"Did your father not mind you marrying me?" She sounded subdued.

"Oh, not really," Harry said cheerfully. "My older brother will inherit anyway, and that means I have more leeway in choosing a bride. Your family is well favoured with lands and perhaps that's why he thinks you are acceptable." Harry chuckled softly. "Or perhaps he thinks I shall be able to control what goes on here. That's if we choose to live at Aydon."

"I doubt it." Alina's voice was soft in the darkness. Harry wasn't sure if her remark applied to his controlling events at Aydon, or where they should live. "Have you made love to other women, Harry?"

"What?" She had surprised him the first time they met, and now she was doing it again.

"You heard me, I think."

He coughed and cleared his throat. Jesu, no woman had asked him that before. He nodded, and then remembered she could not see him in the dark. "Yes."

"Yes? Is that all?"

"What do you want?" His voice, like his thoughts, hovered between irritation and amusement. "A strict accounting? A tally sheet?"

"No," she said, wriggling closer to him in the straw. "I wondered if you knew what you were doing. You don't seem keen, to be honest. I thought men were always as keen as dogs with bitches."

Harry spluttered, caught between outrage and laughter. "You want me to show keenness, then?"

"Of course," she said. "Why else did we come here?"

Harry hesitated. "You had doubts, if you remember. I am trying not to rush you."

Her hands sought his chest, moved to his shoulders. The straw creaked and rustled. "My doubts have gone, Harry. I know who you are, where you come from, that you want to marry me and that my father does not terrify you."

He was not sure of her last phrase but he had no argument with the rest of her statement. Her fingers traced his throat, found his jaw, his mouth and then her warm breath reached him. She kissed him so delicately he did not respond in case he frightened her away. Her lips remained closed. Had she ever been kissed by a lover before? He didn't think so. Errington had stuck to the formalities, then.

He cupped the back of her head in his palm, and let the fingers of his other hand stray over her. Words echoed and ricocheted around inside his skull. "I love you," he whispered.

He felt her stiffened in his hands, heard a hiss of sound as if she sucked air between her teeth. Her arms sprang around his neck and almost choked him. The rest of her pressed against him and Harry fell back in the straw. "Alina—"

She kissed him, pressed against him. Sounds of happiness poured from her throat. Harry grasped her face between his palms and kissed her back. This time he sought her open mouth and she recoiled.

An open-mouthed kiss must be new to her. He held her gently and did not stop her lifting her head. She did not retreat far, for her breath still fanned his cheek. "This is how lovers kiss, Alina."

Her head moved slowly in denial between his hands. "Truly?"

"You will like it," he added, and waited. His fingers held her with the lightest of touches and he knew the moment she decided to try again.

The softness of her mouth on his delighted him. He matched his lips to hers, tilted his head so that their mouths not only met, but melded, melted and joined. Tantalising her lips with the tip of his tongue, elation surged through him when her mouth parted for him. Teasing, tempting, Harry moved slowly. His reward came when she ran her tongue in swift exploratory ventures across the divide.

"What an apt pupil you are," he breathed against her ear, and sought her mouth again.

"I like it, Harry, but it is making me feel breathless, as if I have run a long way."

"M'mmmm. Exactly as it should." He half-smiled as he met her hot, eager mouth.

"But you aren't breathing hard at all."

"You might think that, but my heart is racing. Feel."

Her hand touched his doublet. "I think…"

He brushed her hand aside, opened the hooks and thrust her hand inside, laid it flat against his skin. He shuddered, and she started at that first contact. He heard her swift intake of air and held steady.

"Now, can you feel it? Tell me quickly, otherwise I might think I've died."

Her fingers spread, the pads pressing against his skin, moved slowly to the place where his heart thudded. "It beats so fast, Harry. Perhaps mine does too. If only we had light, I should be able to see you."

He wondered at her thoughts. Did she want to see his body? One day, he promised himself. One day she would tell him exactly what she wanted of him.

He rose to one elbow. "Enough. I want to kiss you again." He pushed her back in the straw and proceeded to show her how varied and magical a kiss could be. In no time at all her skin grew hot and her breathing ragged. Laying a fingertip at her throat, he traced a line slowly down to the drawstring of her linen chemise, found the bow that tied the strings, jerked it loose and pressed the edges of fabric apart. His mouth wandered over her skin.

"Harry...oh, Harry..." Her voice lingered over his name. He found the laces of her bodice, loosened them and let his fingers trawl the sweet mounds of her breasts. "I did this before. Do you remember?"

"M'mmmm." She sounded amused. "In the dark, when you were in the dungeon...and Matho was pacing up and down above us."

Harry let his tongue circle her skin until she groaned and moved restlessly beneath him. Hot, urgent, eager to move, to invade, it took all his determination to hold back. He wanted to judge the moment and make it perfect for her. If he got it right the first time, then everything would be all right later.

The straw rustled and their breathless laughter turned to gasps and moans. The world might have stopped turning but Harry did not notice as Alina trailed her mouth over the smooth skin of his shoulder. In turn he licked the salt off her skin, nipped the softness of her belly. When he touched her thighs, she let them fall apart.

Harry had made love many times. No young man refused an offer if the lady was suitably attractive, and offers came his way frequently. Delightful they may have been, but there was more to this encounter than mere pleasure. He had never found bedding a maid so all encompassing, never suspected how demanding and delightful it would be to have someone want all of him; his mind, his heart and his body, all at the same time.

Not that he objected. It deterred him not in the slightest. He doubted he would ever be able to explain it to any one, perhaps least of all himself, but as he moved over her in a blur of anxious desire, he prayed that she would not reject him at the last moment.

She was ready for him, begged him to go on. With his blood roaring in his ears, he found and thrust into her. Aware of an obstruction and her sobbing breath in his ears, he stayed motionless. Her nails dug into his shoulders but her small whine of pain hurt him more. "Alina?"

Her head jerked to one side. "We can't stop now!"

He hardly dared move. Slowly, little by little, her muscles relaxed around him. "Shall I...?"

She urged him on with tiny thrusts of her hips. "Slowly, Harry, slowly!"

He loosed a gasp of laughter against her cheek, braced his elbows more firmly in the straw and set off in a slow, languorous rhythm that all too soon, and without his permission, increased.

"I shall...I—"

It was impossible to get the words out. He wanted to tell her he must go faster, for that imperative ache was gathering, swelling and about to burst and he could not control it, not this time. He could only hope that she was with him as he rose on the wave that would carry him on to that deep boneless beach of oblivion. He crashed down with a sound that echoed like a growl around the stable loft and dimly, from somewhere close to his ear, heard a short, sharp cry and then a diminishing echo.

He was hot and slick with sweat. His head rested against her cheek and the thunder of her heart frightened him. He lifted his head, suddenly impatient with the darkness that had been their friend until now. "Alina?"

His senses cleared. When he shut his mouth, he heard her panting for breath. She must have enjoyed it, or she wouldn't be breathing as if she'd run up the hill from Corbrige. But he had to make sure. "Alina? Tell me…" He swallowed hard. "Have I hurt you?"

"It's gone now. Harry?"

He found her hand and kissed it.

"Harry, I love you."

Relief and joy swept over him.

Chapter Eighteen

Alina opened her eyes on blackness, cold air and the sound of a horse snorting somewhere close by. Something was wrong. Her fingers clutched the thick heavy cloak covering her. Wide eyed, she gazed into the darkness, listened for the smallest sound. Straw prickled and rustled beneath her.

Memory flooded back. She was in the stable loft, and Harry was beside her…. Her hand wandered, searching for him and found nothing but cold straw.

"Harry?" She called again, louder, but received no answer. Surely she had not imagined his warm bulk, his breath cool on the back of her neck as his large body cradled her in their straw nest?

She sat up and pushed the cloak away in one sharp movement. Cold air rushed in and goosebumps sprang up on her arms, attacked every inch of uncovered skin. Scrambling to her knees, Alina fumbled the edges of her chemise and bodice together.

Where was he? She shuffled forward. No, stop, there's a gap in the floor somewhere. Unable to orientate herself in the blackness, she could not decide which direction to take. It must have been the same for Harry and he was stranger here. Had he fallen to the stable below? The horse snorted as if something disturbed it. Was Harry lying injured somewhere beneath the loft?

The thought was enough to bring her to her senses. She crawled forward until she found the sawn edge of the boards announcing the open square in the floor. A soft breath of warmer air, smelling thickly of horse, came up from below. The stable was as dark as the loft.

She sat back on her heels. She was alone in the dark. He had left her.

She put her head back and screamed. "Harry!"

The horse snorted, iron shod hooves clattering on the stone floor below. The sound of the heavy body thumping into the wooden stall brought Alina to her senses. Mortified by her moment of panic, she leant forward. "Steady, girl, steady. It's only me being stupid." She rubbed her face with both palms, dragged her fingers through her hair. "I'm panicking because it's dark and I can't see and I don't know where Harry's gone. There are steps into the loft, I know that. I've often used them. But I cannot see them in the dark." She clenched her hands into fists and beat them against her thighs. "Think, Alina, think."

Slowly a picture formed in her mind. Since she knelt by the loft opening, then the stairs were on the far wall behind her. Of course. She remembered them clearly. Now all she had to do was make her way over there.

Looping her skirts out of the way as she crawled across the straw slowed her progress, and she uttered a sigh of relief when she reached the steps. One hand to the wall, she felt for the first step, and moved slowly down.

Alina froze in mid-step. Her breath sounded loud in the silence but did not mask the faint sound of footfalls outside. Something creaked and a brief glimmer of light flashed and grew stronger. What if it wasn't Harry? What if Father had suddenly remembered her fondness for Grey House? A dark shape turned the corner of the stable door, lantern in hand and headed for the stairs where she crouched.

"Harry!"

Weak with relief, she sagged to the wooden step.

Harry held the lantern high. "What's the matter?" He bounded up the steps and crouched on the step below her.

Alina blinked in the weak candlelight. "I woke and found you gone. I thought—Oh, Harry! Where did you go?"

"You were coming to find me? Alina, you might have hurt yourself. Let's get back to bed."

"You mean our nest in the straw?" Already she felt better.

"Yes. Our wonderful makeshift bed."

She heard the laughter in his voice, and it warmed her. "Where've you been? What's that?" She pointed to the bundle in his hands. "Can I smell bacon?"

"I went over to keep the fire going," Harry said. "While I was there I thought I might fry a slice of bread. I don't know about you, but I'm starving."

She giggled. "Oh, Harry! You are amazing. I'm hungry, too."

It was easy, in the candlelight, to find their way back across the loft.

***

At first light they went back to the still warm kitchen fire and ate what little there was for breakfast. Alina cleared away the crumbs on the breadboard while Harry crouched by the hearth and built up the fire. Her gaze lingered on him while her hands moved automatically over her tasks. The once-white shirt sat easily on his broad shoulders and his hair glowed in the new flames creeping around the twigs he laid so carefully.

This was a taste of how it would be if she and Harry were married. She smiled dreamily. One day, perhaps, there would be children, too. A girl and boy, if the good Lord deemed it so, each with Harry's wonderful blue eyes and dark hair.

She stared down at the empty board and frowned. It was no good dreaming. "Harry, what will we do now the food is gone?"

"There'll be rabbits in the fields. According to Matho you're a dab hand with a bow."

Lifting her head, she looked at him. "So you talked about me, then, the pair of you? Did he tell you about me shooting at Stagshaw Fair?"

He grinned at the fire and did not turn. "He said you beat all the lads and they hated you for it."

"Ay, and did he tell you how hard my father warmed my backside for me after it was all over?"

Harry laughed. "Let me guess…He said it was unladylike behaviour. How old were you?"

"I was ten," she admitted. "Mama tried to teach me to be a lady, but I was slow to learn."

"You mean you're still a hoyden but with redeeming qualities? I can send you out to shoot a rabbit for the pot when times are hard?"

"Oh, no. I'm fine with the target but I can't kill things."

"So you'd starve rather than kill a rabbit or two? What an odd creature you are."

Alina watched him scrape ash from under the grate. "If I had to, I suppose I would. But until then, rabbits are safe from me."

"It won't come to that," he said easily. He glanced at the window, where the pink clouds of dawn gave way to a bright blue sky. "I think we should go soon."

"It's still early." She followed his glance "Where to?"

"Back to Aydon Hall and your father." He broke a stick across his knee and laid both halves on the flames. "I won't build this up if we're leaving soon, but it would be good to wash in warm water. What shall I use?"

She handed him the old patched cauldron Mama had left behind and he took it outside to fill at the water butt. She went back to sweeping the table clear of crumbs and considered his words. As he came back inside, she looked up, the crumbs in her fist. "Father's not going to be pleased to see us."

"He'll be reasonable, I'm sure." He put the cauldron on the trivet over the fire and stood up as she tossed the crumbs into the fire. "Do you know you have straw in your hair?"

"I'd be surprised if I didn't." She turned her back to him. "Can you take it out?"

"I don't suppose you have a comb?" He ran his hand down the ruffled, tangled fall that reached her hips.

"No. Use your fingers."

Cold air struck the back of her neck as he lifted her hair. "M'mmm. Perhaps I should go and look for a curry comb in the stable."

His fingers ran through the long strands. Bits of straw fluttered to the stone flags at her feet. She tilted her head back, enjoying the sensation and thought she heard the jingle of metal outside.

"Harry, I—"

The door burst open with such violence it rebounded off the wall.

Alina gulped. Harry's hands stilled and then settled on her shoulders.

She was familiar with her father's temper but the man with bloodshot eyes in a twisted snarling face who stood in the doorway seemed a stranger. He looked ready to tear someone limb from limb. Lionel, his expression wary, stepped in after him, closed the door and stood behind him. He offered her a fleeting smile, but remained silent. Some part of her brain registered that Lionel was now as tall as Father. Both men carried swords and wore the sturdy leather and fustian they kept for hunting.

Father's eyes widened on Harry. "Scott!" A tide of crimson rose to the roots of his hair. "We've got you now, boy." His hand clamped on his sword hilt.

Alina squawked in fright. Lionel blocked his father's sword arm.

"Get out of my way!" Carnaby roared.

Lionel stood firm, and refused to be shouldered aside. "Father, you cannot fight an unarmed man with a sword in your own house."

"Give way! Leave me be!" But her father stopped struggling, as if the sense of Lionel's statement reached him.

"How...how did you know I was here?" Alina did not move.

"The smell of bacon on the wind," Lionel snapped over his shoulder. "Drifting down to the watchmen at Aydon in the dead of night. It wasn't too hard to guess who would be hiding out in Grey House since we've all been searching for you most of the day." He nodded towards Harry. "We didn't expect him."

Father's hot gaze remained fixed on Harry while he jerked a thumb at her. "Come here."

Alina remained pressed against Harry.

"Alina! Come to me, girl."

"No, Father. I am staying with Harry."

The fire crackled cheerily in the silence, and a horse snorted outside.

Harry offered a slight bow to both men in turn. "I think it is time I introduced myself," he said calmly. "Harry Wharton, son and emissary of the Deputy Lord Warden of the West March, at your service." He ignored Lionel's surprised gasp. "I know who you are, of course and I offer condolences on the recent death of Sir Reynold."

No one spoke or moved. Alina looked from her father to her brother, gauging their expressions. Did they believe him? She glanced back at Harry. Though he stood straight and tall, stubble shadowed the lean planes of his jaw, and his dark hair tumbled untidily over his brow. The loose ties of his shirt revealed the strong musculature of his throat.

Yet things she had not noticed last night now struck her eye. His shirt had lace edging the collar, and his aiglets sparked in the firelight. His dagger hilt was jewelled. Such subtle changes to the Harry she knew previously. She glanced at his grey doublet hanging over the chair and noticed the silver buttons running from neck to hip. Now he dressed as though he was the Deputy Lord Warden's son. She glanced at him, and saw pride and confidence in his stance and good-humoured smile.

Surely Father would believe him.

"You gave me your name as Harry Scott." The dull red receded from Carnaby's complexion but a vein throbbed on his forehead and his voice held a threat.

Alina drew a breath to speak but Harry forestalled her. "Ah, yes. I fear I lied."

Carnaby's voice sharpened. "You use insolence to me?"

Alina clutched her hands together beneath her breastbone and took what comfort she could from the fact that Father's sword remained in its scabbard.

Lionel shot a sharp glance at his parent. "How do we know," he asked, turning back to Harry, "that you give your true name now?"

Her brother was growing up at last. She sent him a swift smile.

"I have the proof you need in my saddle bag." Harry gestured to the leather satchel on the scarred table and when neither man objected, stepped up, opened the saddlebag and extracted a bundle of papers. He was two steps closer to her father and Alina held her breath in case of an attack. Harry seemed confident as he selected and placed three folded missives on the table. Each bore an impressed blob of crimson sealing wax, still unbroken.

Lionel drew off a gauntlet, stepped forward, scooped up the papers and offered them to the older man.

Father made a swift, dismissive gesture. "You read them." He went on watching the young man he had tried to execute.

Red wax cracked and fell to the flagstones as Lionel broke the seals. Father backed, folded his arms and leant against the vast wooden dresser. "Well?"

Lionel scanned the pages rapidly. "It is from the Deputy Lord Warden at Carlisle, sir. We are to extend the watches. There are details—names, dates, times and penalties for non-compliance. They are direct orders with Wharton's signature." He held the papers out but Father waved them aside.

"They don't prove he's Wharton's son," he growled, still glaring at Harry. "Merely that he is his messenger."

"Of course he is," Alina gasped. "Father, why don't you believe him?"

"Why should we?" Lionel turned to her. "He's lied once and he'll likely lie again to save his life, like all the thieving vagrants in this region."

"Harry is not a thieving vagrant!"

Harry caught her arm and gently pulled her back to stand beside him. "Wait," he murmured against her ear. "It will of course be clear to you gentleman," he said "that there are many men who can identify me. Sir John Forster or John Heron of Chipchase, for example. I think you would believe them, would you not? They reside not too far from here." He smiled at Carnaby. "Come to think of it, I believe your father, sir, has met me on official duty."

Silence filled the room for the second time that morning as the four people stared at each other. A branch burning in the fireplace sizzled and whined and hooves shifted restlessly on the cobblestones outside.

"Father?" It was Lionel, obviously uncomfortable with the turn of events, who stirred. "Since we could easily verify what he says, it seems he tells the truth. Shall we return home? Or make for Halton, so grandfather can confirm him to you as Wharton's son?"

Carnaby puffed out his cheeks, glared at Alina and strode to the door. "Aydon. We go to Aydon. Though what we do when we get there is beyond me. I had not thought to have a strumpet for a daughter."

With that he yanked the door open and flung out into the yard.

Alina stared after him in disbelief. He could not have hurt her more if he had rammed his fist into her belly.

Lionel hesitated at the door and directed a small smile in her direction. "Don't worry. He'll get over it. Mama will be vastly relieved to see you safe and unhurt. She feared dreadful things once she discovered you were missing. At one point she thought the Tynedale reivers had you."

Alina blinked back tears. "I long to see her," she whispered.

"Bring them down, Lionel." Their father's bellow came from outside.

Brother and sister locked glances before Lionel shrugged, turned and grasped the edge of the door. Holding it, he glanced back over his shoulder. "Don't argue with him, Alina, or you'll both suffer for it. He isn't thinking properly right now. You may not believe me, but Sir Reynold's death has upset him greatly."

She moved across the kitchen and laid a hand on her brother's arm. "I don't doubt what you say but grief does not give him the right to browbeat me like this, nor to attack Harry as he did. You seem to have his confidence now. What do you think he will do?"

Lionel shrugged and nodded in Harry's direction. "Depends on him, I suppose. Father can't risk running foul of the Warden's son. Father knows it, but he hates it, too. My advice is to tread gently. Very gently."

When Lionel walked out into the yard, Alina turned to look at Harry. "Will you ride to Aydon?"

He had been staring at the flagstones as if deep in thought. At her words, he looked up, and though he did not smile, he did not look overly worried. "I think we could try, at least. Let me go and get Bessie saddled and we'll be on our way."

***

"Alina! At last, you are safe!"

Alina saw genuine delight in her mother's face as she rose from her chair and rushed across the hall. Eyes brimming with sudden happy tears, Alina surrendered to the comfortingly tight, warm hug, banged her cheek on her mother's gable hood and tried to speak through a throat suddenly grown tight. "Mama…"

Mama drew back and gazed into Alina's face. "Daughter, are you well?"

Alina nodded. "No harm befell me, Mama. I am well."

"Come sit beside me." Mama led her across the room and sank back into her chair with a happy smile, black skirt belling out around her. The light, gauzy veil of her headdress fluttered and settled at the nape of her neck. "Where have you been, Alina? You have been gone a night and a day!" She shook her head. "Such a to-do with the Erringtons. You have no idea of the fuss they made—"

If Mama thought she left early on Friday morning, Alina saw no reason to disabuse her of that idea. She sank to the stool at her mother's side, coughed to clear the constriction of her throat and glanced back at the doorway where Harry hesitated.

"I went to Grey House, Mama. I have been there all the time." She offered a small, tentative smile. "I did not expect it to be quite so bare and cold. I had forgotten we brought my bed here."

"Oh, daughter! You'll be lucky if you don't catch a chill! Why did you go?"

Alina looked down at her clasped hands. "I could not bring myself to marry John Errington."

Her mother's eyes widened. "And you thought that if you disappeared for a day, the problem would go away? The wedding will be re-arranged, you must know that."

Chapter Nineteen

Harry, waiting patiently in the archway, chose that moment to cough gently, and move into the room. Margery turned. "Who is this?" She frowned. "He looks familiar."

"Mama, allow me to introduce Harry Wharton. He is the second son of Sir Thomas Wharton, the Deputy Warden of the West March. This is my mother, Harry; Mistress Margery Carnaby."

Harry bowed from the waist, rose and offered a smile intended to charm. "Mistress Carnaby." He stepped forward, ready to take her hand. "We met briefly in Corbrige market some weeks ago."

Margery Carnaby looked him up and down.

He had washed his face that morning, but he looked rumpled and untidy. With a twinge of regret Alina remembered John Errington's impeccable tawny velvet and silver-stitched gauntlets. Harry's sober grey clothes were far more suited to rough riding than exchanging pleasantries in a lady's solar, but the cloth was heavy and expensive and the silver buttons sparkled in the sunlight. Mama was sure to notice them. "Do you not remember Harry, Mama?"

Margery studied him and condescended to offer her hand. "No, but I met your father once, young man. You have a look of him, perhaps, across the cheekbones."

Harry bowed once more and brushed his lips across her knuckles. "I believe there is a distant connection through marriage between our families."

No one had ever mentioned in Alina's hearing that Lord Wharton was connected to the family. Wide-eyed, she watched her mother indicate the recessed sunlit window with its chamfered stone seat. "I can offer you nought but a cushion on the window seat, young man."

Alina seized a cushion, plumped it and handed it to Harry with a bright smile. He gravely placed it on the central stone square and sat down. In order to fit comfortably, he was obliged to place both forearms on the higher square of stone at each side. He looked vaguely magisterial and most uncomfortable in his stone chair. Alina hid a smile and looked down at her slippers.

"I suspect that this young man has something to do with your refusal to marry John?"

Alina jumped. Jumbled emotions stopped her thinking clearly. Of course Mama was right to grow suspicious. "I'm sorry, Mama."

"It is no good being sorry, daughter. Tell me what I ought to know."

Glancing at Harry, Alina knew she must say nothing that would endanger Harry. But what to tell, and what to miss out? Mama would not be pleased to hear her daughter had spent the night in Harry's arms. Alina took a deep breath. "We met Harry in Corbrige market weeks ago, Mama. Perhaps you remember him now?"

Margery Carnaby's dark, unfathomable eyes considered Harry anew and then suddenly narrowed. "Ah. The young man purchasing a gift for his sister?"

"The very one." Alina smiled. "And you remember I told you he saved me from the bull that broke loose in the market square that day while you were in church?"

Her mother nodded briefly. "But his name...that was Scott? Surely that was what so incensed your father when he heard of it?"

"Yes, well, I was coming to that. Harry was on business for his father, the Deputy Lord Warden. It was secret, and important, so he told everyone his name was Harry Scott. He did not know it was the one name Father hated above all others, nor did he know he was going to meet me." With a swift glance at Harry she rattled on. "He had the ill luck to fall from his horse and lay there unconscious for some time."

"The same day your father rode out after the reivers?"

Alina nodded. Judging from the sharp glances and lack of smiles, Mama had an inkling of where this was leading. Her shrewd dark gaze swept to Harry. "Why were you riding so close to Aydon, sir? It is far from the normal route north."

Seated with his back to the window, the sunshine rimmed Harry with a faint gold line. To Alina's eyes he appeared relaxed and smiled easily. "Pride would have me spin a yarn, but the truth is, ma'am, I wanted to know where your daughter resided so that I might visit her when my business was done. I thought I might ride close by and satisfy my curiosity without exciting any attention." His voice, mellow and soothing, reached them without effort.

He laughed quietly before continuing. "As it was, I gained far more attention than I wanted. A band of rough looking men were in the act of raiding your cattle, saw me and sought to slit my throat. I ran, they gave chase and the result was a collision with the tree. I'm lucky they didn't stop to finish the job." His sapphire blue eyes were full of self-mockery. "I had a bump the size of an egg for days."

Alina relaxed. He was handling things very well. How could Mama resist him?

"You do not know then, that the reivers move at night rather than daylight?" Her mother's acid tone jolted Alina's eyes wide. Mama seemed unimpressed by Harry's charm.

Harry's mouth pulled to one side. "I am learning quickly, but that I did not know. I've spent years in London, ma'am. My father was keen that I should have a good education, and then I served in several important households. I know the ways of King Henry's court better than I do the ways of Borderers."

Mama fell for the lure. One brow arched, and her face softened into a smile. "You must tell us of King Henry's Court one winter's evening. I would like that. I believe Alina would benefit from it also."

Hastily Alina nodded. "Most assuredly, yes." Was her mother warming to him?

"It would be my pleasure, ma'am." Harry's blue glance was sincere and full of respect.

Mama turned to her daughter. "Go on with your tale, Alina."

It had been a temporary reprieve. Mama had not been sidetracked and was still in full control of the conversation. Hastily gathering her wits, Alina saw her mother's eyes widen as a thought occurred to her. "You hid him, didn't you? In Dragon's old stable? Am I right?"

Alina could not deny it. She nodded.

"I knew it." Her mother fished for a handkerchief in her sleeve, found it and held it beneath her nose. "You hid him, you lied to me—all those visits to the horse—the boys found out, revealed your secret to your father and Harry faced the Leap."

She glared at her daughter. Two spots of angry colour sprang to her cheeks and her lips compressed. She swung around on Harry, who straightened abruptly on his stone seat, his face wary. "I heard that you were seen in Corbrige weeks later, and there was a fracas involving my husband and my son. No doubt you were also there. You are nothing but trouble to this family, sir."

Hands flapping at the air to try and stop her mother's tirade, Alina bleated "Father picked a quarrel—"

"I believe he wished to re-capture me," Harry said smoothly, his deep voice pitched to override Alina's alarmed squawk. He rose to his feet and paid his hostess the compliment of walking around to face her so that she did not have to stare into the sun to look at him. "I, of course, had no wish to face him at that point." He smiled. "After I made good my escape, I believe Footless Will Dodd and Dandie's Hob took it upon themselves to annoy your husband."

"Annoyance! I call it a good deal more than that!" Mistress Carnaby drew herself up in the chair, eyes blazing in her thin face. Sunshine caught the gold cross at her throat and flashed light across the solar. "A sword fight is neither an annoyance nor amusing, sir."

Harry sobered and looked down at his boots. "Of course, I have no idea what happened after I left. I believed they sought to divert his attention from me and perhaps pay back old scores at the same time. I am sorry if it got out of hand."

"Out of hand!" Margery frowned. The force of her breathing trembled the soft linen pleating that filled the low, square neckline of her gown. "How is it that you have Border ruffians aiding you?"

"Mama, Harry could not help it." Anxious to defend Harry, Alina broke into the conversation. "Father attacked him and was in such a temper he would have killed him if he could. Harry *had* to escape."

Harry matched his calm gaze against her mother's angry glare. He clasped his hands behind his back and inclined his head deferentially. "I do believe, ma'am, that your husband would have run me through given half a chance. I know that Sir Reynold's relations with Tynedale men are not of the best. Footless Will and Hob hardly know who I am, but would seize any opportunity to make mischief for the Carnaby family."

Mama stiffened in her chair. "What do you know of my husband's relations with Tynedale men? I thought you were a stranger to the ways of the Border?"

"My father knows more than most about the men of the Border, and I have long known of the major feuding families." He looked at Alina. "It is a pity I did not remember that when I selected the name Scott as my alias."

With a sigh, Alina's mother conceded defeat. "Of course your father knows, better than most, those who cause so much trouble." She gripped the arms of her chair as if steeling herself for the worst. "Why are you here, sir? As I said earlier, trouble follows you into this house. What is it you want of us now, Harry Wharton?"

Harry's gaze flew to Alina. She opened her palms and shook her head. Where they went from here she could not guess.

Harry cleared his throat. "I wish to marry your daughter, ma'am."

Mama looked puzzled. Alina did not see why his statement would be so unexpected. She went to stand beside him. "I love him, Mama."

Margery Carnaby's brow creased. She looked from one to the other, a faint smile on her face, and then shook her head slowly. "You cannot marry him, Alina."

"Why not, Mama? Sir Thomas has agreed."

"That is true, ma'am. There is no objection from that quarter."

"The objection will come from your father, Alina. You know he has contracted you to John Errington."

"But…" Alina clung to Harry's arm. Her thoughts spun dizzily. She might have to confess that she had spent the night in the stable loft with Harry in order to get what she wanted. "I cannot marry John Errington when I love Harry."

Her mother's gaze moved beyond her and fixed on someone standing in the hall doorway. Alina looked over her shoulder, and froze. Her father stood there. He must have heard everything.

Alina's father marched into the solar, stood with his back to the window, clasped his hands behind his back and glared at her from beneath lowered brows.

"You shall marry Errington, if he'll still have you."

Alina gripped Harry's hand and shook her head. It had all been going so well, and now this. "No, please, Father."

Father swung around to glare at Mama. "I don't care what cock and bull story they've been telling you, but Errington wants his bride. I've come directly from Sandhoe. The wedding's set for tomorrow."

"No!" The word ripped from Alina. "I can't marry John!"

Her father turned and the ugly twist of his mouth betrayed his temper. Alina quailed beneath the dark-eyed glare and stood rooted to the spot. "I have given my word to Errington," he declared. "Would you make a liar out of me? Have me foresworn?"

Hidden within the folds of her skirt, Harry's hand tightened around hers, warned her to say nothing.

"She wishes to marry me, sir." Harry's voice was calm and clear. "I believe the match to be a good one from your point of view."

Carnaby's gaze travelled to Harry. "How so?"

Harry let a small pause develop. "So far," he said calmly, "I have not revealed your mistreatment of me. My father does not know, for example, that you threatened to pitch me off a rock and let me shatter on the stream bed below." Harry's mouth stretched in a grim smile. "I should imagine," he said, watching Carnaby's face slowly turn red, "that he would be exceedingly angry to learn of such a thing. He might even demand retribution."

Alina stood rigid, fearful and elated at the same time. Harry's threat ought to stop her father in his tracks, but lately his temper had been wound so tight that she feared he would take no heed even though the Lord Warden, one of the King's senior officers in the Border Marches, was far too powerful an adversary to ignore.

She imagined her father's mind ticking over the myriad ways the Lord Warden might choose to make his life a misery should he ever hear the tale of Harry and The Leap. His chin rose. Heart pattering beneath her bodice, Alina waited. Father's breath issued more softly as he hesitated, caught with no answer to Harry's gently made threat. Notch by notch, his breathing calmed as his passion lessened. "So you'll hold this over me to my dying day?" Resignation laced his voice.

"If I have to," Harry said peacefully. "I would rather never have to mention it again." Harry raised his hand, brought Alina's knuckles to his mouth and kissed them. For a brief instant his glance met hers and one eyelid dropped in a wink. "If your daughter still chooses to accept me, I suggest she and I make good use of the priest you have already engaged and we will marry as soon as possible."

Alina suppressed an urge to grin. Smiling up into Harry's eyes, she said swiftly, "I do so choose. Tomorrow, Father. Can we marry tomorrow?"

As swiftly as it had arrived, the colour receded from her father's skin, leaving it pale. Compassion prevented her laughing with joy as she watched her father try to hang onto the last shreds of his dignity by glancing sideways at his wife. "Does this meet with your agreement?"

Margery Carnaby smiled, rose and walked to his side, where she laid her hand on his arm. "It may prove a most advantageous match, husband. A better match, I believe, than with the Erringtons." Her face was grave as she turned to Harry, but a spark of laughter appeared in her eyes. "I fear we will have a great deal of leisure to learn of the ways of King Henry's Court, sir."

Carnaby glared at his wife in disbelief. Shaking off her hand, he snorted with disgust and strode from the solar.

***

Harry listened to the subdued chatter and whisperings as he awaited his bride and caught the occasional jingle of spurs and the thud of a scabbard hitting the woodwork. Men had come to church armed. He shot a surreptitious glance over his shoulder. The well-to-do half of the congregation looked back at him with open curiosity. The feathered hats, rich velvet cloaks and wide shouldered tunics and doublets of the local gentry contrasted sharply with the drab homespun and fustian of the few local folk squashed into the back of Halton church.

None of his relatives were here, but it did not matter. His father would arrive when he could contrive a space in the constant press of business. The Carnabys made up for the lack of Wharton relatives. They lived closest and received the news soonest. Sir William of Halton, splendid in brown velvet, took pride of place at the front beside Alina's mother.

Several Erringtons had turned up, which was puzzling. No one dared turn them away. Perhaps Carnaby had invited them, and if he had, Harry was not going to let it spoil his day. It was possible the news of the change in bridegroom had not reached everyone in time.

A mutter of sound rippled through the church and told him his bride had arrived. He looked around and experienced a rush of delight as Alina, escorted by her father, paused at the church door. Her blue silk gown, already sewn with marriage to John Errington in mind, enhanced her small waist and he saw that for the first time since he had known her, she had adopted the court fashion for a stomacher. The flat front pushed her breasts high, and gave her that elegant outline so beloved of the court ladies.

Richly embroidered girdle cords ended in silver tassels to match the tiny silver cords that tied across the slashed and padded sleeves. As she walked forward the overskirt rippled back to reveal the pale silk underskirt with every step.

His years at court had taught him to appreciate good tailoring, but this time he forgot tailoring as his gaze ran over the square-necked bodice and lingered on the expanse of creamy bosom, barely disguised by a glowing amber pendant. Her newly-washed hair, brushed smooth and caught back from her face by a chaplet of flowers, hung loose to her waist.

She walked eagerly down the aisle to join him beneath the Norman chancel arch, her face alight with joy. Cuthbert Carnaby glowered, said not a word and joined his wife and sons. Alina reached Harry's side and against the background of simple white painted walls her chestnut eyes glowed in the candlelight. He had never seen her look happier.

Her glance took in his new dark blue velvet doublet slashed with gold and her smile told him she appreciated the fact that he had chosen blue to complement her dress. Harry let his happiness show in his eyes and saw her breath catch in her throat. The rest of the world faded away into a blur of strangers. A faint hint of colour stood in her cheeks. He could not stop, indeed did not wish to stop smiling. He took her hand, they turned to the priest and Harry concentrated on the important words that would make them husband and wife.

A latecomer let the church door bang shut. A moment later a deep voice rang through the church.

"That woman is affianced to me!"

The priest stopped in mid sentence, his mouth slack. His gaze lifted from the page of his missal, roamed between the young couple before him and came to rest on someone at the back of the church.

Harry wheeled around, eyes narrowed. Alina turned more slowly. They both recognised the voice.

John Errington, magnificent in crimson velvet, stood in the centre of the church, his hat with its large, curling white feather gripped loosely in one hand. He stalked a few paces forward, halted in the middle of the church and regarded them both. The congregation swayed like trees in a high wind, mouths agape, seeking a glimpse of the intruder. The whispers broke out, a sibilant hiss that rose to the rafters.

Alina's fingers grasped his arm, edged closer to him.

Harry locked glances with John Errington. Carnaby shot a dour glance at Errington and turned back to the altar with an expression very close to complacency.

John Errington ignored Harry. He looked only at Alina.

"You are engaged to be my bride, Alina. I ask that you honour our agreement."

His deep voice battered the stones of the church and bounced back to echo around the congregation. Harry looked down, saw the blood drain from Alina's cheeks as she stared, blank-faced, at John.

Harry glared at Errington. Surely the man could see she did not want him? Would he not see sense, and leave? She turned, darted a swift glance at her father, who stared at the great ceiling beams with a satisfied smile. Had he planned this? As if Alina shared his thought, colour flooded back into her face. Her brows drew together.

"Will you join our guests and allow *our* wedding to go forward sir?" Harry spoke quietly. If news of this ever got back to London he'd be the laughing stock of the country.

John's glance flicked briefly to Harry, then returned to his original quarry. Offering a sad little smile he held out his hand to Alina.

Alina pressed close against Harry. Both her hands curled around his forearm.

Errington shook his head. "With apologies, I fear I cannot," he said with every appearance of sorrow. "I have a signed contract that Alina shall be my bride. I must insist that it is honoured."

Chapter Twenty

Harry hesitated. Aware that the entire congregation hung on his answer, he saw how Alina glared at her father as if willing him to do something. Carnaby sat with a smirk on his swarthy face, an expression that made Harry long to throttle him. Biting back his frustration, he half-turned and raised his brows at the priest.

"It is your bride's affair, sir. I can do nothing."

No help there, then. Harry turned to the girl at his side. "Alina?"

Her eloquent gaze warmed him. "I wish to marry you, Harry." She looked at John. "He must find another bride."

It was all Harry needed to know. Inflating his chest, he turned to face the crimson clad figure. "I regret, sir, if you feel somewhat ill-used. Alina and I will marry today, with her full consent and that of her father. If you will give way, the ceremony may proceed."

"Absolutely not," John Errington said. He waved an elegant hand around the church congregation. "I have many friends and relatives here. They arrived to celebrate *my* wedding to Alina Carnaby. It is you, sir, who must give way."

An indrawn breath shuddered through the congregation. Errington moved a step closer. He looked only at Alina. Once again he held out his hand, and smiled as if he expected her to change her mind. "I would have you for my well-beloved bride, Alina. Will you not come to me?"

The tenderness of that rich voice, pitched for her ears rather than the congregation, must have touched her, for Harry saw her swallow swiftly. She cast a swift look at him and their glances met and held.

"He means it," Harry murmured. "It seems he has a real affection for you." Her hand tightened on his arm as she turned to face the other man.

"John," she murmured and then ducked her head and swallowed hard. Harry wondered what she could say that would not make things worse, but remained silent. Let her deal with it in her own way. "John, I'm so sorry. I don't want to hurt you but....I wish to marry Harry."

Harry watched Errington's hazel eyes darken and realised he was not about to give way. "I am afraid I cannot accept that, Alina," Errington said. The white feather twitched by his thigh. His voice revealed nothing but courtesy, but his expression hardened as he regarded Harry. "I see that this man has coerced or compromised you in some way—"

"No, never!" Alina's denial rang out. Harry shook his head, watching Errington closely.

"Father!" Alina held a hand to her father in supplication but Carnaby, damn him, went on staring at the ceiling.

It was Alina's grandfather who shoved his way to the front of the crowd and stood midway between Errington and Harry. From there he glared at his son. "Get on your feet, man. We can't ignore this. What do you have to say in this matter?"

Carnaby shook his head, folded his arms and nodded towards Harry. "This is not what I wanted," he growled. "And Errington is right. He has signed papers."

A jingling of spurs drew Harry's attention. Several tall, richly dressed gentlemen rose to their feet in the mid-section of the church. Harry glanced back at Carnaby. "Perhaps you forget our earlier conversation, sir? Surely you recall my father's interest in this?"

Carnaby's head jerked back. The glare he directed at Harry was filled with loathing. "Damnation," he muttered. "Errington, I must withdraw from the arrangement. You have my apology, sir."

Harry glared at Carnaby. He suspected Errington had been encouraged into this confrontation so that Carnaby might gain his own way and still be able to claim that but for Errington, he would have married his daughter to Harry Wharton. Now he must hope that Errington would take it further.

Sir William looked from one to the other, and then back at John Errington. "Your supporters may stand down now, sir."

John twirled his hat in front of him, spinning it round and round between his fingers. "My cousins came to attend my wedding. Should they return home unsatisfied?"

Sir William's face grew pink. "Damn it, this is not your wedding, sir! The wedding is between Harry Wharton and my granddaughter."

"Ah, yes. The Lord Warden's son." Errington's glance mocked Harry. "It helps to have relatives in high places, does it not?"

"Now look here," Harry snapped, and surged forward intent on inflicting damage to Errington's sneering face. Alina dragged on his arm. "Harry!" The congregation sucked in an audible breath. Harry clamped down on his temper. "My father gave us his blessing, nothing more."

Carnaby directed a loud "Hah!" at the ceiling.

Errington nodded. "And your father's blessing appears to have cheated me out of my chosen bride. You will therefore forgive me if I wonder at its shape and form."

Sir William shot a baleful glance at his son, who ignored him and remained silent. "There was no coercion, Errington," Sir William growled "if that's the way your thinking runs. I think you must accept what is happening, young man."

John's brows lifted. He gazed down at his hat and ran his fingers, over and over, down the length of the white feather plume. He shook his head. "I fear I cannot. If I am not to have Alina by fair means, then I must use foul." At his words, the young men behind him moved forward in support, and the congregation swayed back to make room for them.

"Gentlemen, gentlemen…" The priest bustled forward, hands raised, palm out. "There must be no unruly behaviour in the Lord's house."

Errington brushed the priest to one side and continued towards the bride. Alina retreated and Harry stepped in front of her.

"Out of my way, Wharton." John's voice boomed in the small church. Harry felt Alina's hands grip the skirt of his doublet just as

Errington's fist reached out and grasped the front of it. "I will have my bride."

Harry lunged forward, grappled Errington and shoved him back. Errington did not let go. They staggered together, lurched from side to side and scattered the Errington cousins and the closest members of the congregation.

***

Hands to her mouth to suppress her cries of horror, Alina backed towards the altar, unable at first to tear her gaze from the sight of Harry fighting John Errington. When she did seize a moment to glance to one side, Grandfather shook his head over the struggling men and her father laughed.

The sight shocked Alina. She straightened, her hands clenched at her waist. Instead of protecting his daughter or helping his prospective son-in-law, her father sat there and laughed. A spurt of rage overrode her wariness. She stalked over and stood in front of him.

"Father!" She flung a pointing finger in Harry's direction. "That is the man I love before all others! Do you want to see me a bride or a widow before the day is out? *Help him!*"

He regarded her without moving, but the smile slowly died on his face. Something must have touched him, for a moment later he rose to his feet and muttered to Sir William. Both men moved forward, arms outstretched and chivvied the two struggling figures down the short aisle to the back of the church.

Alina watched their jerky progress. At some point her mother rushed to her side and gripped her daughter's hands, but Alina could not tear her gaze from the two young men who traded punches before the church door.

The priest called "Gentlemen, gentlemen—"

Sir William's voice echoed hollowly from the back of the church. "Now, lads, lets stop all this hoo-ha and sort this out like gentlemen."

"Errington, you must give this up," her father roared. "Everything is null and void."

Harry landed a blow to Errington's chin. John stumbled back against the wooden font, surged back to his feet and rubbed his jaw where Harry's blow had landed. He lips drew back his from his teeth. Alina had seen dogs do the same thing just before they attacked.

His hand dropped to his sword hilt.

"No!" Alina's shriek soared over the sudden jostle of benches pushed back and the stampede of men to the door. Women's hands clapped against their mouths and three or four stumbled to their feet to follow the menfolk outside.

"Remain inside ladies, where it is safe." The priest scuttled to the door. Alina gripped her skirt and launched forward.

The priest caught her arm as she went by. "Stay, my dear."

Alina glared and shrugged him off without a word.

"Fine how-de-do and no mistake." The strident voice rang in Alina's ears as she ran the length of the church and turned towards the door. "The family's too hoity-toity by far. I always said it and now, Constance Carnaby, maybe ye'll believe me!"

With her hand on the door Alina shot a glance at the speaker. Aunt Agnes, recently widowed, who thought herself superior to everyone by virtue of being a daughter of the Shaftoes of Bavington. She might have guessed it would be Agnes's nasty tongue. Alina threw back the church door, ran across the gravel path and onto the grass of the churchyard.

Surprisingly, she found herself alone. Frowning, she spun round, uncaring that the blue silk of her gown swirled against the ancient gravestones as she searched for Harry and John. A burst of laughter drew her glance to the west. They'd gone through the churchyard and into the Halton grounds rather than towards the village green as she'd expected.

Hands clenched, she watched the men form some sort of square in the open space before Halton Tower. If the bursts of merriment were any clue, they were enjoying themselves hugely. Why were men always so anxious to spar and fight or watch someone else do it? Somebody would be killed.

Her lips thinned and her chin came down. Not on her wedding day, and not with her bridegroom. Alina lifted her blue silk skirt in both fists and plunged towards the gate intent on giving the protagonists a piece of her mind.

A hand grasped her arm and a gruff chuckle sounded in her ear.

"Nah, nah, had up, me beauty. Ye're wi us!"

***

Harry had no time to look for his bride. Swept at great speed out of the churchyard and into the Halton lands, Harry's blood ran hot. Trapped within a horde of jostling Carnaby and Errington men, he caught no more than a swift glimpse of sunshine on the honey coloured stones of Halton Tower and the stables where he'd left his horse two hours ago. The outbuildings formed a rough natural square and the men slowed as they reached it.

The sun sparkled on Errington's blade as it slid from the scabbard.

Harry's muscles tightened. To interrupt a wedding and demand that the bride honour a previous commitment was outrageous and

Errington's taut, frowning face worried him. For the space of a heartbeat Harry rued the day he met Alina Carnaby in Corbrige market square, then his blade leapt to his hand with a chilling, ringing hiss. He was not going to lose her now.

A sigh of expectation whispered around the watching circle.

Harry flicked the hair out of his eyes and bit back a grin. Would his children, assuming he lived to have any, ever believe him when he recounted the tale of a swordfight to win his bride?

Errington attacked with unexpected flair and vigour. Harry found himself driven back against the circle of watching men and sobered instantly. A chill ran through him. His opponent intended to make this a killing game.

The human buffer did not give as Harry skipped away from the attacking blade, but formed a warm, noisy barrier that gave off odours of sweat, musk and civet. Harry slid to the right. Jocular insults filled the air. His sense of foreboding faded. No one else expected this to be a fight to the death.

One of Halton's terriers rushed between ankles and barked around their feet. Someone grabbed it by the scruff of the neck and sent it packing.

Errington's pride was undoubtedly hurt, and perhaps he loved Alina. Harry could understand that. The man needed to make some sort of grand gesture to clear his feelings, and he'd gone too far to back down without some sort of token, some final flourish. Hopefully his pride hurt more than his heart.

On that thought, Harry treated the battle as a weird kind of tournament and prayed he was correct as the silver blades cleaved the sunny air. The spectators roared, swords slid and whined against each other. Sweat slid from his temples. Hair flopped across his brow and more than once Errington's blade came perilously close to a hit.

The man was good. No doubt he too had suffered relentless hours of practice under a skilled teacher.

Harry looked for a weakness and found none.

He noticed that the comments, good, bad and sarcastic, were aimed at Errington and thought it strange until he realised the Errington clan did not deem Harry worthy of insult. No one knew him. He was naught but some jumped-up popinjay who had stolen Errington's bride and must be taught a lesson.

Harry did not care for that assessment. He gritted his teeth, glared at his opponent and redoubled his efforts. Air sawed in and out of his lungs. Their blades caught, clung and brought him close to Errington, so close he felt the man's warmth, smelled his sweat. They glared at each other. Harry thrust Errington away from him.

"Come on Errington! Finish him!"

Harry glared in the direction of the voice. He was tired of the barracking, tired of the whole thing. He should have been married by now except for this man's stupid pride. He fixed his glance on Errington and moved forward.

Harry's spurt of irritation gave an edge to his swordplay. The watchers noticed. Calls began to come for Harry. One got carried away, and offered advice.

"Come on, Wharton! Keep that arm up, don't let him get under—argh!"

Harry grinned. His feint had fooled the watchers as well as Errington. He forced his opponent back a pace or two, his blade whipping against Errington's in a blaze of light.

"Hey, the lad's good," remarked his lone supporter. "Watch how he…"

Harry lunged, his sharp blade caught the skin of Errington's forearm and a spurt of blood flew high into the air.

Harry drew back, chest heaving. Satisfied with his performance, he watched his opponent. Would Errington's honour be satisfied?

"A lucky blow, I think." He offered a public salve to his opponent's pride but he knew deep down that he had taught young Errington not to trifle with the Lord Warden's son. They could both retire with dignity intact if only Errington had the sense to see it.

Errington shook his head, dropped his sword point and allowed a cousin to bind a handkerchief about his arm. Breathing hard, he glanced over at Harry with an odd look in his eye. "More good play than luck, sir."

Some of the tension left Harry. He dipped his head. "Thank you."

The ring of men remained quiet in the sunshine. A wood pigeon fluttered heavily across their heads. Errington patted the makeshift bandage, looked up and seemed surprised to see Harry still at his side. "Still here, Wharton? I thought you came to get married?"

Harry grinned. "I was. I shall, if my bride has not disowned me."

A smile broke across Errington's lean face. "The sooner we get the ceremony over, the sooner we can repair to Aydon and enjoy the feast good Mistress Carnaby will have waiting." He looked around the encircling crowd. "Off to the church, lads. There's to be a wedding." With a roar of approval the whole group broke away in the direction of the church, leaving them to follow as and when they would.

Errington's smile faded when he thought himself unobserved. He rubbed his bandaged arm. Lines of discontent marred his face. Harry could see he was unhappy with the outcome, had expected to win the bout and claim his bride. Honour demanded he maintain a brave face in public.

Some women had drifted out onto the green. Harry looked for Alina, hoping to see admiration in her eyes. She was not there. His gaze slid back to John Errington. On impulse, he offered his hand to his opponent. "I'd be glad to have you as a friend, if you will."

Errington's hazel eyes flickered in surprise. He hesitated a moment, gauging Harry, then flung out his undamaged hand. "I'm not such a fool as to hold grudges, Harry. And if I'm any judge, I'd be the one to suffer for it if I did."

A faint cry rang out. Still clasping hands, they both looked towards the church. "Now what?" Harry groaned.

Faint cries came to them. "Here, where's my horse gone? Hey! They've all gone!"

"What!"

Cries of outrage hit the air. Men ran to the horse lines beneath the yew tree at the church wall and more cries erupted. "They've gone, every bloody one!"

Harry and Errington exchanged glances and hastened towards the church, where frustration and rage laced the cries that tore the air.

"Where the hell's that little bugger I left to look after them?"

"There! Look, is that him?" The man pointed to a small figure racing back down the gentle green slope from the Wall.

"Aye, that's him right enough." He cupped his hands around his mouth and bellowed. "Where's my horse, young Will?"

Less than a minute later, poor Will staggered to halt, palm pressed to his side, very nearly spent. He pointed west. No more than eight years old, pink cheeked and hardly able to breathe, he gasped words rather than sentences. "Reivers…that way…took horses…" He looked at Harry. "Alina as well!"

"What?" Harry sprang forward, knelt and grasped the boy's shoulders. "Will, is it not? Well, Will, nod your head until you can talk properly. You saw Miss Alina ride off with the men who stole the horses?"

Will nodded.

"You are certain it was Alina?"

Will nodded. "Blue dress," he gasped. "Bride."

A chill hand settled around Harry's innards. He glanced up at Errington. "Any idea where they'll have gone?"

Sir William appeared at their side. "Bewcastle's where they take horses stolen hereabouts. Noted for it. Bewcastle's west of here." He glared at them. "If the two of you'd not started footling about with swords my granddaughter would be safe…"

Harry's answer was sharp. "She is my bride, sir. Believe me, I will find her."

"She's not your bride yet, Harry!"

Harry heard the jubilation in Errington's voice. If the man was going to propose a race with Alina as the prize, he would kill him. He got to his feet and hesitated long enough to send a swift wink to Young Will before he turned and ran for the stables.

Footsteps pounded after him. "Do you have a horse? We have to save her!" It was Errington.

"In the stable. I'm family now. What about you?"

They reached the stable door together. A wry grin crossed Errington's heated face. "I came late, remember? My horse went with the rest. You go on, Harry. I'll gather men and mounts and follow you as soon as I can."

"Do that. But don't think you're going to steal her from under my nose, Errington." Harry disappeared into the gloom.

Someone, thinking to add to the romance of the knight and his new lady, had caparisoned his mare fit for a royal tourney. Swearing, he tore flowers from the brow band and reins, ripped the gaudy fabric from Bessie's rump and tossed it over a straw bale.

"She wouldn't come anyway, I can see that now." John's voice came from the doorway. "Will you be able to track them?"

Harry ground his teeth together. Jesu, did the man think he was incapable of following the trail a dozen horses would leave in soft ground? "Childs' play," he snapped.

Harry led Bessie out and mounted in one fluid movement. Errington headed back towards the church, but Alina's father strode towards him across the cobbles.

Carnaby put a hand on the reins. "Will tells of half a dozen raiders and nearly twenty horses. It should be a plain trail." His tone suggested that even an imbecile like Harry could not miss it.

Harry restricted himself to a sharp nod of the head.

Carnaby moved to one side and gestured for Harry to ride on.

"Fetch her home, lad."

Harry heard the soft comment, and glanced back, frowning. He urged his horse towards the open hillside and wondered if he had imagined Carnaby's gruff words.

Chapter Twenty One

Twenty horses on soft ground made a trail as plain as day.

Hoof prints pocked the meadow on a diagonal course up towards the old Wall. Harry drew a deep breath, urged his mare up the slope and scanned the bare landscape ahead. The furious energy of the last half hour still ran through him and anger warred with fear for Alina.

He knew, thanks to his father, how reivers infiltrated the local populace seemingly at will. But how had they known of the wedding? He supposed they'd heard of the proposed Errington match. Or was it pure chance that they rode this way and couldn't resist stealing the horses while everyone was occupied in church?

Or outside it. If they'd stayed inside, they'd have lost the horses, but he and Alina would be safely married by now. The two of them could have feasted at Aydon without a worry in their heads except how to escape to privacy. Stolen horses would have been someone else's problem.

Horse theft was one thing but taking Alina was quite another. He wished he'd told Errington to alert the Lord Warden. Her life might be in danger, though more than likely there would be a ransom demand. Sickening fears stole into his mind. Would those ruffians be able to keep their hands off such a pretty girl? She would be terrified but she had a temper and it was her wedding day. High emotion might lead to angry words. Would she be able to hold her tongue? He growled. If one of them so much as laid a finger on her, he'd kill him.

"Come on, Bessie!"

The mare snorted, flicked her ears at him and thundered on up the slope, shedding a rose from her brow band as she went. She was a good mare but she couldn't keep up this pace forever. If he could get a glimpse of them, if she could get to the crest of the hill, he might be able to see....

What had surprised him was the affection he'd seen in Carnaby's face. Had he mistaken it? It had been only a fleeting glimpse. The wistful expression seemed so very unsuited to Carnaby's heavy features and yet it had been there. The man must have some feelings for his daughter after all.

The slope levelled out, and he let the mare pick her own gait while he searched the land ahead and to either side of the dark, muddied line of hoof prints. The trail rounded a rocky outcrop, followed the outer rim of a copse, then disappeared over a dip in the land and carried on up the rising green slope beyond.

The reivers covered the ground fast. Harry squinted ahead and in the far distance saw the horses travelling west at a steady pace across the bare ridge. With a crow of delight Harry settled down to ride as unobtrusively as possible and still keep them in sight.

Sweat dampened his spine and anxiety tightened his muscles. Bessie responded by speeding up. Controlling the tension that gripped him was difficult. They couldn't do anything to Alina while they moved at speed. The danger would come when they stopped. Gritting his teeth, Harry intended to be right there with them when they reached their destination.

***

Alina prayed they would stop soon. Her captor rode a shaggy pony with short legs at speed over rough ground and held her face down before his thighs. The smell of horse, grass and stream, bog and stone clogged her nose and knee high clumps of wiry grass whipped her face raw.

The pony broke from a canter to swift, bone-shaking trot and soft, soggy ground slowed the animal to a walk. Hairy fetlocks splashed black odorous water into her eyes.

If only she had not been so intent on reaching Harry she might have heard the reiver's unshod pony pattering up through the churchyard behind her. His evil smelling hand had gagged her and he dragged her across his pony as if she weighed no more than a child. With her as the bull's eye in a round ring of stolen horse flesh, the reivers pounded across the hillside.

The pony lunged forward, jolting her across a trickle of muddy water. Her long hair swung forward and blinded her, the precious amber pendant smacked against her nose. Bracing one hand against the pony's shoulder she gripped the rider's ankle with the other, and swore when the pendant struck again. Joggled and dizzy, she shut her eyes, but that made the dizziness worse. Opening them again, she forced her head up and focussed on a distance clump of grass.

It was better than looking down at the ground.

The rough, uncouth voices around her gradually shaped words and phrases she understood. "Got yersel summat to play wi t' night, Johnnie?"

Laughter followed. "His missus'll tak a butcher's knife to his privates if'n he does."

The pony jerked to a halt. Alina squeaked at the jarring impact. Before she caught her breath, the pony walked into a sluggish stream. Gobs of dirty water struck her face. Yowling in outrage, she got a mouthful of mud. Spitting and retching, she heard howls of laughter around her.

"Sit up then, ye ninny." The voice sounded amused and not unkind, but even when she braced both hands against the pony's shoulder she could not lever herself into a sitting position. Her captor seized and yanked her upright. Alina clawed the wet, muddy hair from her face. Then she looked down at her wedding gown, blotched with wet, stinking mud and choked back the sob that rose in her throat.

"Aye, she's a looker allreet. Mebbe worth a bit o' marital strife, eh?"

Alina lifted her head and looked straight into the beady eyes of the nearest rider. He grinned at her, grizzled whiskers moving back over yellow teeth and his sharp blue eyes glinted with amusement.

"Less o' yer lip, Geordie." The growl came from the man behind her. "This one'll earn me mair gold than ye've ever seen. She's Carnaby's lass. Him that dinged us over at Jedburgh."

Alina did not dare turn and stare at her captor, but she stole glances at him from the side of her eye. She knew the tale. Something as trivial as the price of a tankard of ale had stirred men into a fight a year or two back in Jedburgh. Archie Elliot of Thirtleshope had not taken kindly to having a front tooth knocked out and retaliated with a foray against her grandfather's land at Halton. Cowsheds, barns and haystacks blazed, cattle had been stolen and never recovered. Could this man be Elliot?

It was difficult to speak against the jolting motion, but she managed it in short bursts. "Is your name...Archie Elliot of...Thirtleshope, sir?"

A guffaw of laughter went up around her and the riders closed in to hear more.

"Man, she's polite an' all!"

"Ye be famous, Archie! The lass knaws ye!"

"Geddaway and keep them hosses runnin' in a bunch." The man behind her did not waste words and his stern tone did not spoil the men's good humour, for they rode off, still laughing, and rounded up the two runaways that had made a bid for freedom.

Alina sneaked a sly glance at the whiskered jaw of the man whose corded forearm held her close against him. She judged him to be in his mid thirties. His skin was pockmarked, ingrained with dirt and his clothes were ill-matched and of poor quality but he rode with an easy grace, surveying what his lads were up to and managing his pony with consummate skill. "Na, lass, I'm not Archie Elliot, but he'll tek these 'osses for a good price."

"Who are you, sir?"

"Me name's Johnnie Hogg, not that it'll mean owt t'ye."

"Why then did they call you Archie?"

A huff of laughter gave her the courage to glance back and she caught his considering brown gaze.

"'Cos them daft fools think it's ower funny to call any man Archie if they think he'll be rich someday soon."

"But....Oh, I see. It's because Archie is rich?"

"Aye."

Conversation ceased as he guided his pony through a rocky decline and up the other side but once they reached the open ridge once more, Alina tried again. "Why have you kidnapped me?"

"Sit straight," he commanded.

Hastily she turned to face the pony's ears. "It's supposed to be my wedding day."

"Aye," he said. She heard the grin in his voice. "Heard aboot it in Corbrige."

"What do you hope to gain? Oh!" She grabbed at the pony's mane as it leapt across a ditch and raced on.

"Gold," said Johnnie Hogg, his gaze on the horses his men drove across the shoulder of the hill.

"But Father won't pay! Right at this moment he's probably glad to see the back of me." She bit her lip, but the jarring ride made her wary of biting clean through it. "If you think my father is rich, you are quite wrong. I doubt Sir Reynold's death will make him a rich man, either."

Johnnie's voice sharpened. "Then mebbe we'll gie 'im yer 'ead in a basket."

Her eyes widened. Horror warred with disbelief and absolute acceptance of his laconic words. Alina swallowed hard and tucked her chin down. Her stomach rolled until she feared she would vomit. If she did, she'd likely choke to death, for she didn't imagine he would stop riding. Employing every ounce of common sense and courage at her command, she breathed long and deep through her mouth and exhaled slowly.

Surely her head in a basket, as he had so neatly phrased it, would be Johnnie's admission of defeat when all else had failed? There was a long time, surely, before they reached that point.

But she would have to endure this, somehow. Did Harry know she'd been taken? Surely he would, unless John Errington had killed him. That was the worst of all the miserable thoughts that scurried through her mind. She had to believe Harry had survived and would ride after her. She could hardly expect John to show much interest in what happened to her when she had turned him down so publicly.

What if this went on for days? What if Harry really were dead? Her stomach rolled. Be sensible, Alina. They wouldn't kill each other. Neither of them was so stupid, and surely Father and Grandfather would have stopped it before it got to that point. Or if they didn't, Mama would have done something. Or bossy Aunt Agnes, who thought she ruled the roost. A weak smile crossed her face at the thought of domineering, loud-mouthed Agnes beating the opponents apart with her walking cane.

Alina stared at the land ahead through a blur of tears. The green slope rose slowly and steadily towards the neck of England, where the rocks pushed through the rough grazing. She clung to the thought that Harry would be riding not far behind her and it helped.

While her captor held her so close, there was little chance of escape. Even if she managed to break free, she faced miles of desolate moss and rock before she stumbled across some remote cottage or farmhouse. Reivers rode well away from dwellings unless they wanted to relieve a farm of an animal or two.

Out here on the uplands the breeze was cool. Gooseflesh rose along her arms. The thin silk of her dress offered no protection. She moaned at the thought of her wonderful new gown, now besmirched with filthy, stinking mud. She lifted her head, set her jaw and stared at the sky.

Easy enough to make another gown once she was home again.

The only source of heat was the body of the man behind her. Tempting though it was to lean back and let his warmth soak into her, pride kept her spine rigid and her teeth clenched together.

***

So cold she could barely feel her limbs, Alina stared up at a sky clustered with stars. She kept her hands tucked in her armpits, but it did not help much. Wood smoke tickled her nose and soon the ponies slowed and picked their way downhill.

Johnnie cleared his throat and spat into the undergrowth, then half turned in the saddle. "Tak the beasts ower t' Fat Johnnie's place. Ah'm ganning' doon wi the lass."

The men wheeled off across the open hillside. She was alone with Johnnie. He guided the pony down a dark, shallow incline among shrubs and trees. What would happen now? Nervousness gnawed at her. Appalled, she heard herself say "You'll be taking me home to your wife, I suppose?"

"Aye."

His reply lacked bite. Emboldened, Alina ventured another question. "What's she like?"

"What's it tae ye?"

He sounded indifferent rather than annoyed. Like Lionel when he was tired and hungry. "I'm curious," she said. "I think I know how my mother would react if Father brought a strange young girl home one night."

A single snort of laughter encouraged her. "And 'ow would she greet him, then?"

"Oh, there'd be the civilities, then a frosty silence, and after that the questions would start. That would be in public. Actually," she added slowly, "I can't imagine what she would say in private." It was fear that made her talk like this, but it was better than silence. *Curry favour with your captor while you can.* "Your wife isn't going to like me, is she?"

"Aye, she will."

"Why? Why should she?"

"'Cos ye'll bring in silver, and she'll like that fine."

"She won't beat me, then?"

There were things she feared more than beatings but she wasn't going to voice them in case it gave him ideas. All day long she had squashed the word rape to the back of her mind whenever it appeared, but the thought chilled her even more than the wind. She supposed she ought to give thanks that she wasn't a frightened virgin. At least she had that glorious night with Harry to remember. Even so, now the threat crept into her mind as a very real and possible danger, her stomach shrank into a hard little nut.

"Nah, lessen ye dae summat stupid like."

"That's a relief. What would you—she, rather, call a stupid thing?"

He didn't answer. He was guiding his pony towards a dark building not far ahead, and as she spoke, the door opened and a stream of light shone across the darkness.

"Da!"

"Whose that?"

"M'lad." He raised his voice. "Jack, cum an' tak t'pony."

A lantern, not very high off the ground, bobbed towards them. The pony and the lantern converged and Alina looked down at a small boy somewhere between Lance and Cuddy's age. "Hello," she said without hesitation.

The boy's upturned face was yellowish white in the light of the single candle. He held the lantern higher, and his eyes opened wide. "We'se this, Da?"

Johnnie pushed her through the door of the dwelling. Alina blinked. After the cold and windy darkness, the pungent aroma of warm wood smoke, tallow candles, boiling mutton, dogs and animals was welcome, though the air was so thick her eyes smarted and her hand went to her nose. She sneezed.

"We'se this, Johnnie?"

The speaker was a well-built, comely woman with powerful arms and a face flushed from the heat of the fire. She handed the ladle to the small girl at her side and walked forward, her calm eyes inspecting Alina from head to foot before she looked at Johnnie. "Well?"

"Cuthbert Carnaby's lass."

"An' what's she daein' 'ere?"

Alina bobbed a stiff curtsy. "Good even, ma'am. I am so cold! May I sit by your fire?" She stepped forward, edging towards the welcome warmth.

"Ay, let 'er get warm, Meggie." Johnnie rapidly stowed his gear on hooks by the door. "She's had a long, 'ard ride the day."

Meggie's eyes widened at the rustle of expensive silk as Alina sidled by her to get to the fire. "An' a dirty one, by the look of 'er." She turned back to her husband. "And what do we do wi 'er, then?"

Chapter Twenty Two

Johnnie walked over to the fire and ruffled the curls of the small girl sitting there. The child grinned, revealing a wide gap in her front teeth and leant confidingly against her father's thigh. Alina thought of her own father as she sank down at the side of the hearth and could not remember him ever greeting her with such affection.

Johnnie and his son headed for the door. Alina waited until the door banged shut and then turned to meet the curious gaze of her hostess. "He hopes to extract money from my father," she told Johnnie's wife. "I told him I doubt that Father will pay out as much as a groat for me and that I could be here forever. You know what men are like about daughters."

Meggie nodded towards the girl on the stool. "There's one might not agree wi ye."

Alina followed her glance.

"Why doesn't your father love you?" The child's blue eyes looked worried.

Alina managed a choked, feeble sort of sound and hoped they thought it laughter. "Oh, he does, I'm sure. But he loves my brothers more." She looked up, and her glance met and meshed with Meggie's thoughtful brown gaze. Perhaps she ought to stop chattering. It might annoy these people and that would never do. "Am I in the way here?"

Meggie stirred, widened her eyes and shook her head. "Nay, you stay right where you are and get warm. Ye can keep yer eye on the stew while yer at it." She turned to the deeper shadows behind her and lifted several wooden bowls from the crude wooden wall rack.

Alina smiled at the child beside her. "My name is Alina. What's yours?"

"Mary."

"Ah, such a pretty name. Like the princess."

Mary's mouth dropped open, revealing a gap in her bottom teeth. Hesitantly, she asked, "D'ye *knaw* a princess?"

Meggie plucked the ladle from her daughter's hand, bent over the pot and doled stew into bowls. "Mary, ged up and tak these bowls to t'table, there's a grand lass. Jack and ye Da will be back in a trice." The child scrambled to her feet to do her mother's bidding.

It wasn't long before Johnnie banged in through the door with his son trotting at his heels. "Summat smells good," he muttered, rubbing his palms together.

The family clustered about the table and ate the stew from steaming bowls. Alina's mouth watered but she stayed by the fire and said nothing. Perhaps they didn't intend to feed her, or perhaps there wasn't enough to go around. Johnnie bolted his share and scoured the bowl with a hunk of bread. "By, that were grand."

Stretching her neck, Alina peeped into the blackened pot hanging over the fire. It looked empty. Resigned to a hungry night, she watched with little interest when Meggie seized her husband's bowl and rose from the table. She walked to the hearth, filled it from the pot and thrust it at Alina.

Surprised and grateful, Alina took it in both hands and closed her eyes as she breathed in the meaty aroma. "Thank you," she said, smiling at Meggie. "It smells delicious. I know I shall enjoy it. Thank you."

Johnnie grinned and flicked a glance at his wife. "So ye should. The meat's from one o' the best farms around."

Alina swallowed a mouthful and scooped up more. "I did not hear that remark," she said softly and kept her eyes on the bowl.

Jack gazed at her with a look that clearly said she was stupid. "Da said the mutton came from—"

"I know what he said, Jack."

The boy left his empty bowl on the table and came to the hearth. "Then why—"

Alina eyed him over a spoonful of fragrant stew. "I have two younger brothers. Cuddy is seven and Lance is nearly fourteen. When they are told something they don't like, they pretend they never heard it. Sometimes they clap their hands over their ears. That way they keep their consciences clear."

Jack's eyes gleamed. "And they don't do whatever it is they didn't like!"

"Exactly."

He regarded her with calculating eyes. "So…you don't want to know the mutton was stolen but you want to go on eating it?"

She sipped broth from her wooden spoon. "I am devilish hungry."

He laughed, Johnnie snorted and Meggie looked amused. "I should have been at my bridal feast tonight," Alina murmured, "I was so nervous this morning I couldn't eat more than a mouthful."

Meggie's spoon sank back to her bowl. "You got married today?"

Alina shook her head. "Not quite. The service didn't…it didn't go on long enough. I'm not married, though I should be…*Je suis desolee*," she whispered. It wasn't hard to pretend that she might cry at any moment.

"Ah, ye poor thing," Meggie cried, gathering up both spoon and bowl and coming to the hearth. "Did ye want to marry the lad? It wasna a forced match?"

"No. Indeed, I desperately wanted to marry Harry."

"Marry Harry," chortled Jack. "Marry Harry, marry Harry….Ow."

His mother's elbow in his ribs put a sharp halt to his litany. Meggie nodded towards the ravaged blue gown. "That'll be why ye all dolled up, then."

Alina nodded. "Well, this is my wedding dress. Not that it did me much good."

"And what's he like, then, this Harry?"

"Oh, he's tall, dark—"

"And handsome, o'course!" Meggie grinned. "Gan on, gan on." She slurped the last of her stew off the spoon, handed her bowl to Mary and nodded at the table. The child obediently replaced the bowl while her mother turned to her brother. "Jack, clear the table. I want to talk to…"

"Aw, ma."

"Dee it, Jack, before ah clip ye ear."

Alina suspected Meggie wanted to talk of the outside world and happily obliged her. "My name is Alina, and yes, Harry is handsome." She clasped her hands about her knees and smiled. "He has wonderful blue eyes that match the sapphire he wears on his right hand. We only met a few weeks ago quite by chance in Corbrige market...and then only because I was rather forward."

"Ah can well believe that," Johnnie remarked dryly. He got up, and went to sit in the only carved wooden chair by the fire.

Alina pulled a face. "Mama rebuked me later. Shall I tell you what happened next?"

Meggie nodded, round face aglow in the firelight. "Aye, it's as good as a pedlar's tale." She let Mary climb onto her lap and settle down. "We don't know this one, do we, lovvie?"

So Alina told the story of the bull, Harry's encounter with the reivers and his subsequent lapse of consciousness. Meggie hung on every word, so Alina embellished it as much as she could. When she described her father's return, the discovery of Harry and the confrontation in the hall, even Johnnie listened. By the time she got to the tale of Harry's Leap, Meggie's eyes widened and Jack bounced up and down at the news Harry had escaped.

"He's a brave lad and no mistake." Meggie cuddled her little girl and rocked her. "Then he came back? There's more?"

Alina nodded. "Oh, yes"

Meggie nodded at the girl in her arms. "But the little one's very nearly asleep. We'll hear the rest tomorrow."

In no time at all, the children and Alina were bundled up a rough ladder to the half-gallery floor above, where straw and a couple of rugs made a bed for the children.

"If ye squeeze in wi the bairns ye'll stay warm enough." Meggie waited till Alina lay down and then retreated, taking the candle with her. Darkness settled over the gallery. Alina snuggled in next to Mary, though Jack insisted, with manly dignity, on maintaining some distance between them. Alina didn't mind. She was so tired she could sleep on a pikestaff, as she once heard her brother Lionel remark.

When silence settled down over the barn-like dwelling, there was only the breathing of the children to keep her awake. No sounds came from below, where Meggie and Johnnie no doubt had a bed in one of the dark recesses on the ground floor. She wondered if, given a little time, she might make a friend of both Mary and Meggie. Judging from the worn appearance of Meggie's woollen kirtle and the darns in her shawl, the family was not earning enough to live comfortably. The children's clothes were little better, for Jack's shirt was far too large for him, and had to be a hand-me-down from an older boy. Or perhaps a shirt of his father's, cut down to fit him. Mary's kirtle had been roughly cobbled together by someone not too experienced with a needle, as if the seamstress knew the garment would not last long.

Alina sighed. Life was hard for these people, and yet they were generous with what they had. Johnnie had stolen her, and yet even he had offered her no violence, and owned a dry humour she found amusing. She stared up into the rafters. Telling of Harry's Leap had woken her own fighting spirit and her last thoughts before she fell asleep were that she must look about her for a way to escape and get back to Harry.

Happily dreaming of his blue eyes and warm smile, she vowed that she would be off and on her way home by midday tomorrow.

***

Harry tracked the reivers to Bewcastle, watched the bulk of the group peel off and herd the horses north across the fell, then followed Alina and her captor down through the wooded dene. Lurking in the deepening shadows, he watched Alina enter the building and observed the boy stable the man's horse. Assuming no further action until daybreak, Harry retreated, rode to Bewcastle castle and demanded access.

The guards were leery of a stranger arriving after nightfall, but Harry used his father's name and was duly allowed in and escorted to the commander of the garrison.

Harry ducked under the door lintel, walked into a small panelled room with a fire burning in the hearth and smiled with relief when he recognised the stout, middle-aged figure and florid features of Henry Burton.

"Harry!" Burton looked up, full of surprise. "My dear fellow, what brings you to this neck of the woods?"

"I need your help, sir." In swift, concise sentences Harry outlined his predicament and watched Burton's expression change from surprise to outrage and then to concern.

"You don't know, then, precisely who has her?"

Harry shook his head. "No, but I know exactly where she was taken. A small dwelling built onto an old tower down in the dell below the church."

"Ah! Then that would make it Johnnie Hogg who has her. He's a cunning fellow, but not vicious. He'll not harm her, you can rest assured on that score." Wreathed in wrinkles, his eyes twinkled. "Besides, his wife would have something to say about it if he laid a hand on your young lady."

"Sir?" Harry gaped at the older man. "Surely we should take men and affect her release at once?" Burton seemed unconcerned at the thought of a young girl in the reiver's clutches.

"Time enough tomorrow, I think." Burton smiled. "It's nearly midnight, and you look exhausted. If you set off after these fellows mid-morning, you won't have eaten all day." He walked to the door, opened it and bellowed for food and ale.

"But she could be in danger at that man's hand—"

Burton closed the door and shook his head. He walked forward, stood beneath a candle stand unaware that candlelight revealed the pink scalp through his thinning hair. "She'll come to no harm in Hogg's house. He has a wife and two small children. Take my assurance, lad, she'll be in no danger. All Hogg wants is money."

He sounded convincing and Harry could hardly force him to rouse the guard. A tap on the door brought a plateful of cold beef, pickles, bread and a brimming tankard of ale. Harry's mouth watered and his stomach rumbled. He took his place at table, and let the heat of the fire sink into his bones.

***

Alina awoke in darkness for the second time in three days with the unsettling feeling that she couldn't remember where she was. This was not the hay loft at Grey House. Nor could she recall why there was a small, warm body on either side of her. Blinking, she felt straw beneath her. That felt familiar, but the rough, scratchy wool blanket, swiftly and loosely woven, held an odour that was new and different. It scratched her chin. Her eyes felt gummy and sore, as if she'd spent far too long in a smoky atmosphere. It was hard not to cough.

It wasn't absolutely dark. Light filtered through from somewhere above her head. Lifting herself gently on one arm, she surveyed her surroundings. There was a raftered roof and thatch above her, and stone walls.

Memory filtered back, slowly at first, and then at great speed. Today she should have awoken in Harry's arms as his legitimate wife, duly witnessed and attested by all in front of the Lord. Her father had no control over her now.

She grimaced. He did, of course, for the marriage was incomplete. A wave of regret swamped her, swiftly followed by a wave of something hotter, stronger and much more urgent.

She must get out of here and find Harry.

Such joy as they shared was a rare gift and not to be wasted. Looking about her, Alina determined there and then that no one would ever say she lacked the courage to get off her bottom and find her way home.

Where was Johnnie Hogg? Peering down to the floor below, Alina understood all too well that Johnnie needed gold to keep and feed his family. She was to be his means of achieving the money but she didn't think he would harm her. She suspected he was one of those men whose bark was far worse than his bite.

The children slept on. Gazing at them in turn, she smiled. So much for Jack's protestations about sleeping alone last night. Here he was, curled in at her side, one palm beneath his cheek and with the hint of a smile about his mouth.

If she could extricate herself from the blanket and the straw without waking either of them, perhaps she could sneak down the ladder and leave before any one woke. No sound came from downstairs. Once outside, she would walk until she found someone who could help her. The castle must be nearby, and she could ask for help there. Or perhaps she could take one of the ponies they'd stolen yesterday. If she headed south from here, she would find the line of the Wall and then all she had to do was ride east until she found the river. It couldn't be too hard to find her way home.

Slowly, inch by inch, she drew herself up from between the children. Straw creaked and rustled, and every sound seemed magnified in the silence. Hardly daring to breathe, she got to her feet, backed away and then stepped carefully towards the ladder. Small twinges ran through her muscles from the exhausting ride yesterday but she gritted her teeth and carried on.

Someone thundered on the door below. Instinctively Alina sank to her knees with her heart leaping in her chest.

"Wake up, Johnnie. It's a fine bright morning and we've business afoot."

Alina peered over the gallery. She heard a grunt from Johnnie and watched a leather boot fly through the air and thud against the door.

"Now, Uncle, that's nee way to greet ye nephew."

A rustle of straw announced Jack's presence at her elbow. "Da! It's Uncle Tom!" he called.

Alina thought of ducking back to bed and then thought better of it. It would be natural to be alarmed and awake.

"As if ah didn't knaw that," Johnnie muttered, staggering across the floor in his shirt tails. Alina watched him heave the drawbar into the tunnel and open the door. Daylight flooded inside and struck the wooden ribs of the dwelling. A tall young man strode inside.

The children yelled a greeting but Alina sank back into the straw as the newcomer swivelled on his heel and lifted his gaze to the gallery. Such a fanciful name for such a rough wooden platform, but what else could she call it? The young man's bright blue eyes found her.

"Morning Jack and Mary. Who is that I see beside you?"

Alina did not like the way the young man's bold eye scoured her. Nor did she like the extravagant curled feather in his black hat, the dashing swagger with which he moved or his attempt at gentrified speech. His grubby hands and dirty nails, which she could see from several feet away, proclaimed him less than a gentleman.

"Oh, it's only Alina. She came last night."

"Mistress," he said, sweeping off his headgear and making an extravagant leg in her direction. "Tom Scott at your service."

Jack exploded in a burst of giggles. Alina took one look at the sly face, registered the name and shuffled behind Mary. "Hush, Jack." It was a reflex reprimand, one she would have given her younger brothers. Sounds of movement drew her attention and Meggie walked into view, a woollen shawl pulled close about her shoulders. Johnnie, now fully clad in fustian doublet and grimy leather breeches, followed her. He did not look happy.

"Get yersel' doon 'ere," Johnnie roared, glaring red-eyed at the gallery.

"Does he mean you or me?" Alina asked.

"All of us," Jack muttered. "Come on. He's awful tempered of a mornin'."

On the ground floor, Alina felt less safe. Instinctively, she moved over to Meggie, offered to help with the pot of oats and water and found herself in charge of the big ladle. Jack squatted beside her and a few minutes later Mary came to her other side.

"I heard you took the lass for hostage yesterday, Uncle." The young man seemed to have no fear of his uncle's morning dourness. "Is that the lady in question?"

"Aye, if'n it's any business of yourn."

Alina's hand shook as she stirred the porridge. Furtive glances at the young man told her he watched her with a decidedly lascivious glint in his eye.

Oh, Harry, where are you? Alina gripped the ladle and stirred the porridge rather wildly. Why couldn't Harry have marched in as bold as brass like this young….She hesitated, unsure what to call him, glanced over her shoulder and met another unsavoury leer.

"No business of mine, Uncle, except that she's a bit of a beauty, and I like the look of her. I could keep her busy for the day, if that would be to your liking."

Air hissed between Alina's teeth, and Mary bit her lip.

Meggie banged bowls down on the table with a resounding clatter and shot a venomous look towards Tom Scott. Coldness settled in the pit of Alina's stomach and worked its way up until she shivered violently.

"Woman, woman, can a man not have a bit o'peace in his own hame?" Johnnie sounded petulant. He pulled his jack over his shirt and stabbed a blunt finger in his nephew's chest. "Gan on hame, Tom Scott. When I have summat for ye, I'll let ye knaw."

There was a moment's silence in which Alina did not dare look round.

"Gan on, lad. There's nowt for ye 'ere. She'll gan back to her father the way she came and ye'll not be putting ye clammy hands on 'er."

Alina's relief was such that she dropped the ladle in the porridge and Jack had to fish it out for her with a bit of stick.

***

Harry woke to something shaking his ankle. Alarm ran through him and then he recognised the voice that growled at him in a monotonous undertone.

"Wake up. Wake up. For the love of God, Harry, wake up. Do ah have to drag ye out by ye feet?"

Lifting his head, he squinted at the burly figure at the end of the rough soldier's cot allotted to him. "Jesu, Matho, it's not light yet."

"Sun's up. Open your eyes, man."

Harry yawned, sat up, stretched his spine and concentrated on Matho's rough northern speech.

"'eard what happened to ye yesterday." He grinned. "Reet performance that was an' no mistake. Thought ye might need a bit o' help again, an' Carnaby 'ad nah objection like. Errington's no' far behind me. They stopped off at Lanercost, said they'd come on at first light. Ah came straight ower Black Rigg and Side Fell, mesel', thought ah'd find ye first like."

Dragging the fingers of both hands through his hair, Harry swung his legs out of the narrow cot and stood up. He looked Matho up and down. "You look as if you slept rough last night."

"Aye. A haystack makes a nice warm bed when ye stuck. D'ye knaw where she is, then?"

Harry dipped his face into the bowl of cold water, shuddered and patted his face dry on a square of linen before he turned to the redhead. "She's in an old barn-like place built onto a peel tower in yonder dene."

Matho's grin disappeared. "There's business there already. A rider came in from the north as ah scouted around the castle to find ye."

"Alone?"

Matho nodded. Harry flung the linen aside, and as one, they headed for the door and ran the quarter mile from the outer bailey to the Kirk Beck. Harry checked both up and down the sides of the sloping dene, and saw nothing untoward among the trees. Matho nudged his arm and pointed. An over dressed young man rode a flashy chestnut up the track towards the lip of the dene.

"That's 'im. Didna look ower pleased, did 'e?"

"No," Harry said thoughtfully, looking back at the square stones of the tower by the beck. "But I think I have a plan."

The sun caught Matho's red hair as he gave Harry a sharp look. "As lang as it doesn't mean walkin' in there like that lad did, I'm listenin', but mind, that's all I'm deein'. Ah knaw what a mad de'il ye are."

Harry grinned. "You're a mind-reader, Matho. That's exactly what I'm going to do." He took two strides towards the dwelling, and glanced back over his shoulder. "Coming?"

Matho scowled. "Aye. Alreet."

Halfway down the slope, Harry heard muttering behind him. "Having second thoughts, Matho?"

"Aye, damned right. What if there's a 'ouseful o'men in there? Thought of a plan, 'ave ye?"

Harry paused. "My father and Burton, the man in charge back at the castle, are friends. Burton tells me that Johnnie Hogg will not harm Alina and wants only money for her return."

Matho's eyes focussed on something behind Harry. "The door." He pointed, and dragged Harry behind the nearest tree trunk. With a finger to his lips, he parted the leaves.

They both stared towards the small figure in blue sidling out of Hogg's dwelling. The girl reached for the ring to pull the door shut behind her, and then hesitated and peered around the glade, obviously unsure which way to go.

Relief ran through Harry like a wave, and the strength of it surprised him.

"Gan on, man," growled Matho. "Dinna stand there wi a foolish grin all ower ye face."

Harry stepped forward. At that moment the door of the dwelling opened wide, a man's hand clamped on the girl's arm and wrenched her back inside. The door slammed shut with a resounding bang.

"Damn!"

Matho's bleak tones came from behind him. "Aye, well, what's plan two, then?"

His gaze still on the door, Harry straightened his shoulders. "Nothing wrong with plan one, Matho."

"Off ye go, then. I'll watch ye back."

Harry examined the redheaded young man who had become something close to a friend over the last few weeks. Matho had a formidable presence and there was none of the usual servile resentment in the cool, calm eyes that surveyed him.

"You love her too, don't you, Matho?"

Matho opened his mouth as if to spit out a pithy remark, and then hesitated. A wry smile touched one corner of his mouth and he nodded briefly. "Aye, you may be reet at that." His grin widened. "But for the Lord's sake don't tell 'er. A man's got to 'ave some pride. Anyroad, ah'm not breaking me heart ower it."

"Come with me. You can watch my back far better in there than out here."

Matho glared at him. "Ah canna think o anything mair stupid than gannin' in there."

But when Harry walked boldly up to the door and used his fist on the worn boards, he knew Matho was right behind him. Around them the sunlight strengthened and leaves rustled in the breeze sweeping down the dene. Sharp movement, hastily cut off, came from the other side of the door and a thick, throaty voice demanded "We'se there?"

Harry looked at Matho with raised brows and an expression of annoyance. "Can't these people speak English?"

"T'is English, man. They talk like that around the east end of the Tyne. Ye'll get used tae it."

Harry frowned, and stared at the door. "Open the door, Hogg. I've a proposition for you."

A light feminine squeal of delight from inside sounded as if it was cut off before the owner intended.

"Did you hear that? Sounded like Alina."

Matho raised his brows in a question and nodded towards the door.

Harry shrugged. "Go ahead." It made sense that the man Hogg would speak more readily to Matho than himself.

Inflating his lungs, Matho bellowed. "Johnnie, me name's Matho Spirston and we've a deal for ye. Money for the lass." The redhead turned to Harry. "How much have ye got wi ye?"

"Enough."

"'e'll be greedy."

Harry's brows rose. "If he's too greedy," he said softly, "tell him I'll go back to the castle and borrow Burton's troops for half an hour."

"Who's wi ye, Spirston?" A man's voice growled the question.

Matho chuckled. "The bridegroom, that's all. He's daft enough to pay siller for t'lass ye've got in there."

There was a lengthy pause in which Harry suffered agonies of frustration. Alina was so close and yet he could not see her, touch her or hold her. Suddenly the need to hold her took precedence over everything else. He glanced at Matho. "Get on with it!"

"Dinna git yersel in a fettle man."

Harry looked at him blankly. "*What?*"

Matho shrugged. "Don't be so impatient, that's all."

"Stand in t'middle of the yard so's ah can see ye," commanded the voice on the other side of the door.

Harry looked up. There was a small open square in the wall above their heads. A piece of sacking stretched across it. The thought of a pistol or a bow poking it aside as they walked across the open space chilled him. Matho followed his glance. Harry shook his head, and Matho bawled at the closed door.

"Open the door, man and stop being so bloody cagey. D'ye want the gold or not? The man'll gan and find another bride if'n ye tak too long."

Harry mimed what he wanted. Matho understood, linked his fingers and propelled Harry up to reach the window above their heads. Harry balanced on the protruding door lintel until Matho pounded on the door, and then wriggled headfirst through the small opening. It was a tight fit around his shoulders. As his palms touched the gallery floor he heard the sound of a sneck lifting on the inside of the door.

"About bloody time," snapped Matho.

The narrow gallery was only three feet below Harry. He softened the sound of his entry as much as he could and looked around. Straw and rugs gave evidence that someone slept there on a regular basis. Staring straight ahead over the empty space beyond the gallery, he saw the massive stone blocks of the old peel tower dominated the room. Harry crept to the edge and looked down.

Sacks and barrels stood against the huge baulks of timber that held up the stout roof beams and one corner of the room was penned off for animals. There was little furniture. A scarred table and a wooden bench, a few crackets and one carved chair. A stream of sunlight ran from the open door to the bed tucked against the stone wall that joined the old tower.

Then Harry's heart lurched. Alina stood in the middle of the room, surrounded by Hogg's family. Though a woman held her by the arm, Alina stood straight-backed, her head high, and a rush of pride flowed through him.

"Ach, dinna fash yersel, man." Hogg's words drifted back into the house, and the tone suggested that he surveyed Matho with acute dislike. "Thoo's at fault, fer breakin' a man's sleep."

While Matho argued with Hogg, Harry cat-footed his way to the stairs.

"And here's me thinkin' ye were a man that knew a bargain when it pitched at his feet." At Matho's uncompromising answer, Harry's grin broke through. "But mebbe ah wus wrang."

"Stop yer bletherin' man and get the tale tell't. Where's the bluidy bridegroom, then?"

Harry put one hand on the rail and vaulted the eight or nine feet to ground level. "Here," he said, landing in a crouch.

Alina saw him first. Shock widened her eyes and then she flung herself towards him with such force that the woman could not keep hold of her. Harry kept one eye on Hogg as he and Alina came together in the beam of sunlight. She clung to him, a glorious armful of femininity and he looked down and forgot his plan.

Something hard crashed against the back of his head. He staggered and then flopped over Alina. She cried out but could not hold his weight. He dropped to the floor, and lay there unmoving.

Chapter Twenty Three

"Meggie!" Alina wailed as she knelt at Harry's side. "What did you do that for?"

Matho leapt forward, encircled Hogg's head and shoulders in a bear hug and dragged him over the threshold and out into the new day. Hogg roared in anger, the children squealed in excitement and Matho bellowed instructions.

"Harry! Get me a rope to hold this bugger."

Alina shook Harry, gently at first and then with increasing strength. Hogg bolted back inside. Matho sprinted after him and then jerked to a stop at her side.

"Harry?" Her voice quivered. "Are you hurt? Can you hear me?" She glanced at the woman standing over him, a blackened iron griddle grasped in one limp hand. "I'll never forgive you if you've hurt him."

The children, wide eyed at her sudden vehemence, vanished behind their mother.

Harry groaned. Alina turned back to him, smiled, touched his cheek and spoke over her shoulder to Matho. "Meggie hit Harry with that griddle pan. It's a wonder his head's not dented."

There was no sign of regret in Meggie's pleasant, homely face and Alina wasn't about to forgive her until she knew how Harry fared. He seemed perfectly content to stay where he was, a silly smile on his face, his cheek tucked against her bosom. She held him within the circle of her arms and crooned to him as if he were a child.

Matho fidgeted beside her. She glanced up, and caught an unguarded expression on his rough Border face that tugged at her heart strings. He knew, as she knew, that nothing could ever have flourished between them. But he looked at her, his eyes filled with such tenderness that her breath caught in her throat.

It was time Matho Spirston found a woman of his own.

Hogg stooped, grabbed Alina's arm, and dragged her, shrieking, across the room. Harry flopped to the floor. Hogg got his back to a pillar. Matho started forward but stopped when Hogg drew a knife and held it to Alina's throat.

Alina gulped, stood absolutely still and swallowed noisily. The steel blade was chillingly cold against her skin. Matho's face had lost the soft look. "Let go of 'er." He took a step forward.

The knife moved against her skin, pressed on the tendons.

"Johnnie, no! The bairns are watchin' ye!"

Johnnie glared at his wife. "What d'ye expect me te dee? Let 'er gan off without a penny piece for me trouble?"

"Da!" bleated the boy.

"Don't hurt her, Da," cried Mary.

Alina locked glances with Matho. She glanced meaningfully at Harry. Matho's glance flicked to the floor.

Harry had opened his eyes. He gazed vacantly at the thatched roof.

Johnnie snorted behind her. "The 'ero wakes. Ger 'im up."

Harry struggled to his knees, shook off Matho's impatient hand on his arm. In two effortful moves, he made it to an upright position. One hand probed his skull, and his fingertips came away bloodstained. He looked from his fingertips to his attacker. "Madam." He swayed but kept his gaze steady on her and struggled to produce his easy smile. "You have an exceedingly strong arm."

Something in her face softened as she regarded him. "Ay. It's all the 'ard work that does it."

Dressed in his wedding finery of slashed blue velvet he looked overdressed in this hovel. Harry rubbed the back of his head, and tugged at his once starched collar to loosen it. "Do you think we can persuade your husband to release my bride?" He hesitated. "I want to take her home. If it is a case of money…"

Alina called across the dark space between them. "Meggie, let Harry pay. He can afford it." She twisted her head slightly, felt the blade slide at her throat. "Johnnie, how much to release me?"

Harry turned, saw Alina with a knife held at her throat and blanched. "Good God, man. Release her! Your quarrel must be with me!"

There was a pause. Everyone stared at Johnnie. "Ah can see yer fond of the lass, but what's her life worth to ye? Enough to keep me family alive for five years?"

It was a huge sum. Alina's gaze latched on to Harry. "Pay him, Harry. He will put it to good use. Meggie will make him, won't you, Meggie?"

Meggie's expression radiated confidence. She turned to Harry and smiled. "Aye, he will that. Ah'll see to it that he does, m'lord."

Everyone turned to Johnnie Hogg.

"Please, Johnnie?" Alina's voice was soft and persuasive. "Let me go?"

Greatly daring, Alina turned her head to meet Johnnie's sharp glance for a brief moment. The knife did not press quite so hard against her throat, but he looked grim and she could not blame him. He had two lovable children and no means of supporting them other than by thievery and trickery. The muscles of his stubbly cheeks worked as he looked beyond her to Harry and Matho. He must wonder if he could trust either of them, if men like Matho and Harry would deal honestly with him.

They, of course, stood there like wooden lumps. Impatience ran through her. Why didn't Harry simply hand over the money? Johnnie was hardly likely to refuse any payment, however small, and he must be keen both for money and to be rid of her. She was nothing but a burden to him, another mouth to feed. Then the knife pressed cold against her throat, and Johnnie's gruff voice snapped out one word. "Well?"

No one answered him.

Alina refused to believe that he would use the wicked blade on her.

He might consider selling her on, like a horse or a cow. That way he would make money. Her heart jolted and then steadied. But if Harry paid him, Johnnie wouldn't need to sell her. Why did Harry stand there, his face wooden, his eyes dark in his pale face and say nothing? The suspense was terrible. "Harry, if you love me, please!"

His troubled gaze came to her at once, a line of anger or puzzlement between his brows. Was it imagination, or did she see a confusion of pity and love in his eyes? If only Meggie hadn't hit him and clouded his judgement. He probably had a horrendous head ache. Her teeth dug into her bottom lip to stop it trembling and prevent words tumbling out. Words that would beg him to get out his leather purse and save her.

His gaze went from her back to Johnnie. His father was Deputy Warden, and knew the King. Harry talked as if he had wealth, certainly spoke like a gentleman. He'd been taught at Oxford and served the Royal Household. Why then did he look at her so sorrowfully, as if apologising or saying goodbye?

In sudden fright, she looked at Matho. The man she had known all her life stood as solid as a bear, his red hair glowing in the shaft of sunlight, his eyes dark beneath it. Were they going to abandon her? She feared they might think she was not worth such a vast sum. Matho couldn't pay. He had never earned that much gold. Her breath came faster and faster as terror gripped her.

"What sum would keep you and Meggie for five years, Johnnie?" She had to know. Her habit of chattering when nervous was unattractive and she really ought to control it. Harry did not move a muscle. She swallowed hard and felt the blade move against her skin.

Why didn't Harry say something? If he spoke, she wouldn't have to.

"Four times fifteen punds a year," Johnnie snapped. His voice hardened. "But judgin' by the face on yon lang streak o' misery, his purse is full o'holes." He snorted a gust of air by her cheek. "Or mebbe he thinks o' choosin' another bride."

Sixty pounds was a large sum, but she was sure Harry could manage it. If he still wanted her, of course. She tried to read his expression. Was he thinking of deserting her?

Harry drew in a long, shuddering breath and looked at her captor. "I don't have the money."

Alina gasped. He had rejected her. Her heart stopped in her chest and tears sprang to her eyes.

The edge of the cold steel slid across her neck and sharp biting pain flared behind it. She squealed and flinched away but Johnnie held her fast. Jack started forward, his eyes huge, and Mary cried out.

Harry's eyes narrowed, his face twisted. He lunged forward, but Matho caught his arm and dragged him back, steadied him. Warm liquid spilled down her throat and pooled in the hollows of her collarbone. Alina, breathing hard, squinted at the spatter of blood decorating her bosom. How much blood was too much? Would she bleed to death?

"Johnnie, Johnnie. Remember the bairns, man." Meggie's voice, laced with worry, came from somewhere behind her.

Johnnie didn't respond to his wife's instruction, but he did move the knife a hand span from her throat. She drew in a ragged, unsteady breath and shut her eyes. Her knees felt weak and it was tempting to lean back against Johnnie.

"Ye were sayin'?" Johnnie shifted behind her, his tone inviting Harry to change his mind. She opened her eyes and gazed at her lover.

The dazed look had disappeared. Fire sparked in Harry's eyes. His mouth formed a straight line and the line had deepened between his brows, but still he said nothing. Alina regarded him with growing horror. So ready with a quip at every opportunity, and now, in her hour of greatest need, he had nothing to say.

"Harry?" Her voice wavered. She cleared her throat. "Changed your mind, Harry?" It came out more aggressively than she intended, and she regretted it when she saw him flinch. She stiffened. Why should she feel sorry? He had no intention of saving her.

His lashes flickered. He shrugged his shoulders, half-turned to Matho, then looked at the earthen floor at his feet.

She choked down the lump forming in her throat. "This is my wedding gown, Harry. Had you forgotten?" She could not believe that he was forsaking her. She gulped in another breath of air. Was she going to have to shame him into saving her?

She could not bear to look at him. It had all been for nought. He never loved her, not really. Closing her eyes, she sagged back against Johnnie. His arm shoved her forward again. She straightened her spine and lifted her chin. She would not show Harry how much he had hurt her.

Johnnie hissed against her ear.

Her eyes flew open just as Harry, his voice raw and angry, broke the silence.

"Damn you to hell, Johnnie Hogg! If you make her suffer one moment more, I'll strangle you with my bare hands! I can't pay you because I have only coin enough for half a year on me. What fool rides the Borders with such a vast amount of money in his saddlebags?"

At the venom in his first words, her eyes widened. Then she broke into a shocked gasp of laughter. He could not meet Johnnie's demands for simple, practical reasons. Dizzy with relief, she grinned at the roof as his words rang around the rafters.

"Aye," added Matho, with a hard edge on his voice. His heavy features and lowered brows added to the menace of his threat. "An' if'n 'e doesn't finish the job, ah will, mak nae doot aboot it."

"Why, Matho..." She couldn't think what to say.

Johnnie spat close by her feet, rubbed the hand with the dirk across his chin and nearly gave her another scar as the cold blade whispered across her shoulder. "Can ye no' get the money in the week?"

It was a practical compromise, but Harry's scorn was withering. "Of course I can. But I will not leave Alina with a worm like you for a week. I would not consider it for a moment."

"Well, ah won't let 'er leave. If'n ah do, ye'll ne'er come back."

"Don't be stupid, man. Do you dare to doubt my word?"

"Ah have'na heard yer word yet," Johnnie said dryly.

Harry coughed and looked at his feet. "Then let me give it to you. I will leave with Alina now and return within the week bearing enough gold to support you and your good wife for five years. You have my word as a gentleman on it."

"Nah." Johnnie shook his head.

Alina twisted her head to meet his gaze. "Johnnie, please!"

He gave her a quick shake. "Gold's nee damn good. Silver'd be better."

A faint grin crossed Harry's face. "Then silver it shall be. I swear it." He looked around the strange room. "If you own a Bible I'll be happy to put my hand on it."

Johnnie considered. Then he let go of her arm, put a hand between her shoulder blades and shoved her forward. She ran into Harry's arms and buried her face against his throat. Gasping, laughing without enough breath to do it, she pushed deeper and deeper against him. Weak with reaction, she remained there, her face against the pulse in his neck, pulled the warm spicy smell of him deep into her lungs and fought the urge to sit down and cry.

"Does he mean it?" she whispered, forcing herself to stand up straight. "Will he really let us ride away?"

"He'd better. If he doesn't, he's never going to be a rich man." Harry snuggled his nose into her hair and swayed her in his arms for a moment. Then he looked up. "Is this your land, Johnnie?"

"Oh, aye. What there is of it."

Meggie's voice came out of the gloom. "There isn't much to gan 'roond when the law divide's a man's lands 'tween his sons."

Harry nodded. "Beggars increase and service decays, isn't that what they say of it? Could you not get service with the garrison? I could put in a word for you with Henry Burton."

Meggie stepped forward, a child on either side. "That would be reet good o' ye, sir. Johnnie's a good man, but he's lucky 'is neck's no' longer than it is."

Alina looked at the children, and saw that they had not understood the reference to hanging. She looked at Johnnie. "Will you allow him to do that, Johnnie? To speak for you at the castle?"

The reiver looked at his wife, and then back at Harry. "Aye, if'n ye like."

***

Sitting sideways across Harry's thighs as Bessie walked back to Aydon gave Alina the opportunity to lay her cheek against the tickling velvet of Harry's doublet. She passed both arms around his chest in order to absorb his slightest movement as they rode east across the wide fell. The sun shone warm on her spine, but a breeze cooled her front and gave her an excuse to shuffle closer still.

After the adventures of the last few hours, she was content to measure the rise and fall of his chest as he breathed, inhale the scent of expensive velvet and the alluring smell of his skin and hair. The dark stubble around his jaw made him look like a reiver, but a healthy, expensively dressed and extremely handsome reiver.

Her fingertips absorbed the shape of him, following the flexing of his spine as he rode. The rolling gait of the horse transferred through his thighs and her shoulder moved constantly and rhythmically against his chest. It was comforting, even sensuous. Her thoughts turned to love-making. His heartbeat echoed in her ear, and when he spoke, his voice was a deep rumble that made her start in surprise.

"He's a good man," Harry remarked. "I've come to like him a good deal."

Lifting her head, she saw he watched Matho, who, with a surprising sense of tact, rode twenty yards ahead.

"If that wasn't Matho, I'd say he was showing sensitivity." She angled a flirtatious glance upwards and caught the flash of Harry's smile.

"Sensitive? Matho? He'll never live it down."

"He knows we want to be alone."

"Do we?" He grimaced. "I must get you back to your parents."

Alina sighed. "I suppose we must." She waved a hand over her tattered blue silk. "Mother will have a fit when she sees my wedding dress covered in mud. And blood." She smoothed the skirt with one palm. "And with a rent or two in it."

Harry reached for her hand and kissed it. "Never mind the mud. I love you in spite of it. We can soon get another dress. I could never find another you."

Both hands clutching one of his, she pulled it to her bosom and opened her eyes wide. "Do you? Really? I doubted it when you remained so silent at Johnnie's house."

"I love you." His firm mouth curled. "Do you know you're staring at me like an adoring puppy?" He shook his head. "I wanted to do so many things, but couldn't because he might have used the knife."

Alina lowered her lashes. An adoring puppy indeed. Her hand went unconsciously to the strip of almost clean linen Meggie had bound about her throat. "He did use the knife." She looked up. "But it could have been so much worse. It hurt much more to think that you no longer loved me."

"Don't be silly. Of course I—"

A shout interrupted him. Up ahead, Matho wheeled his horse and pointed. As Bessie breasted the slope, Harry and Alina saw a company of horsemen sweeping up from the south.

Alina clutched a fistful of Harry's doublet. There were a good many men, perhaps twenty, riding at speed across the rough grass. Even at this distance, she could see the glint of armour and weaponry. "Who are they?"

Harry didn't answer. His mouth set in a grim line, he spurred Bessie towards Matho and gestured to the riders. "Do you know them?"

His red hair hidden under a brown cap, Matho wasn't worried. "It'll be Errington, after the stolen nags."

Alina sagged with relief against Harry's chest. "Are you sure?"

"Aye. He's wearing that damned silly bonnet wi the feather again."

His dour, caustic humour made her eyes open wide. Staring out across the hillside, she saw a flash of white about the leader's head and choked back a burst of laughter.

"We're for Aydon," Harry said quietly. "Matho, you are a free agent."

Matho's face was unreadable, but after a moment, he gathered up the reins and sat up straight in the saddle. "Aye, well, ah'll let ye lovebirds gan yeeam on yer own. It's embarrassin' tryin' not to watch ye. Mebbe Errington needs a bit o'elp like."

Alina felt warmth creep into her face, and tried not to laugh at his disgruntlement. "Then we shall see you back at Aydon, Matho. Thank you for saving me."

He looked at her. "Seem te me ah've been pullin' ye out o'scrapes all me life. Why should now be any different?"

As she drew a swift breath to object, Harry waved him on, and Matho, with a grin and salute, rode away.

They watched the whole company, including Matho, veer off at a tangent across the vista of green and brown fells towards Bewcastle. Matho would steer them away from the dene towards the fields where the stolen horses would be resting and with any luck they wouldn't find Johnnie, for he had an appointment inside the castle with Mr Burton.

Chapter Twenty Four

The sun warmed the air and fitful little gusts of wind blew across the long slope of the hills. At midday they rounded an outcrop of rock by a small stream, unsaddled Bessie and let her graze the sweet, luscious grass. Harry rummaged in the saddle bag and unfolded the square of cloth that held the bread and cheese Meggie had put up for them.

He drank from cupped hands, rested his back against a stone warm from the sun. Long legs stretched out and crossed at the ankle, he tore off a chunk of bread and spoke around a bulging cheek. "She's a good sort."

Alina dabbed a wet handkerchief at the blood stains on her gown. She looked up for a moment. "Meggie? She's certainly strong enough to keep Johnnie in line. She says he's a softie at heart."

Harry snorted. "And you believed her?"

Hands stilled, Alina tilted her head back and thought about it. "Yes, I think I do. There are so many things Johnnie could have done, but didn't." She shivered in the sunshine and went back to her work. "Meggie said she comes from a village on the coast south of Newcastle and she met Johnnie on a visit to a cousin's wedding. They fell in love and ran away. His father was so angry he gave Johnnie no help. That's why they struggle. He must have been handsome ten years ago but they live such a hard life it would destroy anyone's looks. Even yours," she added, with a swift, teasing glance that made Harry smile.

He licked the crumb of cheese off his fingers and lifted his brows. "Are you not hungry? I'll have to go back there soon. You could come with me, if you've a mind to."

Alina spread the hankie on a rock to dry and reached for the food. Busily stuffing cheese inside the bread, she frowned. "We've business to settle first, Harry Wharton. Johnnie can wait."

"He won't wait ower long, as Matho would say."

Alina chewed and swallowed. "How long does it take to get married? A day? Half a day?"

"An hour would do it."

"Well, then, that's what we must do first."

Harry grinned. "Impatient, are you?" The blue sky behind her was a paler echo of her once splendid gown and emphasised the coppery glints and darker strands in her chestnut hair.

Alina wiped crumbs from her rumpled skirt. "My first really expensive gown," she sighed. "Ripped, torn and bespattered. Mama will be furious. Father will rue the expense." Her fingers went to the amber pendant at her throat. "At least I didn't lose this."

She went on eating, but Harry sensed she was not as confident as she wished to appear. "Don't worry. You are my bride and he cannot touch you now."

Instantly she faced him, wide eyed. "He never beat me, Harry."

"Did I say that he did?"

She ate the last mouthful and wagged her head from side to side. "I thought you suspected it."

"I wondered," Harry admitted. "He has a temper on him that would have scared me at twelve years old. I'm still full of admiration for Lance and Cuddy. Did he vent his temper on them when I escaped?"

Alina folded the cloth and stuffed it back in the satchel. "They got a beating, but I didn't find out until later. They never complained."

"And what about you?" For some reason, she would not meet his eyes.

"He ordered me to marry John."

Harry felt strange. If he had stayed away a week longer, she would have been married to another man. It would have been too late. Their glances met and held, both aware of how nearly they had missed each other. They should have been married by now, but for Johnnie Hogg and his disreputable band of reivers.

A lark sang somewhere in the sky. The soft breeze nodded through the bog cotton and bracken but blew over the top of the small hollow by the stream.

Harry reached for her and pulled her close. He lifted her hand and sucked her fingers clean. She caught her breath and gazed at him.

He tightened his arm around her. "I think of you as my wife. When I saw that man hold a knife to your throat…" His fingers touched the strip of white cloth.

Her eyes glowed in the sunshine. "What did you think?"

He shook his head. "I didn't think, I couldn't think. I wanted to rush him, throw him to the ground...I would rather have died myself than have him hurt you."

"But you couldn't do that for fear he might kill me." Slowly she moved closer, touched her lips to his. No more than a feather light touch, it was both a promise and an assurance.

"You love me, don't you."

She did not say it as a question, but more as a statement of fact. He watched her eyes close, saw the dark lashes clustered on her lightly flushed cheek. Already his blood ran faster, his fingers ached to touch her. Her eyes opened showing him a dark, languorous gaze that fastened on his. Her lids half closed as she focussed on his mouth. The tip of her small pink tongue peeped between her lips and without conscious thought his mouth closed over hers.

"I adore you," he said. "I want you for my wife before the world. I love you Alina."

The long ride, holding her so close to him, had already roused his senses. Hers too, it seemed, for she moved closer, tilted her head, traced his underlip with the tip of her tongue. His heart thumped in response. He leaned forward, grasped her temples between his palms and drew her alongside him without breaking their kiss.

***

Danger had not altered her feelings for Harry. Without a qualm, she reached for him as eagerly as he sought her. When he pulled down the neckline of her gown, let the sun find the curve of her pale flesh before his mouth, hot and wet, covered it, she flung back her head and gloried in the sensations that rolled through her.

Her breath came in short, hard gasps. Her eyes closed against the sun, she sought his mouth by touch, found his shoulders, his throat and finally his mouth. She rose to her knees, heard the rustle of silk as he scrabbled beneath the layers, felt cool air on her thighs.

Following the pressure of his hand at her back, Alina arched closer, absorbed in the delight of his mouth. The tight bodice cut across her breast, but did not lessen the pleasure as his hand arched over her, traced the outline of her flesh. Aching to touch him, she grasped the edges of his doublet and tugged, forced her hand beneath the white silk of his shirt.

His skin burned beneath her searching fingers, and he groaned. Alina opened her eyes. Harry freed himself from his breeches while desire soaked into the air around them. Larks trilled, high in the sky, and the scent of pollen, buttercups, dandelions and daisies filled her nostrils. When she looked down at him, she caught her breath. In the darkness of the stable at Grey House, she'd known him by feel and pressure alone. Now, she could see him in full daylight.

Hesitant, but curious, she reached out, touched him. Harry shuddered, caught her hand and held it there as desire smouldered and flared. Between them they wrenched his doublet free and her hands slid inside his shirt, caressed the roll and ridge of his chest until he clutched her to him.

Fingers sliding into his thick hair, she pressed against him, enticed him, licked his mouth and pressed her forehead against his. She lost herself, found hunger welling within her and breathed his name as she took his lips.

Senses raging, greedy, she wanted more. "Harry—"

He caught her tight in his arms, rolled her to the grass and settled between her thighs. "I know," he muttered. Sweat beaded his hairline.

She waited, panting, gazing up at him. His entry brought shivers of joy. She yelped in delight, curled her knees along his flanks and let her palms skim the smooth skin of his spine beneath the loosened doublet. Her gaze locked on his, she revelled in the love she saw in his eyes. She urged him on. "Harry! Oh, Harry—"

He groaned. "If you don't—"

Her hips pressed upward in soft, enticing flicks, and she laughed, sobbing with eagerness. It was over in moments. He rolled onto one hip, and she followed him. Tracing a finger across his moist brow, she watched him pant like a racehorse that has run a long, hard race.

"Harry…?"

His eyes flickered open. "Give me a moment." He laughed without any breath to support it.

"It is…" Her hand went to her chest. "My heart will explode."

He shook his head. "No, it won't." He sat up, shuffled back to the boulder and leaned against it. She crept into the circle of his arm and snuggled against his chest. A little while later, when she had breath enough to speak, she looked up.

"I wonder…I still don't know you well, Harry Wharton. Do you like custard, for example? Duck eggs?" She smiled, thinking how she would learn every thing about him. "And at the same time, I feel as if I have been waiting for you all my life."

He grunted, and dipped his head to her shoulder and licked the moisture from her skin. "I have to admit that you were not in my plans." He lifted his head, and stared down into her face. "But those plans seem unimportant now. They belong to someone else, not me."

"What were they, these plans of yours?"

"Oh, to find and marry an heiress."

Safe in the knowledge that he could not see her, she pulled a face. "Money or land?"

A bead of sweat from above dripped onto her hand. "Both."

"A grand plan indeed." She rose and faced him. "I apologise for not being rich, but I will have lands once I marry."

"You will?"

"I will. But that's not important, is it? I'll make up for being poor with kisses every day. If kisses will make you rich, then rich you shall be."

"Once I would have laughed at that. Now I know differently. You have changed me, altered my view of life."

"You mean you'd rather live on love than seek a rich heiress?"

His arm encircled her and he pulled her so close his nose touched hers. "Indeed I will. Don't let the supply ever dry up." His finger traced the bandage at her throat. "If I needed to have my feelings sorted out, it happened back there in Johnnie's home, when I thought he was going to cut your throat." He swallowed and glanced aside. "I thought it was bad enough when you disappeared from our wedding and I followed the trail for hours thinking all sorts of dire things. But when Johnnie held you, I couldn't have felt worse if it was my own throat he was proposing to slit. Life without you seemed impossible."

He looked so vulnerable that she tilted her head and kissed him lightly on the lips.

"You mean you would have missed me?"

"I remember the moment when your blood spurted under his knife. Words I'd never thought I say rushed through my mind. Totally unhelpful and wonderfully surprising, words."

"What words ?"

"*I love her, I love Alina.* They've echoed in my mind ever since. How it happened, or when, I do not know."

"Oh, Harry. I love you, too. You must have missed me, then?"

His mouth pulled to one side, and his eyes changed shape as he smiled. "Missed you? A bad-tempered harridan with big brown eyes and the courage of a grown man? Never."

She laughed.

***

"Alina!" The roar came down from the alure of Aydon Hall and bounced off the stones of the curtain wall. It was a voice she recognised.

"I daren't look," Alina whispered. She shut her eyes and clutched Harry's doublet.

The roar came again, with even more annoyance laced into it. She opened her eyes and looked beyond the guard post above the gate to the wall-walk.

Cuthbert Carnaby glared down at her. "That's Father."

"Jesu!" muttered Harry. "That's my father standing next to him. I wonder what they've found to talk about." He grinned at her and pulled a face. "Never fear. They can't touch us now."

He guided Bessie through the gate, dismounted in the outer bailey and held out a hand to Alina. She slid down into his arms and together they turned to face the two middle-aged men walking out from the inner courtyard.

Cuthbert Carnaby's face was mottled red, but the man next to him, a superbly dressed grey-haired man in grey tunic and matching hose, looked as if he struggled to restrain his amusement.

Suddenly aware of her bedraggled appearance, Alina dipped a hasty curtsy in their direction. "I'm safe and well, as you see, sir. Harry rescued me from the reivers' band."

Carnaby cleared his throat, but said nothing.

Puzzled, she stared at him, waiting for him to speak. Groping for Harry's hand, she gripped it firmly. Her father did not utter a word.

Sir Thomas Wharton took control of the situation. He inclined his head politely to Alina. "Well met, Mistress Carnaby, I am Harry's father, as he has no doubt told you. Harry, I came in order to greet your new bride and heard only the story of her abduction. It seems your life is full of adventure these days. How are you, lad?"

Harry let go of her hand and stepped forward, smiling. The two men met in a brief embrace. "I am well, Father, as you see."

"Alina, Alina!" Lance ran up, threw his arms around her waist, buried his face against her and then backed off, red-faced. "'Lo, Harry." He looked at Alina. "Cuddy's gone for Mama."

Wharton looked at his host. "Perhaps we should go inside?"

Carnaby jumped. "Of course, of course."

Alina glanced at Harry and waggled her brows in amazement. What on earth was matter with Father? It was most unlike him to remain silent.

Carnaby led the way but Wharton hung back and addressed his son. "I take it you were heading for Aydon with the hope of completing the marriage ceremony?"

"Of course. As soon as it can be arranged."

"I see no reason to delay." Wharton glanced at the man hesitating at the bottom of the steps. "What do you say, Carnaby?"

Alina squeezed Harry's hand, hidden within the folds of her skirt. "Just what I want," she whispered. "I like your father, Harry."

Carnaby grunted. "To be sure. The sooner she's married and off my hands, the more delighted I'll be. We can soon rouse the priest from his quarters at Halton."

Sir Thomas had a glint in his eye as he surveyed his son. "Mount up, Harry. We've a wedding to attend."

"No!" Alina headed for the stairs to the hall and then hesitated. She half-turned, and dimpled a smile at Harry's father. "I do not wish to seem rude, sir. But I cannot get married looking like this!" From the first step she glanced down at Harry, eyes pleading. "I must see Mama. Give me but a little while and I shall be ready."

Sir Thomas smiled. "Perhaps Harry could also benefit from a change of clothes. How fortunate I had his wardrobe brought with me."

Harry leapt up the stairs behind Alina and ran straight into a flurry of feminine cries as Mistress Carnaby and Cuddy burst out of the hall. The two women hugged each other and Cuddy's face, already beaming, lit up. "Harry!"

Squealing, the boy flew across the square landing and threw himself into Harry's arms. "You're back!"

Scooping him up and holding him with one arm, Harry continued up the last stairs to the landing. "How are you, lad?" He listened to Cuddy's excited voice but stared at the picture of mother and daughter in each other's arms. Eyes closed, tears glinting on her cheeks, Margery Carnaby murmured words Harry could not hear while Cuddy lisped questions in his ear. Finally they released one another and Alina scrubbed her sleeve across her face before she swooped across to Cuddy and kissed his cheek.

Margery Carnaby blotted her face with a wisp of lace-edged linen and took a deep breath. "Please come inside, sir."

Harry put Cuddy back on his feet and grasped Alina's hand. Following his hostess inside, he smiled at Alina. "All seems well?"

"Oh yes, but what's happening, Harry? Father seems afraid to say a word! Has your father threatened him?"

"At this moment, I do not know. I shall find out later."

The south window in the hall was open to the gentle breeze and as they walked through to the solar, voices from outside drifted up to them. Harry recognised his father's cultured speech and nudged Alina towards the window embrasure. Grinning, eyes alight with mischief, she tiptoed into place beside him.

"Do you not find the ravine a dangerous thing to have on the doorstep, Carnaby? Children could vanish in a twinkling." There was a pause. In a thoughtful tone, Harry's father added, "Easy to get rid of a few unwanted guests, or enemies, for that matter."

Eyes widening, Alina clapped a hand over her mouth. Harry held a finger to his lips as he peered out of the window.

"Oh, I can't believe anyone would…" Her father's voice petered out. Harry and Alina exchanged glances and watched as Sir Thomas walked forward, stood on the extreme edge of the Leap.

He peered over. Hands clasped behind his back he stared around him.

"I heard tell once of a Scots baron similarly situated, except that the drop was into the sea. He gained a fearsome reputation for tossing enemies over the cliff. He laughingly called it The Leap, I believe. It's still known as Harry's Leap." He chuckled, glanced back at Carnaby. "Of course, I don't know that the tale is true, but it gives rise for thought, don't you think?"

Alina closed her eyes and struggled to hold in her laughter. Harry grasped her wrist intending to drag her from the window, turned and found her mother behind them. She too had been listening to the exchange below. Her gaze still focussed on the treetops, she shook her head and stepped away.

Once in the solar she sat in her favourite chair. "Your father is clever, Harry."

Harry bowed his head. "He is, ma'am."

Alina came to rest with her hands on the back of her mother's chair. "He knows what Father did and he's let him know that he knows. I think you are quite safe now." Alina looked down at her mother and back at Harry. "He won't dare touch you now and we can get married right away with a single worry."

"I hope Cuthbert is wise enough to understand he must accept you, Harry," added Mama. She smiled, reached up to touch her daughter's hand. "Why not take Harry to my room, Alina. I shall have hot water brought to you, and a change of clothes."

"Thank you, Mama." Stooping, she pressed her lips to her mother's cheek, then whirled to grasp Harry's hand and led him beyond the curtain. Her parents' four poster crouched in one corner, its rich red hangings soaking up the available light. There was only one lancet window. A large carved oak chest stood beneath it, with a matching chair and stool alongside. The room was gloomy, but at night candles would make it a comfortable and private place.

"A bed," Harry said softly behind her, his eyes alight. He kept hold of her hand when she would have let go and swung her around to face him. "May I help you with anything? Take off your gown, roll down your hose. Unlace you?"

He stepped behind her and already his fingers were busy with the pins that held her stomacher in place. Alina flattened her palms against it as it fell away. "Harry! The maid will come at any moment—"

His lips caught her ear, then her shoulders and her heart thundered. "The maids," he said calmly, "can await our pleasure."

"But they won't," she said, backing away from him. "They'll barge straight in. And anyway, Mama sits just beyond the curtain."

Harry walked over and twitched the heavy velvet aside with one finger. "Would you believe me," he asked, glancing over his shoulder, "if I said your mother has left the solar?" He grinned and walked towards her. "A most sensible woman."

The End

But will ye stay till the day go down
Until night comes o'er the ground,
And I'll be a guide worth any twa
That may in Liddesdale be found.
Hobbie Noble, English reiver, planning a foray